Handbags and Gladrags

Also by Sally Worboyes

CHR
3.16
CHR
12.19.

WO

23. MAY 08

28. OCT 08

BARBER

14. JUN 08

21. NOV 08

10. JUL 08

17. FEB 09

10. JUN

446

Handbags and Gladrags

Sally Worboyes

First published in Great Britain in 2008 by Orion Books,
an imprint of The Orion Publishing Group Ltd
Orion House, 5 Upper Saint Martin's Lane
London WC2H 9EA
An Hachette Livre UK Company

3 5 7 9 10 8 6 4 2

A CIP catalogue record for this book
available from the British Library.

ISBN (Hardback) 978 0 7528 7553 8

Typeset at The Spartan Press Ltd,
Lymington, Hants

Printed in Great Britain by
Clays Ltd, St Ives plc

The Orion Publishing Group's policy is to use papers that
are natural, renewable and recyclable products and made
from wood grown in sustainable forests. The logging and
manufacturing processes are expected to conform to the
environmental regulations of the country of origin.

www.orionbooks.co.uk

Acknowledgements

I would like to thank Charlotte Plater and Mark Dickenson at Hudson Property Services for coming to my rescue with this book when my printer stopped working. They were my knights in shining armour.

One

1959

Coming out from under the railway arch and into a quiet and familiar cobbled turning which led out onto a main road, shy and sensitive thirteen-year-old Nathan Cohen screwed up his eyes against the glare of the bright July sunshine. He pushed his round, loose National Health glasses up onto the bridge of his nose and did his best to focus on a small group of lads who attended the same school as he – lads who were known as bullies. In the midst of them was not one but two local ruffians who loved to pick on boys who were loners through no fault of their own, and who unintentionally invited humiliation of one sort or another any day of the week.

Too late to turn around and make a cautious retreat. Nathan, who was overweight and a touch short for his age, felt a rush of fear sweep through him as he realised that he was already the focus of the gang's attention. His lips beginning to quiver, he felt his throat go dry. The boys were forming a kind of human chain across the worn cobblestones and each one, arms folded, was grinning at him – bar one, who hunched his shoulders and splayed his arms, palms upwards, as if to mimic a distinguishing posture of an East End Jewish elder. Clearly, he was mocking Nathan's grandparents, who ran a small local grocery shop-cum-Jewish delicatessen in a back turning.

Nathan knew from experience that it would be folly even to try and retrace his steps, never mind run for his life as he had done before, only to be chased and caught. It was certain that there was going to be no escape from humiliation of one sort or another, perhaps a good thrashing, for they saw only that he was faint-hearted and fat and an easy target. So, trying to act natural and friendly even though beads of sweat were breaking out on his forehead, Nathan did his best to keep an easy pace as he strolled closer to his five would-be tormentors, who were at a loss to do much else with their time other than taunt those weaker than themselves.

On his way to visit his grandparents who lived close by, Nathan was in his faded spinach-green school blazer and an open-necked cotton shirt tucked into his grey school trousers. These were the clothes he wore day in day out, come rain or shine. His only pair of stout black shoes was a touch shabby but, as ever, had been highly polished by himself that very morning while his mother, Lilly, was at work in the local umbrella factory. Nathan's father Jacob, an accomplished tailor, worked in a small sweatshop in the back and beyond of old Aldgate East and had done for several years. Jacob had always taught his three sons and his only daughter that they should make the best of whatever talent they had and work hard so as to achieve a more comfortable way of life. He had also drummed into them the most important thing of all – that they should take pride in having been born Jewish.

Nathan's elder brothers had taken their father's lessons to heart. They had gone into the print business together some years back, and had managed to climb the ladder of success. They both now lived in Golders Green on the border of Hampstead, and only came into the East End to be with their parents and younger brother for Sabbath on a Friday afternoon or evening, depending on the time of the year. Of course they would then stay overnight because of the strict rule of no travelling after the sun had set. These close-knit family gatherings were part and parcel of the Orthodox Jewish way of life, as was the written law of not working on a Saturday.

Their observance was also something that rewarded Jacob and Lilly for having been good parents.

Sadly for Nathan, his sister was no longer a part of the gatherings. Jacky Cohen had married an American Jew when she was only eighteen and had gone to live in the States. Nathan had missed her so much at first that he had cried into his pillow night after night, but now, six years later, he had learned to live without her. She had left the country in 1953 when he was seven years old and just before he and his family had joined in the street parties on the day that a princess had been crowned Queen Elizabeth II. It was a day when there had been a national celebration the like of which had not been seen since VE day. Had it not been for his close friend Charlotte, who lived in the same block as himself, Nathan would not have joined in the celebrations. Charlotte was his one and only best friend and it was she who had got him to join in the spirit of national unity, when Union Jacks decorated every street, every child was given a Coronation mug, and schoolgirls – rich and poor alike – wore red, white and blue ribbons in their hair. Together they had watched the Coronation on a small black and white television set in his living room with his parents, and had sat next to each other at the street party later. The second of June 1953 had been a day to remember always, despite the rain that came down on the spectacle.

Nathan's dad was a young unmarried man during the battle of Cable Street in London's East End in 1936. He joined Jews, and other groups such as communists, in protest against a march by Oswald Mosley's British Union of Fascists, the Blackshirts. That experience taught him a lesson which he now passed on to his son, that he would be better served if he kept his eyes lowered when approaching a group of lads who were not of the same beliefs as himself. And that, even though he should always return a smile, to be on the safe side, he should never invite one.

Good though Jacob's advice was, Nathan knew that it wasn't of much use when a gang such as he was approaching was bored and looking for a bit of fun. The small menacing group was now spreading across the cobbled back turning, which was hemmed in by lock-up storage space beneath the railway line on one side and black iron railings and a park on the other. There really was no choice for the thirteen-year-old in this deserted street other than to turn around and run or steel himself for their goading and then a beating – unless an adult happened to come by.

The sweat trickling down his forehead had all but plastered his black wavy hair flat and his spectacles were more steamed up than usual, but he knew this was no time to take them off and dry them with the big white handkerchief that he kept in his trouser pocket. It was no more than seventy degrees that day, but to Nathan who had never been good in heat, it felt like a hundred. A worried frown creased his forehead but he forced a nervous smile and he nodded hello to the intimidators, who smirked sarcastically.

'Here he comes, the fat Jew boy who's in the A-stream class wiv all the other fucking clever dicks,' said the leader of the pack as his lips parted in a detestable smile. 'Don't he make yer feel sick. Look at him. Fat 'n' Jewish and he stinks of herrings. And he's in the fucking clever A-stream.' He looked from his followers to Nathan. 'I bet you he still ends up in a suit factory what's run by Jews. *You want a good suit?*' He mimicked the lad's father, Jacob Cohen, by hunching his shoulders and splaying his hand. '*If you want a beautiful suit then go see the boy's father. He makes such a beautiful suit you couldn't belief it.*' The boys laughed as Nathan flushed with humiliation and suppressed anger. Still doing his utmost to appear unruffled, Nathan could see the louts closing in with the same menacing look he had seen before. Tears welled behind his eyes and he could feel his heart beating so rapidly that he was afraid they would hear it. Taking a deep breath, he forced back the tears

4

and waited for the assault that would no doubt begin with him being forced to the ground and end with a good kicking, accompanied by insults to do with his religion or his weight.

This was not the first time he had stepped into their realm, only to receive a hiding. From experience Nathan knew that all he could do was clench his fists, close his eyes tightly, and take whatever came. But luck was on his side this afternoon because suddenly another person had caught the attention of Kenny, the ginger-haired leader of the pack. He now peered over Nathan's shoulder with a different kind of smile on his face, and an expression now much softer and, for the moment, quite normal, even warm.

Following his gaze, one of the others – the tallest youth – licked his lips and then quietly chuckled. 'Lucky day . . . see what the wind's blown our way.'

'Charlotte the virgin,' sneered another. 'Charlotte who likes to hang around with weirdos. Given 'er one yet, 'ave yer, Jew boy?'

'Watch your mouth,' said Kenny, glaring at his mate. 'I wanna keep this girl sweet. I've marked 'er out. I fancy 'er rotten.'

Knowing when to keep quiet, Nathan chose to ignore the comment about his best friend. At least the immediate attention was off him and he could breathe a sigh of relief even though he had every intention of staying right where he was. Reaching the gang, thirteen-year-old Charlotte, with her lovely natural blonde hair cut into the new urchin look, narrowed her wide blue eyes as she summed up the situation. She then winked at Kenny, who was wearing his brother's hand-me-down black leather biker's jacket.

'How hot is your blood today, Kenny?' she said, doing her utmost to behave as if she hadn't picked up on what was going on.

'At boiling point, and hot enough for you any day of the week, babe,' was the cool reply.

'Good. Because the leader of the Roman Road gang and a few of his crowd are on their way. You've been a naughty boy and gone and upset them from what I heard.'

Chuckling, and looking from her to the lads and back again, Kenny raised his eyebrows in derision. 'The Roman Road gang? Do me a favour. We saw 'em off wiv a good kicking weeks ago. They know not to come onto our patch.'

'I just did you a favour by telling you, but it's up to you whether you believe it or not. Your mum wasn't best pleased to see them on her doorstep – not from what I could hear from the stairs on my way down from our flat.'

'Listen to it.' The lad with the ginger crew-cut chuckled. 'On my doorstep? No way! They wouldn't dare step on Bethnal Green territory.'

'Please yourself,' said Charlotte, 'but don't say I didn't warn yer.' With that the slim shapely girl, who was tall for her age, slipped her arm through Nathan's and gave a gentle tug. 'Come on you or we'll be late. Move yerself.'

Kenny was by now too preoccupied with what Charlotte had told him to care about his victim any more. 'So Charlie, where are they now then, the cretins?'

'Looking for you lot. And especially *you*. And my name is Charlotte to people I don't like. You'd best get home and find out what's what.' She then pulled on Nathan's arm saying again, 'Come on, we'll be late.'

Staring into her face with a hint of fear in his eyes, Nathan slowly nodded as the penny dropped. 'Time waits for no man,' he said, relieved that he had an escape route. Charlotte had sidetracked the gang with her fib about them having to be somewhere else and he was off the hook. This time . . . Talking over her shoulder as she walked away, she boldly advised the lads to keep a low profile for a day or so. The couple hadn't got far when Kenny's voice pierced through the air.

'If that was a lie and you did it to get the fat Jew off the hook, Charlie, I'll find you and I'll take yer while the others hold the Jew nice and tight. He can watch the free show. I reckon he'd like not having to *pay* for a ticket!'

Charlotte stopped in her tracks and glared at him. 'Go fall in the cut Ginger! And watch your vile tongue or I'll start telling tales. Your dad's fitting carpet in our front room next week. You wouldn't want me to tell him about your strange hobbies, would you?'

'Hobbies? What fucking hobbies? I live on the outside,' said the bully, going pink in the face. 'I hang out in the snooker clubs and on street corners—'

'Whatever you say, Ginger. Whatever you say!' She then quickened her pace, whispering to Nathan to do the same. 'Don't look back,' she said. 'Just keep on walking.'

'I fully intend to,' said her friend, embarrassed at the way she had stood up to one of the most notorious bullies around, making her braver than he was. 'Tell me about his strange hobbies later.'

'I made that up, but from what I heard from the girls at school most lads have the same one. But we won't go into that. He did go red in the face though, didn't he.' She giggled. 'So perhaps I pressed the right button.'

Looking sideways at Nathan, Charlotte could see that he was blushing. 'It's all right,' she teased. 'Just so long as you don't do it in public.'

'I don't know what you're talking about,' he said, a touch haughtily, and then changed the subject. 'Ginger's no more than a little boy in a big boy's jacket.'

'Maybe, but you should try and stay out of his way all the same.'

Nathan shook his head with a jerk. 'I can't believe that you said that to him. The bit about his strange hobbies.'

'Everyone's got a secret. Especially lads of his age.'

Still blushing a little he nodded. 'Yes I suppose so.' He

glanced over his shoulder and drew breath. 'Shit. They're following us.'

'It's all right,' said Charlotte, squeezing his arm. 'We'll be fine once we're out on the main road and by the entrance to the park.' She looked back to see that the boys were now milling around their leader, who stood all macho with his hands on his hips.

'See you in the classroom, schoolboys!' Charlotte called back to them.

'Oh for fuck's sake, Charlie. You shouldn't have said that, you're asking for trouble. I learned long ago not to rise to their bait. It's not a game of tease and chase. I used to have to hide in the boys' toilets. That lot can be right bastards when they want. You should watch your tongue.'

'Don't be mad. I'm a girl! It wouldn't wash if Ginger Kenny were to lift a hand to me. He'd lose too many Boy Scout points.'

Still perturbed by her lack of respect for a gang with a reputation, Nathan glanced over his shoulder again and saw that they were half-loitering, half inclining towards them. 'They're gonna come after us.'

The boy then took a grip on himself and encouraged her to step up the pace. 'You shouldn't antagonise that kind of person,' he said, slipping his arm out of hers and taking off his glasses at last to give them a wipe and dab his perspiring forehead.

Charlotte tenderly punched him on the arm. She could tell by the look on his face just how scared he was. 'They're wastrels, Nathan. Nothing but loud-mouthers.'

'I know that, but they take pleasure in beating me up. You don't know how hard it is for me to stop myself from running but I know that would be worse than anything.'

'Oh come on, you know that I know that. Why do you think I just dragged you out of that little trap? You've got to stop trying to get on their side. They won't let you in so don't even *try* and be their friend.'

He looked back nervously once more. He could still see the lads, but at least the space between them was growing. 'I don't think they *are* going to follow us,' he said, in a tone of relief.

'Seems not.' Nathan looked as if he had just escaped a fate worse than death, and quite possibly he had. Charlotte slipped her arm into his again and they walked slowly along the path. 'I wish they would all move out of our neighbourhood.'

'Me too.' Nathan just about managed to smile at her. 'They were only loitering because they've got nothing else to do.'

'Exactly. Whereas you've always got somewhere to go because of your relatives being close knit. And anyway one day you'll be able to jump all the hurdles that they'll baulk at.'

Nudging his spectacles back into place, the lad drew himself to full height, took a deep breath, and pushed his shoulders back. He wanted to walk proudly beside his friend, who was not only pretty, but everything that any boy could wish for in a girlfriend. She was all that his honeyed dreams were made of, but he had never said so – and never would, because he felt that they would only ever be friends. He was shorter than she, he was fat, and he was Jewish. Mixing religion when it came to marriage wouldn't go down well with his parents, never mind hers. He had felt warm and brotherly love towards her since they first got to know each other at the age of five, when his family moved into the block of flats where Charlotte was already living. On the first day that he started at the same school as she, they had partnered each other when forming a queue to move from their classroom to the art room. It was one of her favourite places; there, they were allowed to use primary colour powder paints and were given their own paintbrushes to clean and keep in their school desks.

Aware that he now had sweating armpits, Nathan slipped

his hands into his trouser pockets and kept his arms straight and close to his sides to try and hide the damp patches on his cotton shirt. Certain that the gang really had gone, it was with a thankful sigh that he strolled with Charlotte in the park. They rested for a while on a park bench.

'We're very lucky to have these gardens, Charlie,' he murmured. 'Who would have thought it? A beautiful place like this in the heart of the most feared and dreaded East End.' He quietly chuckled. 'That's what others from better parts of our city think, you know? That here we live as if it's still Dickensian land, but look at our surroundings. What more could you ask for?'

'A pair of slingback shoes and a matching handbag.'

'Oh, not that again. If your parents think you're too young for that kind of thing then that's all there is to it.'

'Others in my school year have got them. I've seen them all done up on a Friday night, going to the local dance halls. Dad doesn't seem to realise that I'm a teenager, he still treats me as if I'm his baby girl and I'm not even allowed to wear stock- ings. Mum said she'd buy me some, and a pretty suspender belt to hold them up once I've turned fourteen, but that's nearly a year away.'

'I'm not interested in girls' fashion fads, Charlie,' said Nathan, a touch self-conscious to hear her talk about her underwear. 'And anyway, you shouldn't walk through the back streets by yourself at night and you would have to if you were going to any of the youth clubs that hold dances. It's dangerous. Especially in old Bethnal Green, around by the old Jago.'

'The old Jago? I wouldn't go there anyway. It's all old factories and workshops now. But it's all right where my great-aunt and uncle used to live. Broadbent Road is okay, and there's a smashing dance hall for young people close by. I went there one summer evening to see what the girls at school were getting excited about.'

'And was it any good?' he asked.

'From what I could see from the doorway it was fantastic,' Charlotte replied. 'It was dark, with red and blue light over the dance floor, and there was a stage where a band was playing and singing songs from the hit parade.'

'Why didn't you go inside?' he said, his elbows now resting on his podgy knees and his hands cupping his face.

'Because I was wearing my gingham check frock with the white Peter Pan collar that would suit a six-year-old. My parents just won't accept that I'm a teenager. That's what comes of being an only child, I s'pose, but I *will* get my slingbacks even if I have to get a Saturday job and buy the shoes myself.'

Charlotte turned her head towards the open gateway to the park, and felt an icy chill shoot through her: the boys were coming their way. 'We might be through the gates, Nathan, but we're not out of the woods, as my grandparents would say. They're still hanging around. Let's head for the park-keeper's little wooden hut and hide in there. Come on.'

'Won't he mind? The park-keeper?'

'I doubt he'll be in there on a sunny day like this. And anyway, no, he won't mind, he's nice. I often sit with him when he's in Queen Victoria's open-fronted shelter.'

Nathan laughed. 'Queen Victoria? I doubt she ever sat in our park.'

'Course she didn't, but it was built to commemorate her coronation so the adults have always referred to it as her shelter.'

'I know that. I know my local history.'

'So you should. Come on.' They made their way to the little tucked away place where the kindly man in his uniform and peaked cap usually sat when having his packed lunch or taking a tea break. They passed through heavenly flowerbeds where scented roses, ranging from pale apricot to deep velvety red, were in bloom. They could see that the hut door was open but there was no sign of the keeper.

Charlotte turned and looked to the entrance again. She could just see through the shrubbery and the iron railings that the gang was either about to enter the park, or carry on across the main road that led to the Mile End Gate. Whatever the case they were hovering, and clearly looking for something – or someone – with which to kill time.

Not wishing to risk any trouble for Nathan, she turned her attention to her friend, who was now sitting on the bench inside the hut. He was in full view of any passers-by, and she quickly went to him, pulling at his arm and ordering him to get behind the shed and duck down behind the thick foliage. The thicket, with its leafy screen, had always been a favourite of Charlotte's when she was a child playing hide and seek with friends.

Doing as he was told and once hidden, Nathan didn't move a muscle as they watched from their hiding place. The gang were now sauntering along in their direction and Charlotte's own heart was beginning to beat faster. She clasped her hands together and silently prayed to God to make the boys turn back or walk by without searching for them. They were now sitting targets and it had been she that had led them into this corner. Nathan, realising that this could be the lull before the storm, removed his glasses and rubbed his eyes but gave nothing of his terror away, and Charlotte couldn't make out from his expression whether he was troubled or not.

But she *could* see the lads were looking about them and sniggering at a tall, upright man with greying black hair slicked back. Definitely a gentleman, he was wearing a shabby, old-fashioned suit, frayed at the edges, with a gold fob watch and chain in his waistcoat pocket. He had the air of a man who had once had money, but it was impossible to tell if he was from a posh or poor background. Linking arms with him was a woman of similar age; her thinning, almost transparent, blue-rinsed hair shone in the glow of the afternoon sun. The boys did no more than snigger at the couple, and Charlotte could see that Kenny was peering in their direction but, fortunately, didn't spot them through the screen of foliage. 'I think they're going to turn around,' she whispered.

Nathan wiped his brow with the back of his hand and breathed a sigh of relief. 'Yes, I think so too.' The boys sauntered away, going back through the open gateway and leaving the park with an air of despondency. This patch of greenery was not one they could be bothered with.

'The trouble with that lot is they're now finding out about the birds and the bees at school and it's messed up their thinking. They don't know what to do with themselves now that they're meant to be thinking about the facts of life,' said Charlotte.

'What are you talking about? I don't understand.'

'Well, up until recently any talk about sex at home just didn't happen, but not any more. Our parents are being encouraged to talk to us about things, aren't they.'

'I don't know,' said Nathan, 'but then my dad never held back where sex was concerned. I know most of what I need to know already.'

'Perhaps Jewish families are more open about that kind of thing. But now that we've got this education at school, these boys don't know whether they're supposed to be kicking a football or kissing a girl. Before now we were brought up to be ashamed of puberty. My mum still hides her box of sanitary towels even though I'll soon be starting my periods.'

Nathan was aghast at the thought. 'Urrgghh. You're making me feel sick. For God's sake, shut up.'

'Why? We shouldn't be ashamed. I read an article about it in a girl magazine. It all made sense so my fivepence wasn't wasted.'

'My grandmother once told me that I was never to have

anything to do with girls and I passed out when she explained what she meant and why she had said it.'

Charlotte laughed. She could see that Nathan was embarrassed and tried to think of something to change the subject. But then, all of a sudden there came from the overgrowth a pattering of warm raindrops that had settled on broad leaves earlier on after a light July shower. Laughing as they came out into the open to shake off the rain, they dusted themselves down then strolled through the grounds towards the public library. There, a glass of Welfare orange juice and a biscuit was served at this time of the day to school children, pensioners and tramps.

'I really wish I didn't have to hide from those fucking bastards,' said Nathan, pulling both hands into tight fists. 'It's bloody well getting on my nerves. I'm sick of them calling me a fat Jew boy and then putting the boot in.' He looked sideways at Charlotte to see that she was trapping laughter.

'Well, three cheers that you find it so amusing.'

'Oh shut up. Of course I don't. I'm just relieved that they've gone and you've got away without a kicking. It's when you swear that makes me want to laugh. I can't help it. You're just like your dad when he sounds off at you sometimes. And something else – I think you should tell your parents what's going on with the bullies.'

'There's no point. I think if I told Mum she might feel that I was making up stories and if I told Dad he would want to go up the school and let them know what's going on, and I don't want that.'

'I don't know about your dad, but your mum would never think you were making it up. She's not like that.'

'I don't care what you say, I don't want them to interfere. And as for swearing, my dad hardly ever says fuck in front of me and would go mad if he heard me saying it. He only does it when my brothers come. They sit and talk in the kitchen and swear. My mother would go potty if she heard what I hear at times.'

'Men always do that when they're together with no women about. You hear it going on all over the place. It's the way it's said I s'pose. Not angry but just part of the language.' She smiled. 'You did remind me of your dad though when you said it.'

'Well, I'm *bound* to, Charlotte! I'm his son! The only difference is that I'm a young Jew and he's an old one.'

'Oh, for Christ's sake! Will you let go of all of that Jew boy stuff? And it's not because you're Jewish that *they* start on you, it's because you react as if *that is* what they're doing. I remember right back to when we were six and you had a row with one of the boys in the playground. He called you a fat Jew boy and you went berserk in front of all the other kids watching. You ranted that if anyone else called you that you would pulverise him or her. So what did they do? They all chanted fat Jew boy. Remember?'

Nathan sniffed. 'I don't recall that. You must be thinking of someone else, it wasn't me.'

'Yes it was. And it was your own fault that they did it more and more. That lot behave like big kids and you should walk the other way when you see them. You should turn around and leave. They'll soon get bored with trying to lure you in. We've all turned thirteen going on fourteen, Nathan. We're not kids any more.'

'Tell me about it. I've not long since been through my barmitzvah.' He held up his hand. 'Don't ask!'

'I wasn't going to. And listen . . . I'm not gonna say it again after this. Right?'

'Whatever,' said Nathan, fed up with it all.

'You can't do anything about your religion but—'

'I don't *want* to do anything about it, thank you,' he snapped. 'I like being Jewish. All right?'

Looking into his face she could see that he was grinding his

15

back teeth and her heart went out to him. 'Of course you do. Why wouldn't you? But you don't like being fat, so do something about that. Every time I see you at school, in the playground or whatever, you're putting something into your mouth – a sandwich, sweets, crisps. You and a bag of chips go hand in hand.'

'That's *my* expression. You shouldn't steal other people's expressions.'

'Hand in hand?'

'Yes.'

'My grandparents have always said it. Don't change the subject.'

'I didn't know that your grandparents also said it. So you think I eat too much?'

'You *know* you do. And I've seen you hiding behind the caretaker's shed at school.'

'What if I was having a pee?'

'The boys' toilets are closer to the school than the caretaker's shed is. And before you make any excuses about the boys teasing you in there being the reason for you not using it, I've seen you go in and out lots of times.'

'So you've been spying on me then? Thanks. And if you really want to know, I would rather die than go on a diet. My mother keeps saying I should and my dad tells her to leave it be. He says that once I shoot upwards I'll be lean like him.'

'Well, it's up to you, it's your body. But I'll help you if you want me to.'

'You don't have to worry over me. You're not responsible for my welfare. It's not as if we're boy and girlfriend, is it?' He glanced slyly at her face hoping that she might blush, which would give him a little hope.

'We're mates, Nathan. Good friends. We go to the same school and we live in the same block and that makes us neighbours as well as best friends. Just because we're the opposite sex it doesn't mean to say that we've got to be going out together.'

'Who said it did? Did I say that?' Shaking his head in despair Nathan then gently laughed, and said, 'You are *so* old fashioned at times. I can't believe that you just said that. You watch too many free films at the cinema where your aunty works. Complimentary tickets might be your downfall.'

'Well, you don't turn down an "entrance free" when I get a spare one, do you?'

'That's true, but it's because I need to study all aspects of drama. I would rather your aunty worked in a local theatre that she could get free tickets for. But we can't have every-thing go our way.'

'Oh, not that again.'

'I can't help it. I've dreamt of being part of that world ever since I helped put on a children's show for parents at our Stepney Jewish club. You know that. I loved it. I was assistant stage manager don't forget. My dad said that that was quite an achievement for an eleven-year-old.'

'Maybe it was, but rather than harp on about it why don't you join a young people's theatre group? They run something like that at a disused church hall in Wapping.'

'We'll see,' said Nathan, 'we'll see.' He then broke into quiet laughter and said, 'Going out together? You and me? As if . . .' He gave Charlotte another sideways look, then, trying to make light of it, he fooled around by holding his arms out to her and singing loudly, 'Let me call you Sweetheart.' This was a line from a song that his father liked to sing to his mother now and then when larking around in the kitchen while she was cooking.

'You're mad, Nathan. Do you know that? Stark raving bonkers, and what's more I've got something to tell you.'

He waved a theatrical arm and said, 'I am all ears, your majesty . . .'

She gently took hold of his hand and smiled warmly. Then, swallowing against a lump in her throat said, 'It's a secret that my mum and dad don't want to get out. Not yet anyway. It's all to do with my grandparents and aunts who might start shouting the odds, saying that family should live where their roots are.'

Nathan showed a puzzled expression. 'Are you mad or what? Who gives a shit about roots? Especially those around this way. We live in a dump, Charlie.'

'It's not a dump but I'm glad you're okay about it.'

'About what? What are you talking about?'

Charlotte sucked on her bottom lip and then said, 'In a fortnight's time we're moving. Out of the East End. We're going to Norfolk. To live in a small country town called Bridgeford.'

'Norfolk? Bridgeford? Where in God's name is that?'

'I just told you. In the countryside, miles away, where they've built brand new council estates for Londoners. And from what I saw of the stuff they sent about it, cheap private houses are planned for people who want to buy their own property.'

Nathan slowly shook his head. 'Bridgeford? It's not even on the map.'

'Yes it is.' She stood looking at him as a few leaves swirled in the warm breeze. 'Mum and Dad are over the moon about it so I'm trying my best not to be down. I won't be going back to our school next term.'

After a horrible silence the two best friends looked at each other while a desperate thought ran through Nathan's mind. *What will I do without her*? 'If the piper calls,' he finally said, speaking in a quiet and croaky voice, 'then the troupe must follow.' He couldn't believe that the same thing could happen to him twice. The only other girl that he had cared about was his elder sister, Jacky, who had left him as well. He had missed her so badly it hurt. Now all that he could hope was that the old-fashioned saying where love was concerned – *Absence makes the heart grow fonder* – was a load of rubbish.

'Some friends of my parents are doing the selfsame thing,' he murmured. 'Except that they're going to Suffolk. To a town called Bury St Edmunds.'

'Well, that's not far from where we'll be living. Dad mentioned it more than once in the past because the firm where he works as an electrician will have a branch there too. Dad reckons that he'll get a bit of private work as well. Because of the new estates that are being built. He wants to work for himself eventually. We're going in for a transfer from our borough to Norfolk, so we'll be on a brand spanking new council estate. Can't be bad, can it?'

'No. My parents' friends will be living on a small quiet estate in a terraced house. They'll be getting a mortgage and all of that stuff. Barratt Homes I think is what my dad said. Maybe your parents should talk to them about where they'll be going?'

'There won't be time, Nathan. There's so much to do and arrange.'

Holding out his hand so as to shake his best friend's he only just managed to say, 'I hope you'll find it over the rainbow. The pot of gold.'

Charlotte pulled back and narrowed her eyes. 'I'm not gonna shake your hand you daft sod. We're friends not business people. But promise that you'll get yourself on a train and come to visit me?'

'I won't make promises. I hate it when people do that. Make them, and then break them.' He pinched his lips together and tried his best to smile as tears welled behind his eyes. With a broken voice he just managed to say, 'God go with you and your family.'

'And I wish the same to you and yours.'

'I think I'm going to need it,' he all but whispered as the recurring thought rolled across his mind. How could he possibly live each day without her being there? 'Will I see you before you leave?'

'Of course you will. We're not doing a moonlight flit. I just wanted you to know before the other neighbours. Mum will only have to tell her friend from next door and it will be all round the block.' She looked into his big, round and doleful warm brown eyes. 'Don't tell anyone though. Because of our relations.'

'I won't say a word. Although I might get the local paper to broadcast it.' He felt like crying but laughed a touch nervously instead.

'I'll write to you. You don't have to write back if you don't feel like it. I won't be offended.'

'I'm pleased to hear it because I won't write back. Old people send letters, not the likes of us. I will jump on a train and come visit you though.' He looked into her face again and pinched his lips together. 'It'll be a nice trip out for me. A few hours in the countryside. That I *can* cope with. Just.' He pushed his hands into his pockets and looked down at the ground as he slowly walked onwards.

'You realise that you'll be leaving all of your old friends behind, Charlie,' he murmured, 'and so will your parents be. But I'm sure they must have considered all of this.'

'Probably, but I'd rather not think about it. I've always hated change of any kind. They plan to get rid of Trinity Square you know. Knock down my aunt Sheila's house.' Her gaze fell to the ground. 'They're going to pull all the lovely old almshouses down to make room for another small council estate.'

'There's nothing wrong with that. It's called progress. We all have to move with the times. As a matter of fact, I'm going to join the local drama group next week, so in a sense I'll be taking a step forward. I've always fancied the idea of being somebody else on stage.'

'I didn't know that – why didn't you say earlier when I suggested it? I think it's a great idea. You'll make new friends.'

'Maybe.'

The two of them went quiet and little else was said as they made their way towards the library, each of them immersed in their own thoughts. Thoughts of how it was becoming a scary and fast-changing world. More importantly, where Nathan was concerned, very soon he would only be able to murmur Charlotte's name to himself because she would be gone. And while he was thinking this, she was trying not to think about the sad fact that she was going miles away – and not just for a fortnight or so, but forever.

A silence hung in the air until she spoke in a quiet husky voice. 'I can't say that I won't cry because I will. I'll miss all of this, Nathan. I'll miss you as well.'

Too gutted to think straight he held firmly onto the only bit of bravery that he could muster. 'Everything, with the exception of a ring, comes to an end at some point. None of us will be in this area for always I don't suppose.' He slipped his hands into his pockets and looked anywhere but at her face. 'And we're all bound to miss each other. You'll be gone for too long but there's nothing we can do about that. You'll be gone forever in fact.'

'Maybe. But I might not like living in the sticks very much.'

'You're bound to like it.' The lad pushed a hand through his short black curly hair and forced back the tears. Write me a letter as soon as you get there.'

'Of course. I'll write straight away. You're my best friend.' Her lips parted in a smile, and Nathan wasn't sure whether this was purely from friendship or whether the expression might possibly be laced with love. But the look on *his* face as they observed each other said it all. He worshipped her.

'The only good thing to come out of this is that Mum whispered to me that if I was good and didn't make a fuss and kept the secret then she would buy me some slingback shoes and a handbag to match – once we've settled into the new house. But what good will they be then? I'd look daft walking along country lanes and rivers all done up with nowhere to go.'

'You don't have to go. You could live with your grand-parents, you know how fond you are of them. And you never know . . . when you leave . . . it might be the last time you'll see them alive.'

'They're only in their early sixties. That's not old.'

'Well, maybe not, but you won't be seeing much of them will you. Not with all of those miles in between. It stands to reason.'

'You don't have to tell me. I already know it. I'm just gonna have to make the most of things. Mum and Dad can't wait to go. I've never seen them so happy as this before, so if they think it's a brilliant thing to do it must be . . . mustn't it?'

'If you say so.' He shrugged exactly the way his father did. 'Then it must be. But don't abandon me altogether.'

Charlotte could see that he was crushed by the whole idea of her not being there for him. She didn't want to leave. She didn't want to say goodbye to any of it. She didn't want to have to get used to different grocery shops and markets and a baker that probably wouldn't be Jewish so there would be no beigels for tea. No more beigels and no more going into the local sweet shop with the wooden floor that she had been in and out of since she could walk with reins. She could hardly bear the thought of it, but she was going to have to. It was now set in stone.

'You make sure you join that drama group like you said. You love being in the school plays and the Christmas shows.'

'That's true. And it's what the drama teacher keeps on saying as well. Maybe that's what I'll do. Act my way through life.'

Charlotte laughed fondly at him. 'No. Act your way through plays on the stage and live your life the way you want to.'

Two

Five Years Later

Enjoying a pint in a nearby pub in Bridgeford where he, his wife Rita and daughter Charlotte now lived, Eddie Blake thought that he recognised someone across the bar from back home in London. Peering discreetly over his pint glass at the lad, who looked to be about the same age as his daughter, he tried to think where he might have run into him.

The tall, skinny youth, with dark auburn hair cut in the Beatles style, seemed a touch on the flash side and wasn't the type that Charlotte would have had as a boyfriend, but for some reason when Eddie looked at him he thought of her. He wondered if the lad had been part of their earlier life in the East End. Resting his elbow on the bar and leaning discreetly forward so as to catch his accent, Eddie smiled inwardly. The kid was a true-blue Cockney all right and a Jack the lad with it, and as far as he could tell he had cold-hearted thief written across his forehead.

'Live and let live,' he told himself as he drained his glass. But then, when he glanced across the bar again, the penny dropped as to just who it was in the same pub as himself so many miles from both of their roots. It was that flash little bastard, Kenny Wood, always known as Ginger, who had lived in the same block of flats as his own little family. He wasn't best pleased to see him there. Kenny's dad was a good bloke, but the lad had spelt trouble since he had been knee-high. Bridgeford was a small town, and Eddie hoped that this young man, who had always been a lying little toad, hadn't settled here. His hair had changed with age and was now a dull red but he still wore the same old troublemaker expression. He decided not to let on to Rita that Kenny used the pub because she would only stop going in there. As much as he loved his wife she was a bit of a worrier, and a snob on the quiet.

Catching Eddie's eye, Kenny peered at him and then half smiled as he showed a hand, saying, 'All right, mate?'

'Good as gold, son. You?'

'Not so bad.' Kenny grinned. 'You look familiar. Do I know you?'

'I don't think so.' Eddie placed his empty pint glass down on the bar and winked at him. 'Stay lucky,' he said and then turned away and sauntered out of the pub. He didn't want to get on friendly terms.

'I'm sure I know that face,' murmured the eighteen-year-old to one of the men that was keeping him company – a professional gangster who wore a dark blue serge suit and heavy gold cufflinks.

'Well, maybe – just like you – he's moved up 'ere to find out what a fucking dump it is,' said the man as he narrowed his eyes and drew on his small cigar.

'Each to their own, Albert,' Kenny chuckled. He was a touch miffed by the way the two men he was drinking with were knocking the town into which he had recently arrived. 'What's it to be then, boys? Chinese takeaway or fish and chips?'

'Neither.' One of the partners in crime shook his head, sighed, and then said with a smile, 'You should 'ave moved to Haverhill, son, instead of this fucking dump. What on earth brought you up 'ere?'

'What brought me up 'ere? What d'yer think? Or can you see the Old Bill crawling all over the place?'

'Get to the point, Kenny.'

'I am getting to the point, all right? The country coppers are just as slow on the uptake as the country bumpkins are. You could rob a fucking bank in broad daylight and they wouldn't notice. And anyway, an old mate of mine who joined the army is stationed close by. He put me on to a cheap flat and I've not looked back.' He grinned. 'I'm on the dole, you know, and I get quite a bit of work painting and decorating, cash in hand. And I do big favours for the local criminal fraternity when they can't find anyone wiv guts and a bit of *savoir faire* . . .' He tapped the side of his head and grinned to get his point across. The point being that he thought he was brighter than they were. 'I pick up a few nice little earners that keep the pockets lined, and as for that shit hole Haverhill, don't be too sure. You can't always tell a book by its cover you know. There are more pubs in this town than there is there.' He saw the guy glance up at a sign on the wall and then smile wryly.

Kenny turned to look at it and then shrugged. 'Who the fuck wants to jive or bop in any case.'

'That's my point, son,' said Albert. 'Even the outdated sign is a turn-off. You need to go elsewhere at your age. This is a pub for thirty-year-olds and over.'

'What, and you reckon that Haverhill's full of night life do yer? You'll be lucky.' Kenny sniggered.

'It's a lot closer to London, son, and that was the point I was making.' Albert checked his gold Rolex wristwatch and then eyed his friend. 'We'd best be on our way.'

'And don't forget boys,' said Kenny with an overly familiar wink. 'If the post office job goes well you can count me in for other work in London or in Essex. I'm not fussy. And I can handle a shooter, no problem.'

'We'll bear that in mind,' said one of the men with a knowing look at the other.

'Good.' Kenny winked again and grinned. 'Because I'm not as wet behind the ears as I make out. I can't please everyone all of the time it's true . . . but can any of us? But I won't let you down.' He smiled at Albert and then gave a cheeky wink at the other, Tony, who was an Italian born and bred in London and who, from the expensive perfumed aftershave he was wearing, Kenny presumed had a penchant for toyboys . . .

'We'll see. You've not got your diploma yet, sunshine.' Albert looked from Kenny to his Italian friend, who was also wearing a made to measure suit and handmade shoes and who now had the look of murder in his eyes. 'In this game big fish eat little fish. Don't forget, it's the way of the world. Take it slow, son, and take it easy with the mouth.'

In the eyes of the two professionals, lads like Kenny were two a tanner unless they showed promise: that they would be able to shoot to kill should the need arise. Each of them was of the opinion that most dogs had the right to at least one bite – but not this flash little upstart. The expression on each of their faces told the other that they should give this one the elbow. Leaning towards his friend, Tony whispered in his mate's ear. 'It's true you can't always tell a book by its cover, but I think we can with this moron. Come on. Let's get out of this pisshole. I'm starving.'

With just one look his friend told him that he couldn't agree more. Leaving the pub, all three of them got into a brand new Jaguar saloon, with Kenny in the back seat. The upstart still had Charlotte's dad, Eddie, on his mind. 'I'm sure I know that bloke from somewhere,' he said.

'What bloke?' Albert asked as he pulled the front passenger door shut.

'The one I spoke to at the bar! Who else? I just can't place 'im. It'll come to me though. In time.'

'If that's the case,' said Tony from the driver's seat, 'you'd best leave Bridgeford. Forget the post office job, you don't want to risk anyone sucking up to the country coppers. The bloke had a good view of all three of us which would 'ave been fine if you hadn't started to rabbit like an old woman. Fancy asking if you knew 'im. You've got a lot to learn, son.'

'Nah, I was acting natural. You two need to chill out a bit more. Take a leaf out of my book.'

Sighing loudly, Tony slowly shook his head and pulled away from the pub car park. The silence that filled the space said it all. The kid was no more than a tadpole in a pool of sharks. He had a long way to go before they would even think of letting him go on a job with them, never mind arranging one himself, which had been the suggestion thrown at them. After this drink with him, set up by the boy's father, they were already striking him off their list. He couldn't even be trusted as a messenger any more. The boy had been useful in the past as a kind of a runner, but it was time to give him his marching orders. It also seemed prudent to give his dad a bit of advice as to the way his son behaved. His dad, who was a distant cousin, needed to be told that his son would be better sticking with the family tradition of carpet fitting.

The flash little sod was, after all, from a different era to these men. They had been through the Teddy Boy period of rebellion; they had drunk at Ronnie Scott's jazz club and smoked marijuana through all-night sessions of trad and modern jazz. In the afternoons they had enjoyed Italian-style espresso in coffee bars while listening to the jukebox or live music. They had been there in the early Fifties at Mocha in Frith Street and then in Heaven and Hell in Old Compton Street. They had mixed with young aspiring actors, artists, designers and students, and the only difference with them and their own kind was that they sat back and inwardly laughed at those demonstrating around Trafalgar Square and campaigning to ban the bomb.

They still drank at Ronnie Scott's and spent time in the all-night coffee bars, rubbing shoulders with the rich so as to be able to steal from them. They pretended to be cool while they weighed up how best to extract wealth from the wealthy –

and it had paid off. And because of all of this, they, and several other gangsters like them, had got used to a certain way of living and their standards were high. Fledglings like Kenny from the old East End were seen as boy servants until they had proved themselves, and very few ever did. To make it as professional and respected criminals, who could mingle with society and the famous, it took more than a decent suit and polished shoes. Men and women of their ilk had to have that extra something that couldn't be bottled or go on sale in a supermarket. And the kid didn't have it.

The telling thing about Kenny as far as they were concerned, was that he had told them in the pub that he liked the old town of Bridgeford and loved the ancient buildings and narrow back streets. He had whispered that it reminded him of Dickens and pickpockets and Fagin. He was no Oliver Twist, he had said, but he fancied himself as Fagin, all nicely set up with a team of thieves to steal for him. Even apart from these infantile fantasies, he was right out of the picture where they were concerned.

But Kenny wasn't quite as wet behind the ears as he had made out. The two men, comfortable in the front of the dark blue Jag with the leather seats, had not picked up on the fact that he had no intention of working for them. It had been enough for him to be seen in their company in that popular pub where some of the flash boys drank and the old locals kept away. He felt that he had notched up a gold star or two by drinking with London gangsters of their ilk.

He had had no intention from the start of arranging a post office break-in, but had simply dangled the idea as a carrot. He had merely been laying the foundation for his own plans. He wanted to be in on their little meetings when strategy was being worked out and listen and learn from it. Then, after a short spell, he could back down and show fear and trepidation or whatever else would convince the jerks that he was too young and too chicken for them. He had wanted to spend as much time in their company as he could. Then, when the time was right, he would grass on them before an important bit of illegal business took place. He would take a nice little earner from one of several palm-greasers in the London force. Men who he had been tipping off about certain planned robberies since he was fourteen, and from whom he had received decent pocket money for his efforts. And the best of it all, to Kenny's mind, was that he knew he had one up on the flash boys who saw themselves as top-notch gangsters. Yes, he had every intention of grassing on them when the time was right. How could he be blamed for grinning into their faces in the pub? He had been one step ahead of them all along.

Smiling in the silence that the two in the front were creating, he had to stop himself from laughing out loud. He knew that their minds were turning over the question as to whether or not to take him on. The joke was that people in their profession needed faceless risk takers and the stupid bastards, from what he could tell, had him down as someone they could use. Just so as to keep them in an easy mood Kenny sighed contentedly and then said, 'This is a nice car, boys. It's always been my dream to own one of these. I don't care what task you set me. Nothing's too risky where I'm concerned. I respect you two more than I respected the headmaster at senior school. And I'm telling you – he was a wicked bastard with that cane. Hard as nails. I loved 'im.'

This final spurting of verbal diarrhoea from someone who the men saw as a little shit slammed the door shut as far as these two timeworn villains were concerned. They glanced at one another and then at Kenny via the rearview mirror to see that the lad was, in his own pathetic way, gloating.

'How's the carpet-fitting business going, son?' said Tony as he glanced at him in his rear mirror.

'It's all right. Keeps a bit of butter on the bread and the law off my back.' He grinned and then chuckled in his usual irritating way. 'It's an honest to goodness trade, innit? And an easy way to suss out who's got what tucked away in the bottom drawer. Some of them Jews that me and Dad work for are fucking loaded. Wads of notes in the bottom drawer. Money they've earned but not paid tax on. I do all right on the quiet. Don't tell the old man though or he'll cut me dead. Too fucking honest for 'is own good at times. He'll die a poor man if he don't wise up a bit.'

The somewhat hushed atmosphere in the car, reminiscent of a church before a service, was sending the wrong message to the eighteen-year-old. He actually thought that he was winning the hardened criminals over and that they were all ears. 'I'd rather work for you two than fit carpet for Jews. Their houses stink of fried fish. But there you are. If I hadn't of been born on the border of Stepney and Bethnal Green I would never 'ave met the likes of you two. We're third cousins removed, ain't we?'

'If it wasn't for your old man, son,' said Albert, 'you wouldn't be sitting in this car. Show a bit of respect.'

'My dad's all right,' he said, missing the point. 'Goody two shoes, but there you go. Someone's gotta walk the straight an' narrow, ain't they?' He went quiet and thoughtful. 'Mind you, he and Mum are not as innocent as he likes to make out. The cupboard in their bedroom would make your eyes pop out at times. A dozen solitaire diamond rings was brought in last year. I sold on three of 'em in a week. I 'ave to be careful though. I'm the sort that them fucking newspaper writers love to get an angle on when they wanna write about the criminal fraternity in the East End. Dozy bastards.'

'They weren't diamond rings, son – they were zircons and sold out at a fiver each.' The driver quietly laughed. Tony and Albert knew his dad well and liked him. They glanced at each other and contained their frustration with each of them thinking similar thoughts, that Kenny was either a penny short of a shilling or totally full of crap. 'I don't know why I've lost my appetite,' said Tony, 'but I have.'

30

'Me as well,' said Albert. 'We'll eat once we get to Haverhill.'

'Ah well, you'll 'ave to count me out on that little trip. I can't stand that place. Fucking Haverhill, do me a favour.' Kenny started to snigger again, and when he heard the despairing sigh of the driver he let it go over his head. He was enjoying his own little bit of games playing with two men who could put the fear of God into the criminals in the underworld but couldn't ruffle his feathers. He returned the sound of clearing of the throats from the elders with more irritating quiet laughter and only just stopped himself from calling them jerks.

Needless to say he wasn't in the least bit put out when the car pulled up outside the dingy wireless shop in a side street beneath the run down self-contained furnished flat that he was renting. A flat that consisted of a box room with an old-fashioned bed and sagging mattress and a single wardrobe, as well as a tiny sitting room and a makeshift kitchen on the landing. This was his home. His castle. A place where he could be self-sufficient and answer to no one, and be able to pay in advance the rent of two pounds a week all inclusive. His dad, not knowing that his son earned a decent bit from grassing to the law, had been more than pleased to lend him some money to start a new life in Norfolk. Or Suffolk. Or Kingdom Come. He had been glad to see the back of him in the same way that he had been glad to see the back of his mother when she walked out on them earlier on in life. She soon drifted back into the fold, though, once she started to miss her son and heard that he had been pining for her. Kenny had been a bit of a mother's boy and still was, if truth be told.

Kenny had loved his mother so much when he was small and it hurt worse than anything could when she left him. He was just seven at the time. The only reason he caught the train back to old Bethnal Green now and then was to see her. His dad was all right. He liked him well enough, but he just couldn't forgive him for encouraging his mum to go out on the game earlier on in life. She had earned good money though – before age caught up with her and younger prostitutes took over her patch.

Looking from one of the London gangsters to the other Kenny detected a sense of boredom. He knew that the swanky bastards were about to dump him without an offer to work for them, but decided he didn't give a fuck. To his mind they would always be morons and not worth his time and attention.

Coasting past the Bridgeford post office about which he had already given them details as to when cash was normally delivered, the two men burst out laughing. It was useless information and a joke as far as they were concerned, but the trip had not been a complete waste of time. They had wanted to check out this small town that was now being whispered about as being the next generation small-time underworld and a place to lie low when the need arose. It was no more than a backwater town as far as they could see but they weren't sorry that they had made the journey. The men owed a favour to the lad's father, who sometimes did a little bit of work for them on the quiet and had asked if they might think of using his son Kenny for better paid work. They had seen him, bought him a drink or two and had a chat, and that was more than enough. They didn't like the way he was turning into a self opinionated little upstart and they couldn't wait to get on the road back to the East End.

Three

One week later, and Charlotte was waking up to the familiar sound of a squirrel that came and went from its nearby habitat, the grounds of a boarded-up mansion house that had seen better days. She smiled sleepily and peered at her bedside clock. It had only just turned seven a.m. and she still had thirty minutes or so before her alarm went off. Snuggling down into her bedding she slipped back into a light sleep. She felt sure that she had been dreaming about the little furry creature, as she had done several times before at this time of the morning. She knew that it was a squirrel scrabbling on the roof tiles that had woken her but she didn't mind in the least bit. The furry creatures that reminded her of the Beatrix Potter picture books was something that had helped her bond with her surroundings ever since the day that she and her parents had moved into this old Victorian terrace house, three up, two down. A house that had an old-fashioned kitchen with a scullery attached.

Charlotte made a mental note to place a few more dried shelled walnuts, left over from the previous Christmas, into a cracked dish that she had placed at the very end of their back garden, and then pulled her white cotton sheet over her head. She wanted to stay in this cosy half awake mood, trying to picture what her surroundings might have been like when the grounds on which her parents' house now stood had been part and parcel of a mansion house – a building now in a dire state and badly in need of restoration. The one good thing that she could say about the small town in which she now lived was that it was steeped in history and, from what she had read and heard, it had once been a much livelier place.

She had learnt from an old boy called Eric, who was born and bred in the area, that there had once been a theatre in the centre of the town, opposite the Queen's Head pub, which had been built in the distant past by a large family of actors and comedians. Her thoughts turned to Nathan, and she recalled how he had often said that he would rather be involved in the unreal world of theatre than the cruel world of real life. The last time that she had heard from him a couple of years since, he had written to say that he had joined another theatre group and spent his free time and most weekends working with actors and others involved in little theatres. He had started as a runner and was, according to his final letter, an assistant stage manager during weekends and some evenings.

The lovely small theatre in Bridgeford had closed down a century and a half ago, but by all accounts it had boasted a good company of excellent actors from all over the country. She hugged her warm pillow and tried to imagine her lovable friend in costume, giving his all on stage. She made a vow there and then to get in touch with Nathan sooner rather than later to see what he was up to. She wondered if he was now frequenting discotheques and nightclubs like others of their age who lived in the capital. She couldn't imagine him on a dance floor. The thought of it made her smile.

With one picture of her old life coming after another, she felt a glow spread through her. No matter how unhappy she was at times, nothing and nobody could take away Charlotte's memories. Even though she had been out of the East End and living in Norfolk for five years, she still pined for everything and everyone she once knew. The truth of the matter was that she had never got over having to leave

London, but she did have those treasured memories. They were hers, and they were tucked in a safe place inside her head and in her heart. Wrapped in her warm bedding and submerged in reminiscence, she didn't hear the bedroom door open. It was her dad coming in to get her up.

'Time to get up, sweetheart. I've just made a fresh pot of tea. D'you want your mother to fetch a cup up?' Eddie said with his usual smile on his face and warmth in his voice, even though his thoughts were with work and the jobs that he had lined up for the day: fitting in private work in between the hours he put in for the company he worked for. His dream was to be his own boss and have his own successful business one day.

'I'll be down in a sec,' said Charlotte, slow and sleepy and not best pleased with the intrusion. 'Is there any cut bread for toast in the bin?'

'No. Your mum used the last of it for my sandwiches, but there's still a loaf of uncut that she bought at the bakers yesterday. You're a big girl now. You can cut a couple of slices with the big bad bread knife.' Quietly chuckling he left her to her early morning pillow.

Downstairs, Eddie downed the last drop of tea from his cup and checked himself in the large modern mirror on the wall in the passage. He had fitted it himself, and loved the way that it reflected light from the stained glass panels in the top half of the old pine front door. He was smartly dressed and smelt of decent after-shave; he took pride in his appearance and outfitted himself according to the day and the customers that he would be looking after. He was also proud that his daughter, his only child, took after him where looks were concerned. His blond hair had of course darkened a little over the years, but there was no doubting as to where his Charlotte had got her colouring and her light blue eyes.

Always ambitious and heading for the top of the tree, Eddie

had been pleased enough about his recent promotion to a managerial position for the electricity board. Even so, to him this was just another stepping stone to the top. He spent most of his working days going from one site to another, inspecting the work of less experienced electricians until his day ended around four o'clock. He would then return home and change from his suit into smart casuals and spend another three hours or so with his private customers. After that, he would pop into his local and favourite pub for a pint or two before going home for his evening meal. This was Eddie's routine and this was what kept the bank figures in the black.

Rita, his attractive wife, had lovely green eyes and dark auburn shoulder-length hair, and was employed as a receptionist with plenty of clerical work to keep her busy. She loved her work at the nearby Bridgeford Cottage Hospital. When the family had first moved into the small town, Rita had passed an interview for the position with flying colours. She almost lived for her work and, more than anything else, had enjoyed going around in her free time to chat with and cheer up the in-patients. Then, a year previously, the wards were closed down to allow the hospital to cope with the ever-growing influx of outpatients who were coming with their families to settle in the town.

Still in her dressing gown, Rita was carefully painting her nails a creamy orange. Glancing at her wrist watch to check that time was not running on too fast, she went to the bottom of the staircase and was just about to call up to Charlotte when Eddie said, 'I've already nudged her, she'll be down in a minute. I'll see you around seven.'

'No you won't. I'm going to the indoor swimming pool, remember?'

'Oh yeah, keeping fit and all of that. It's a pity you don't get Charlotte to go with you. She spends too much time on 'er own.'

'If she wanted to come with me she would, Eddie. She enjoys her own company. You should know that by now.'

Looking into his wife's face, he sighed then turned to leave. They had been down this road before, but the more often he said that his girl needed to get out and about, the tetchier Rita would get. Just as he was about to open the front door Charlotte came down the stairs and said, 'Hang on a minute, Dad. I've got something for you.'

'Oh? And what's that?' said Rita, who was now standing in the open doorway of the kitchen.

Paying no attention to her mother, Charlotte put her arms around her father and spoke in a quiet voice, saying, 'I haven't got anything other than a kiss for you, Dad, but I wanted to say stop worrying about me. I'm all right.' She then kissed him on the cheek and could see that he was a bit choked. 'Honest to God – I'm fine.'

'I know that, sweetheart.' He smiled and winked at her. 'I'll be in my local around seven if you fancy popping in for a Babycham.'

'All right,' she said, returning his smile, 'I just might do that. If I've not turned up by eight o'clock you'll know I'm not coming. Is that okay?'

'Good as gold. See you later.' With that he nodded at Rita, opened the street door and left the house.

Looking into the hall mirror now that her nail varnish had dried, Rita swiped on her favourite pale apricot lipstick and glanced sideways at her daughter. 'Cheeky sod. As if you'd walk into a pub by yourself as bold as brass. What if you missed one another?'

'You mean if I went in and he wasn't there?' Charlotte shrugged. 'I'd walk out again, Mum. I'm not eight years old, I'm eighteen, and I have got a brain between my ears.'

'And you've also got something between your legs that men in pubs would like to have a go at.'

'Cheers for that. It's nice to think of myself as a walking come-on for dirty old men.'

'A horny young man is what I meant. It wasn't intended as an insult. You're too sensitive, that's your trouble.'

'So you've said. I'm gonna cut some bread and make some toast. Do you want some?'

'No, I had some Weetabix. And anyway I promised to go into work a bit earlier than usual. One of the girls is out sick.' She dropped her lipstick in her make-up bag and snapped it shut. 'Right. Just enough time for me to go up and throw some clothes on.' She gave Charlotte a peck on the cheek and then smiled at her. 'Would you like to come swimming, sweetheart?'

'Maybe. I'll think about it. I used to hate going with the school, you know I did, but . . . now that I'm free of rules and regulation, maybe I would enjoy it. Free will and all that.'

'Well, the offer's there. It's up to you. The group that I meet up with would like to meet you, I'm sure, and a bit of fun gets the boring jobs done – as your gran always used to say.'

'She still says it. And thanks, Mum. I'll dig out my old swimming costume next week and see if it still fits me.'

'Even if it does, Charlotte, I think it might be time for a new one. A good one that shows off your figure. We don't want the swimming club to think that we can't afford to move with the fashion, do we?'

'No, that would never do!'

Tilting her chin, Rita narrowed her eyes. 'Don't be facetious. Your dad relies on the sort of friends I make for us. Some of them have very big houses and some have husbands who run their own companies, and your dad needs all the right contacts he can make.' She then cupped her daughter's chin with her hand. 'One day we'll be living in a big country house, babe. You see if we won't.'

'I like this one. It's homely.'

'It's a stepping stone, Charlotte. A stepping stone.'

That lunchtime, with the sun on her face, Charlotte sat on an old bench on the river bank, eating her cheese and Branston Pickle sandwiches and fancying herself on a narrowboat with a handsome guy at the helm. She imagined herself with a good-looking young man wearing a straw boater and striped jacket, just like she had seen in films. Daydreaming herself into one romantic flight of fancy or another was a way of passing time as well as blocking out the reality of her life in this small town where nothing ever seemed to happen. She was taking her lunch break from the local borough offices where she was employed as a copy typist for little more than half as much as she would earn in London, her hometown that she still so badly longed for. Shuddering as if a ghost had walked across her grave, she pushed all thoughts of her old life from her mind as she had done a thousand times before. She knew from experience that wishing to turn back the clock only served to make her feel as if her childhood and upbringing with her cousins, her aunts and uncles, her grandparents and friends, had been obliterated in one clean sweep.

A touch on the low side for no apparent reason other than that she was lonely she told herself to get a grip. Even though she had been on a few dates soon after a four-month uneventful courtship had ended, she still felt as if there was something missing in her life, but didn't quite know what it was. Looking about her, she tried to shake off another wave of the loneliness that came and went but always left a horrible empty void in her chest. She could see couples, and others in small groups, sitting on the grassy banks on either side of the river and deep down knew then – as she had known for a while – what her problem was. She also knew that wishing was not going to make a dream come true. Ever since she had come to Norfolk with her parents, she had hoped that sooner or later some of her old school chums from the East End would leave London for a new life and come to Bridgeford.

But this, it would seem, was not meant to be. Five long years had already passed and there had been no sign of a familiar face from back home.

When she saw the lovely smiling face of Mavis, a village woman who was strolling towards her and who worked in the same building as she did, Charlotte felt a grey cloud lifting. Smiling back, she raised a hand in greeting.

'I'm just on my way to the post office, Charlotte. Did you want me to get you anything while I'm by the shops, dear?'

'No, thanks,' said Charlotte. 'I thought you was gonna sit by the river and eat your lunch.'

'Well, I should like to, dear, but needs must. I shall tomorrow though, and that's a promise.' With that, the woman who always seemed to be smiling continued on her way with a wistful Charlotte watching her go. So in need of someone to talk to, Charlotte quietly repeated something that she had heard as a child, which kept her going when she was in this lonesome kind of mood. 'No one feels sorry for those who feel sorry for themselves.'

Swallowing against the lump in her throat, she looked around at the trees and the riverside shrubs and reminded herself that she was lucky to be living in beautiful surround-ings in the heart of old Bridgeford. Her grandparents, Nell and Johnny, had told her more than once that, if she found that she couldn't settle in Norfolk, she could return to the East End and live with them in Bromley-by-Bow once she was eighteen. Deep down she knew that they had always felt sure that she would want to return. Just thinking about her nan made her smile, and she remembered what she had said to her on the quiet: 'Even if your mother and father are as happy as pigs in shit living as if they was countryside born and bred, you don't 'ave to put up with it. Get yourself back down 'ere before depression sinks in if you don't like the life up there.' Thinking about the few words that had followed this, Charlotte smiled as it all came flooding back. 'Bridgeford?

It's not even on the fucking map,' her nan had said. But then she always did have something to say.

Of course Norfolk was on the map and of course her Nan knew this. But at the time of their departure, even though on the surface she had shown a temperate face, Nell's heart was breaking. On the occasional visits that Charlotte had made with her parents to London during these last five years, they had gone down in her dad's van and then later on in his new grey Anglia car. It was at such times that Nan had taken her to one side and hammered it home that if she missed the atmosphere that she had grown up in and the people that she had lived amongst, she would get her granddad to wallpaper the spare bedroom. And not only this, but to lay new carpet. This comforting thought of being able to go back home to her roots had kept Charlotte going, but recently it was doing more than this. It was becoming more and more likely. A day didn't seem to pass when she wasn't seeing herself back in the capital, living and working in the centre of things. This dream was consuming her thoughts when alone and was becoming more of a fact of life rather than an option to be considered. Deep down she knew that she was going to have to go back home if she wanted to wake up content in the mornings.

Four

Charlotte was the only grandchild from Nell and Johnny's only daughter, Rita, who had married her childhood sweetheart, the lovely Eddie. Nell was of the opinion that her granddaughter would return, but would not necessarily want to lodge with her and her granddad. She was prepared to accept and settle for this. If her beloved Charlotte wanted to share digs with people of her own age, Nell was prepared to swear with a hand on the Bible that she would not interfere in her life. She might drop in once or twice a week to be certain that the place was being kept clean, and maybe bring one of her famous steak and kidney pies, but this, she had told Charlotte, would be all.

Nell's husband, Johnny, had hardly ever missed a day in Spitalfields where he had worked, man and boy, since the age of fourteen. Now he was more than content to help out locally in the nearby markets – Whitechapel, Roman Road and Bethnal Green – ducking and diving and paying no tax. He always had been, and occasionally still was, happy enough to travel to and from Spitalfields in the wee hours of the morning for cash in hand. Charlotte's grandfather was as fit and active as a man ten years younger than he. He wasn't alone: there were several old boys like himself who, having worked since they were thirteen years old, were now garnering a bit of untaxed money. He had run his own little stall a few years after the end of the Second World War but it was too much like hard work. And now that the mood of being self-employed and independent was creeping through the working-class sector, he was leaving it to the young to go upwards and onwards.

Londoners had been, and still were, uprooting from war-damaged or run-down areas east, south and north of the Thames to go and settle in new houses in new and old country towns where housing estates were being built to accommodate the London overspill. And the evacuation was continuing as families were moving in their droves to Essex, Cambridge, Suffolk and Norfolk.

Even though Eddie and Rita had moved on since their arrival in Bridgeford and were now living in their own Victorian terraced house, they knew very well that Charlotte was not happy. She had said many times that, unlike them, she badly missed the atmosphere and the buzz of London, but for the first few years she had tried to keep up a pretence of liking Bridgeford for their sakes. She knew they were enjoying their new way of life and she didn't want to put a damper on it. They had, after all, joined a few groups and clubs and made friends of their own age and both were working full time. Her dad was taking on more and more private work as well as holding down his position as master electrician with a small team of younger men in his charge.

It had only taken her parents a year or so of living in a council house to save enough for the deposit on the modest house in which they were now living, one that was close to the railway station. Of course, there was still a huge gap between the affluent who didn't have to rely on work, and the rest of the country who did. Nevertheless, the mood was that the dream of a change for the better for the working classes was actually becoming a reality. Charlotte had heard the familiar Cockney accent here and there from the very day they had moved into the town, but still this hadn't compensated for her missing the buzz of things. Back home was where she wanted to be; shoulder-to-shoulder with those she had grown up around. She had tried to stop thinking about the simple things that she had once pined for since the day she left the East End as a thirteen-year-old.

Lying in bed at night listening to the sound of the sleeping countryside instead of the noisy old city, she could so easily bring to mind the faces of the regular London bus conductors; the men and women in their flat caps and uniforms, who were nearly always bright and happy as they dinged the bell just before the bus approached the next stop. She missed seeing her favourite smiling ticket collector with his ticket machine held to his body by a leather strap that went from shoulder to waist. She also missed nipping down the underground to catch the tube to her grandparents' house. And sometimes she longed to be able to breeze in and out of the Bethnal Green museum and the Whitechapel art gallery, where she and Nathan had once tormented the life out of the attendants until they agreed to let them in free of charge when they should have been slipping two pence into a slot in the turnstile.

She hungered for the picture palaces, the youth clubs and young people's lively pubs and, of all things, those familiar red double-decker buses. The epitome of old London town. At least she had come to terms with no longer being able to hear the old steam train on the railway track first thing in the mornings while still in her bed, because they were no longer running. But settling into Norfolk hadn't been easy because she hadn't made a best friend. And she still felt detached from the lifestyle that her parents had taken in their stride.

Rita and Eddie, being social animals, had immediately set about joining a team of card players who came to their house once a week. The only thing that Charlotte had been able to join was the local school. This she left when she was just fifteen and hadn't managed during her time there to bond with anyone. Now that she was earning her own living and could be independent if she wanted, she felt that she was seen by the locals as a mature young woman who should be engaged to be married. Quite a few country-born and bred girls of her age were.

Gazing into the river and settling for the fact that there wasn't going to be anyone around to talk to, Charlotte placed her handbag on the ground to use as a makeshift pillow. She then lay on the grass in the warm sunshine. At least she was making the most of the lovely weather, enjoying the sight of swans gliding lazily by, near where water was falling from sluice gates at the Old Water Mill. The mill had once been used for grinding coffee beans, her favourite beverage. According to the talk of the Bridgeford elders, the rich aroma of the roasting beans had once filtered through the air.

She could hear the laughter of boys who were swimming close by and felt a touch isolated from the life going on around her. The lads were splashing about, yelling to each other that they should make their way down to the wider part of the river where youngsters liked to lark around together and adults liked to sunbathe on the grassy banks. During her lunch break, on nice days like this, Charlotte often sat or lay in this spot where occasionally one or other of the girls or women who worked in the council offices would join her. Nowadays it made little difference whether they did or not because she had got used to being by herself.

She and Nathan had kept in touch by letter at first but this had gradually tailed off. She thought that this was probably because she hadn't anything new or interesting to tell him and her letters were dull. He, on the other hand, from the sound of his occasional letters was now immersed in London life, where things seemed to be changing all over the place. Families were still on the move while the heart of old London was being rebuilt in places that had been wrecked during the war. With her friend in her thoughts, she could hardly remember when their letters to each other had stopped. She had missed his at first, but when four or five months passed by

45

without a word she presumed that he had found himself a new life – perhaps even a sweetheart. She imagined Nathan going off every morning to work in an accountants' office, and smiled at the thought of him rushing to catch the train and dabbing his forehead with his familiar big white handkerchief. She could see him in her mind's eye, anxiously looking out of the window each time the train pulled into a station so as not to miss his stop.

Right up until she had left Bethnal Green her friend had always seemed to be hurrying towards or away from somewhere for no real reason. At other times, when she knocked on his door, she might find him neatly pressing his school trousers in between wiping his steamed-up glasses or adjusting them on his nose. Nathan had always been a good and thoughtful person and someone who shouldn't have been picked on. She recalled one of the worst times, when she had seen him from a distance in the park grounds. He had one hand against a tree and was looking about him when one of the bullyboys had suddenly stepped out, leaned towards him and spat in his face.

Drawing breath as she remembered the ghastly things he had had to put up with, she was warmed by the voice of an old boy drifting towards her. 'Look at that scruffy little old stray, Charlotte,' he said, as he strolled up to her, smiling. 'Course I knew straight away that our little old mongrel was a little too near the side of starving today, so I went up to the butcher's shop. I went in and I say to him, hev you got a few old bones with a little meat on. And do you know what? A new woman who was working at the counter thought thet I was a blooming old tramp. What d'yer say to thet then? Do I look that poor?' He quietly laughed.

'Of course you don't, Eric. And it was a lovely thing to do,' she said.

'Well, you can't jes' let the poor ole thing go hungry. I

46

shouldn't think any one of us would like to be a stray with no home to go to.'

'No, Eric,' she smiled. 'I shouldn't think we would.'

The old boy then tipped his cap at her and continued on his way, and whether he knew it or not he had lifted her spirits. Apart from anything else, she loved the sound of the broad Norfolk accent.

Her thoughts drifted back to Nathan. In a strange way old Eric, who was now shuffling along with his hands in his pockets, reminded her of Nathan – except of course that her friend would have been pretending that his attention had been taken elsewhere. There had been so many times when she had been at boiling point because of the way he had been intimidated. She still sometimes woke in a sweat at night after a bad dream to do with him. A dream of times such as when the leader of the pack would be standing outside the large school gates, arms folded, grinning and sniggering at Nathan. Nathan's only hope of escape at such times, before the boot went in, was that a parent might happen along to pick up an offspring. But seeing an adult nearby didn't always help. There had been one occasion when three goading lads had surrounded Nathan and a tall, well-built sports teacher strolled by. Too deep in a world of his own to grasp the situation, he had simply nodded at the boys and walked on.

Once he was out of sight and roaring away in his car, Nathan, her fainthearted friend, had been on the end of even worse abuse. As usual, he had removed his wonky National Health glasses to wipe them dry of steam and sweat, and resigned himself to an onslaught of fists and feet. On that occasion she strode forward, determined to help, but the boots had already gone in. Her only option then was to run and get help from inside the school building. By the time she had found a teacher and he had come running to the rescue, the boys had gone and Nathan was bleeding on the floor. Bleeding from the nose and doubled up in pain.

Even though Charlotte had managed to wipe most of this kind of thing from her mind, still she would sometimes wake in the night having had another nightmare to do with horrible scenes centred on her friend. Worse of all was the memory of Kenny the bully. Times when he had stared into Nathan's face, saying, 'Can you see us without the National Health specs, Four Eyes? Can you? Can you see us, Jew boy? Will you be able to see my fucking boot when I kick your face?'

'Of course I can see you,' had been his feeble stock answer. On one of those occasions tears had filled Charlotte's eyes when he had said, 'You're in Mr Spartan's class. He's very strict, isn't he?' Nathan's pathetic attempt at trying to befriend the bastards had never worked but simply fuelled their desire to draw blood. She had seen him humiliated at the end of one vicious attack, when he had been booted in the crutch as a farewell gesture, and all he had said was, 'Please may I have my specs back now?'

Pushing one of the boys out of the way, nervous but angry, Charlotte had squeezed herself between Nathan and the bully. She stared into the bully's face saying, 'Come on. Punch me in the face! Come on! You pick on boys with glasses when they're alone, so you're capable of beating up a girl. Kick *me* black and blue . . . and then see what everyone at school thinks of you. You lousy rotten cowardly bastard!'

This had taken the heat out of things, but there had been other times he had suffered just as much when the gang had found him wandering around by himself. But at least the flash boy on that occasion had been belittled by having a girl challenge him in front of his pack. His response had been to walk away, calling Charlotte all kinds of names, then turn and stick up two fingers at her. Once they had all drifted away, Nathan had made a fist and told Charlotte that he had just been about to put the boot in when she came along. His noble attempts at bravery still brought tears to her eyes. But all of this was history, and the last time he wrote, he was fine. He was working as a junior in an accountancy firm in Bishopsgate and of course he was involved in the theatre group.

The more Charlotte thought about Nathan, the more she fancied the idea of paying a surprise visit to see how he was faring. She could afford to buy a second-class train ticket to London and knew that she could sleep over at her grandparents' house whenever she wanted. She wondered what Nathan might look like now, five years on. The only thing about her that had changed was that her natural blonde hair was no longer cut in the urchin style but was shoulder-length with a thick straight fringe to her eyebrows. She was a few inches taller of course, and a little curvier, and she wore eye-shadow, mascara and pale apricot lipstick. But deep down, the same old adventurous Charlotte was in there and desperate to spread her wings.

She wanted to write to Nathan, but felt that no matter how she worded her letter he was bound to pick up on her true feelings, realise that she was getting in touch because she was lonely. She didn't want pity, but she did want to see him again. And she wanted to see his wonderful parents, who had invited her into their home from the first week of the family moving into the block of flats when she and Nathan had been playing jacks on his doorstep. Forcing back tears, she drew breath and ordered herself to stop all this. To stop re-living the past just because the present was so lonely and her only contact with like-minded people of her own age seemed to be through the television. Programmes such as *Juke Box Jury* and *Top of the Pops*. On the walls of her bedroom she had posters of the Beatles, the Kinks and the Rolling Stones. Deciding there and then that this being a Friday, when her parents would be in their local with friends, enjoying their regular end of the working week night out, she would phone Nathan come what may.

*

49

Later, alone in the house again, Charlotte was sipping hot milky Ovaltine from her special mug. She had the television on for a bit of company but with the sound down low. Curled up in an armchair, she was thinking again of her old life and Nathan and was suddenly spurred to take action. She drained her cup, then went to the telephone in the hall and dialled his number, picturing the look on his face when he heard her voice.

She had no idea why her stomach should be churning other than a thought which crossed her mind – that Nathan and his parents, like so many other families, her own included, might have moved out of the East End. And that this was perhaps the reason why his letters had stopped. If this was the case, then she was going to have to face up to the fact that she had lost touch with a close and trusted friend, someone that she had over the years seen as a brother that she loved. The receiver pressed against her ear, she prepared herself for a stranger on the other end of the line. But her fears were groundless because she immediately recognised Nathan's father when he said hello. With laughter in her voice she said, 'Hello Mr Cohen, I don't know if you'll remember me. It's Charlotte.'

'Charlotte sometimes known as Charlie? Skinny Charlotte with the white hair? Of course I remember. How are you, darling?'

'I'm all right. I miss the East End though.'

'You miss it? Do me a favour! Your parents did right to get out. I wish I had done the same. My sister went to live in Brighton and we should have gone too. It's not the same any more.' His voice dropped a couple of octaves as he said, 'I take it you heard about my wonderful Lilly?'

Lost for words the silence that hung between them could have been cut with a knife. 'I've not spoken to Nathan in ages Mr Cohen . . .'

'So then you won't have heard,' he cut in. 'Listen, it was

quick, and you can't wish for more than that other than her still being here, but not bloody well nagging the life out of me. She dropped dead while she was trying on a gown in Mervyn's in Whitechapel, can you believe? Her sister persuaded her that we should go to a posh do, a distant relative's golden wedding anniversary. She was so excited over a gown she'd seen in the shop window she nearly wet herself.'

Charlotte could hardly take this in. Nathan's parents were not that much older than her own. There was an awesome silence between them until she said, 'I don't know what to say to you, Mr Cohen.'

'There's nothing to say, darling. She died happy. The gown I was going to cough up for had a price tag on it to turn both her sisters green with envy. I'm telling you the truth – she died laughing. And even though it's almost six months ago I can still see the look of joy on her face. Standing there, showing off in that frock in that shop one minute and on the floor the next. Thank God it didn't happen at home after I had paid out for the gown.'

Gently laughing at him, Charlotte said, 'I don't believe for one second that you gave a toss whether you'd already bought it for her or not.'

'You see what I mean? I haven't seen you for years and still you know me inside out. And I'll tell you something else. I don't like this bloody flat I'm living in. I shouldn't have let Nathan talk me into it.'

'You've moved?' Charlotte could hardly believe it. 'But the phone number—'

'Nathan arranged it with the GPO,' the old boy cut in. 'He wanted that I should keep the number. I don't know how they did it but they did, and there we are. I'm in a bloody rabbit hutch of a flat but I've got the same phone number. I'm supposed to be thankful for small mercies.'

'So you didn't move far away then?'

'No. I'm in an old Victorian archaic bloody flat.

51

Ravenscourt Buildings in Columbia Road, by the flower market. Nathan arranged it all. He knows somebody in the right place, by all accounts. They're gonna pull this lot down in a year or so and we'll get a brand new maisonette – according to my clever dick son. So for now I must live like Fagin . . . in a dump.' There was a moment's pause but she knew he hadn't finished talking. 'Why don't you come visit us? Bring a bit of sunshine into my life. You always were a little ray of sunshine. Lilly often said that if you had been born Jewish she would have made Nathan marry you one day.'

'So where is Nathan living?' she asked quickly, before he went into another confabulation.

'Where do you think? With me, of course. It's a poky two-bedroom medieval flat. Give me your number and I'll get him to call.'

'He's already got my number.'

'So when did he last speak with you?'

'About two years ago.'

'What? Two years? The little sod. I didn't know that. We could all have dropped dead for all you knew. It's all this bloody theatre business lot he's mixed up in. And now he tells me that we might move out of the East End altogether, one day, that he would like to buy something small and get on the property ladder in a couple of years' time. God knows where he wants to drag us to. It's got something to do with promotion and new towns. He lugs me around from one place to another as if I'm the bloody suitcase.'

'Listen,' said Charlotte, getting in quick so as to get off the phone. 'I've got to go, but get him to give me a call when he's got time. And I'm really, really sorry about your sad loss.'

'Loss? I shouldn't think so. I couldn't lose that woman if I dropped her off in the middle of a bloody desert. She's still around me. Waiting. Waiting for me to die. Waiting to grab hold of me again. She thought the world of me you know.'

'I know she did, and you loved it. Mind how you go.'

'Mind how I go? Go where? I wouldn't go anywhere in this bloody area if I could avoid it. It's a dump. I should never have left our beautiful council estate. I'll tell Sir that you called. But first things first. Give me your address, darling, and your telephone number – in case he's lost it. Otherwise Nathan will cut, hang and draw me.'

'Okay I will . . . but don't put any pressure on him, will you? He might not want to get in touch. It's been a long time.'

'Sure, sure. Just give it to me. I'm ready with a pen and the notepad that my son insists I must keep by the phone.'

Slowly giving him the details so that he had time to write them down nice and calmly, Charlotte felt a glow filter into her heart and was very pleased that she had taken this first step back to her old life. 'If he doesn't call you I will.' With that the old boy replaced his receiver and all that was left was the sound of the dialling tone.

With mixed emotions Charlotte touched up her make-up and then brushed her hair, determined not to let the sad news of Nathan's mother put her in the gloom. After all, if Nathan's dad could be upbeat about it then she had no right to let it bring her down. She knew which pub her parents would be at with a few of their friends and decided to join them. This was going to be a first, and with a smile on her face she imagined the reaction she would get when she walked into the bar. They had tried to get her to go out with them more often but she had mostly turned them down. It just hadn't felt right that she, an eighteen-year-old, should have to rely on her parents for nights out. But this evening it was different. Not only was she fancying a port and lemon, but she was also thinking about smoking one of her cigarettes in front of her mum and dad so as to get the message across to them that she was an adult. She had been keeping secret packets hidden away in a drawer in her bedroom for quite a while.

Checking herself in the hall mirror before she left the house, for once she was okay about what she saw. She looked all right. More than all right. She was wearing her black and white dog-tooth jacket with matching knee-length pencil skirt, which she had bought off a fashion stall in Petticoat Lane on a weekend flying visit with her parents to visit her Gran and Granddad. Picking up her handbag, she left the house and made her way through the small town to the pub. It was a pub where there was not only a juke box, but one that she had been impressed with before when she had on a rare occasion been in there with her parents. There had been a good selection of records to choose from as well as the top ten in the hit parade. This wasn't bad for a quiet little town. It had just turned seven o clock on a mid summer evening, still light outside so she had no fear about walking along an old and narrow cobbled back street.

Entering the riverside pub, she was pleased to hear a favourite singer and a favourite song drifting out from the open doorway of the public bar: Bob Dylan and 'Mr Tambourine Man'. Lifted by this, she went inside and looked over to a small table in a cosy corner where she could see her parents. It being a Friday night the place was buzzing with happy customers.

Easing her way through the bodies in the crowded bar, Charlotte unwittingly brushed against the last person she would expect to find in there – Kenny, the flash lad from her childhood. He recognised her as someone he knew but wasn't sure from where or when. Narrowing his eyes and giving her sideways glances as she joined a couple who he presumed were her parents and who were clearly pleased that she had arrived, the penny dropped. The man was greeting the girl with open arms. To anyone else it would be just another cosy family scene, but for Kenny it was much more than this. A satisfied smile spread across his face as he inwardly applauded himself for never forgetting a face. He had been so sure that he *had* recognised the man when he had been in this pub drinking with the two flash bastards from London.

And now, standing next to the fellow and looking gorgeous, was the girl that he had always had the hots for back in the East End when he was still at school. Charlie, the girl who used to tease him about his private fantasies, was just yards away. He couldn't help but smile at the irony. He had innocently strolled into the realm of the family who had pulled up their roots and just disappeared.

Giving her the once-over from top to toe, he felt warm around the parts that never got to see the sunshine. He had had the hots for the tart right up until her parents had done a moonlight flit and left him feeling angry and swindled. Charlie had been the star in more than one of his wet dreams. She had been the only girl who he had more than once fantasised fucking. Keeping his head down so as to enjoy a private bit of laughter to do with luck, the short fat Jew boy that the girl used to hang out with came to mind. Now he had to stop himself from laughing out loud. Five years had passed by and right out of the blue a little diamond drops from the sky. He couldn't wait to stalk her.

'I'm glad someone's fucking 'appy,' said his friend Steve, who had come into the pub. 'I lost twenty quid to the bookies today, Kenny boy.'

'Not so much of the boy. I'll go six rounds in the ring wiv you any day.'

'So what's the joke then?' said Steve, looking from him to the big blowsy blonde serving behind the bar and trying to get her attention.

'That's for me to know and for you not to,' he said. 'Mine's a pint.'

'Well, fucking order it then and get one in for me, you tight bastard.' With that the spiv swaggered over to the juke box and chose a couple of records: 'You've Lost That Lovin'

Feelin' ' by the Righteous Brothers and 'I Only Want To Be With You' by Dusty Springfield.

Returning to the bar, he sniffed as he looked around himself. 'Busy in 'ere tonight, innit?'

'Yeah. Bridgeford's bin put on the map. Fuck knows why though. I'm out of 'ere and back to the East End. Nuffing much ever 'appens.' Kenny glanced at his friend's face to see that he was chewing the inside of his cheek. 'It's all right. I've ordered you a Light Ale.'

'Good.'

'Oh dear . . . Been dumped agen 'ave yer?' Kenny grinned and then chuckled. 'State of you. If you're not gutted I'm a fairy queen.' His friend raised an eyebrow. 'Don't worry about it. I won't tell anyone.' Kenny's pint arrived and he downed a quarter of it in one. He then placed his glass on the bar and pulled a packet of Rothmans and a lighter from his jacket pocket.

'Women? Bloody pain in the neck,' said Steve.

'Oh right . . . so the slag did chuck you in then?'

'Chuck me out more like. Fucking women. Most of 'em are not worth the shoes they clip-clop around in.' He took a cigarette out of Kenny's pack and, just as he put it between his lips, the record that he had chosen and was playing seemed to get louder. Kenny tried not to laugh. 'So she's lost that loving feeling 'as she?'

'Shut it, Kenny, I'm not in the mood.' The guy then downed the rest of his drink in one and placed his glass on the counter, saying, 'Stay out of mischief.' He then walked out and left Kenny bent over with laughter.

Regaining his cool composure he turned his head to a pair of local girls and said, 'That's nice, innit? Leaving me all by myself like that. He's my best mate as well. Gone a bit soft in the head I reckon. Love's lost dream.' He then winked at the one with the long blackish-brown wavy hair who was playing the little girly bit while craftily inching closer along by the bar to be near him.

'Where's your mate gone then?' said the other girl, a bleached blonde who was a bit too confident for her own good and more heavily made up than the tart who was with her.

Kenny drained his glass and licked his lips. 'Dunno where he's fucked off to and I don't much care. He just mumbled somefing about not wanting to catch the clap from tarts that used this pub . . .'

'Fucking cheek,' said the bleached blonde. 'He'll get a slap round the face the next time I see 'im. And I 'ave seen 'im before, so I know that he uses this pub regular. I'll kick 'im in the balls.'

Kenny burst out laughing and then feigned a look of respect. 'Good for you,' he said. 'It's about time decent call girls stood up to 'im. He had no right to call you what he did.'

'Oh? And what was that?'

'Ah nah, no way. I wouldn't offend a lady. Never 'ave, never will.'

'Well, I'll tell you what. I'll spit right in 'is face next time I spot 'im. Talking about us like that. Fucking cheek.' With that the girl with bleached hair mooched off and headed for the Ladies'.

Kenny winked at the other girl, who looked intelligent enough. 'It's about time some of you girls sorted 'im out. See you around, eh?'

'Oh. You're not going are you?' She spoke in a tried and tested mock posh voice.

'Yeah. Gotta go, sexy. Gotta put my old nana to bed. Poor old girl's nearly eighty and going blind. She lives in one of them old people's chalets. I fitted her little front room out wiv a nice bit of cheerful red carpet today.'

'Is that your trade then. Carpet fitting?'

'Yeah. It's a family business that my grandfather started up

57

years back. It keeps the wolf away from the door, the taxman happy and the law off my back. I dabble in a lot of things on the quiet, but my nana don't know. It would break 'er heart to fink that I'm not straight.'

'Ah . . . honest? Ah. And you have to put her to bed as well?' Sympathy and respect was simply oozing from the girl's pores.

'Yeah. Of course I do. Nuffing wrong wiv that though, is there? Any bloke would do the same fing for 'is nana, wouldn't he?' He then sighed with sadness. 'Poor old girl. It is a little bit embarrassing for me as well as it is for her at times. You know . . . times such as when a woman's help is needed so as to give the old lady a bit of self respect.'

'Ah, you *are* lovely. Would you like me to come and help you? I looked after my gran before she passed away,' said the brunette, lying through her back teeth. She had taken to this good-looking young man and felt as if she wanted to mother him.

'I like old people,' she continued. 'I wanted to work in one of them places for the geriatrics, but my mother didn't fink it would be cheerful enough for a fun-loving girl like me.'

'I think she might 'ave been right, babe. That would be a bit much. My nana's as bright as a new pin. She suffers with rheumatoid arthritis, that's all, but it would be nice if you could come and meet 'er.'

'Ah, what a lovely thing to say. Where do you live then? Nearby?'

'Me? Oh, my pad is just round the corner above a wireless shop.' He glanced at his wristwatch. 'I've gotta go there now as it happens, to pick up a little box of Cadbury's Milk Tray that I bought for 'er.'

'Your own pad, eh? Get you,' said the girl, impressed. 'Bit young to be able to afford your own flat, ain't yer?'

'Course not. Eighteen? That's not young. And anyway none of us is ever too young to make something of ourselves, darling. I do all right. It's not the be-all and end-all but it suits me, for now. I s'pose you could say that it's a state of the art pad. It's a self-contained, one-bedroom apartment wiv a sitting room and a bathroom-en-suite. I make a wicked percolated coffee,' he lied. 'So if you ever fancy a night in listening to my stereo . . .'

'Sounds good to me.' The girl looked into his light green eyes and wasn't quite sure what she saw. This one was a bit of a mystery, but that beat the country yokels by a mile. Some of the other East End boys that had moved up at the same time as her family had were full of shit as to what they were up to. But this one seemed genuine and soft-hearted. Different to anyone she had ever met before, in fact.

'I'm not saying that my pad's a palace mind you, but it's cool.'

'I shouldn't think it would look much like a palace. Not in Bridgeford. Anyway, my name's Rosie, so are you gonna tell me yours?'

'Why not? The name's Kenny. I'm from Bethnal Green. Ronnie and Reggie Kray's patch.' Thinking of his dingy, bare little flat, he couldn't help being proud of his acting ability.

'I work in Woolworths during the week,' Rosie said, and then embroidered her life a little by adding, ' I'm a model for life-drawing classes as well. I'm from Hackney Downs originally.' She smiled at him. 'So what about your family? Did they all move up or are some of them still in the East End?'

Kenny smiled inwardly. He guessed that this one opened her legs to all and sundry but he wasn't all that fussed. And he was up for a laugh tonight for some reason other than being bored. 'Got any paintings of yourself in the nude for me to look at then 'ave yer?'

'One or two. Course I have. But they're hanging on the walls in my flat that's part of a mansion 'ouse so you'll 'ave to come round – if you want to view the goods.' She was just as good a liar as he was.

'Mansion house eh?' he smiled broadly. 'Very nice too.' Up for a bit of adventure, he said, 'I wouldn't mind seeing the paintings. I was praised regularly for my drawings when I was at school. Once I've got the new sports car I've ordered I'll cruise round and knock on your door. Where did you say the mansion 'ouse was?'

'I never said. But I will now. It's a fifteen-minute walk out of town in a little village. I share it wiv artists and a couple of writers that live there. The rent's cheap but it's a nice place to live. It's a commune.'

'Yeah?' Kenny smiled. 'Sounds like a place in Aldgate in London. Roughton House. But women are not allowed in.' He laughed.

'Oh yeah? And they're artists and that as well are they? The men who live there?'

'Nah. They're down and outs. Meth drinkers and drug addicts.'

'You saucy fucker.' The girl laughed. 'We're nothing of the kind.'

'Only teasing, darling. Can't you take a joke then?'

'Course I can. I like a fella with a sense of humour. Too many men are too fucking serious if you ask me.'

Each of them knew that the other was full of bollocks but neither of them could see harm in it. The girl was a storyteller and so was Kenny. He had heard about the mansion house that she was referring to and knew that it was mostly filled with drifters. 'My parents are still back in the East End,' he said. 'The old man's got his own carpet fitting business and most of 'is clients are wealthy and live in London. So he'd be mad to walk away and move up 'ere.' He gave her a corny all-knowing wink. 'Dad lives on the edge but Mum don't mind. She likes a diamond ring and a bit of clubbing even though she's getting on a bit. Right flash pair they are,' he said, getting off on his fantasies. From the expression he saw on the girl's face he felt that he might have gone too far. He wanted to impress her, not frighten her off. 'So you're a bit on the arty side then?'

'I suppose you could say that. I do a bit of drawing and that as well as modelling for other artists now and then as well. Where did you say your nana lived?'

'Just over the bridge in the old people's prefabs.' Another lie.

'Ah, bless 'er cotton socks. They're nice though. And they're little council bungalows, not prefabs.'

'Same thing. My nana calls 'em prefabs probably because that's what she lived in back in Stepney. She's living in the past. She gets a bit lonely sometimes. Not a lot though 'cause the other old people pop in and out. But I'm 'er only grandson who's bothered to move near to the old girl for a while. So she's bound to rely on me, aint' she?' In full swing with his fabrications now, he smiled inwardly and then said, 'She's the only reason I moved to Bridgeford to tell the truth. I wanted to be there for 'er. She won't be around for much longer.'

'But why did she come up here in the first place if your family stayed behind?'

This caught him off-guard but he was soon on track. 'Well . . . I wasn't gonna let 'er go into one of them fleapits in London. No way. Filthy rotten dirty fleapits for my nana? Nah. I wrote off to the Bridgeford council and arranged it all. She loves it an' all. Couldn't be 'appier.' So pleased with his spur of the moment fantasy Kenny could not stop himself from grinning.

'You are lovely. You're a bit of a softie on the quiet, aren't you,' said the twenty-two-year-old as she flicked her long straight hair off her face. 'I think that's such a sweet thing to do. But then you're an Easter Ender, the same as me.' She looked into his face with an angelic expression and then said, 'I'll tell you what. When my friend comes back from out of the Ladies' toilets, I'll see if she minds if I go with yer. She's not bothered about being in here by herself. There'll be more of our friends coming in soon so she won't be lonely for long. Not that she would care anyway, she'll be chatted up as soon as I've gone. It is a Friday night after all.'

'Well, if you're sure you don't mind I will take you up on the offer. My nana don't get any visitors so she'd be really pleased. I'll wait outside, shall I?'

'All right then, you do that. I won't be long.'

'We'll 'ave to pop into my pad though before we go. Apart from picking up the chocolates Nana asked me to dig out some old photos of 'er old house in the East End.' Another lie. 'They came in the post today from my mum. I phoned and asked 'er to send 'em.'

'Ah, bless. And I don't mind coming to your flat first. It will be nice to see where you live. All by yerself. All lonely.' She pouted her lips as she squeezed his cheek between her finger and thumb. 'Even if you never 'ad a nana and you was just trying to pull me, I would come to your flat because I think you're lovely.'

Her phoney little girl voice was driving him mad, but she looked as if she couldn't wait to get her hands on his body so what the hell? Arriving back at the bar, the bleached blonde looked from her friend to Kenny and grinned. 'Go on then you two. I can see you're ready for it.' She winked and then chuckled. 'Lucky cow. If you can't be good be bad.'

'I wouldn't know how to be bad.' Rosie grinned and then mimicked Eliza Doolittle from *My Fair Lady*. 'I'm a good girl I am.' She then slipped her arm into Kenny's and walked out with him as if they had known each other for years. To all and sundry they looked like a young couple who were very fond of each other. With a smirk on her face the second girl now turned to face the good looking barman who had been giving her the eye. This, it would seem, was going to be a night for a bit of old-fashioned romance all round.

Five

Walking through the back streets towards his pad Kenny was a true gentleman when guiding the girl across a narrow road. He was in seventh heaven. No matter what happened tonight with the slut, who was clutching his arm as if they were man and wife, the finger could possibly point at the guy he had been having a drink with. The idiot who, when in the bar, would have been heard to say, in a nasty derogatory fashion, that this girl was a cheap slag. So depending on the way she came across once in his pad it didn't really matter. He was Kenny and could do what he wanted. He had a choice – he could choose to go one way or the other. Keep her as his bedding whore if this was what she wanted or take her more than once if she refused to come across. He felt that she deserved a good shagging for being a teasing scumbag if nothing else. If he chose the latter then he would make the finger of suspicion point to his flash drinking partner. Joking and laughing, they soon arrived at the old small door in the flint wall that would lead up into his pad.

Once inside, the girl was surprised at how perfectly clean and tidy his little place was. It was no palace but neither was it a shit hole. 'This is really cosy,' she said, a little on the worried side. Something didn't seem right but she was unsure as to what it was.

'It'll do for now,' Kenny winked at her and grinned. 'My pad in London's better than this.' He was embellishing the fact a little. The fact being that he didn't have a pad in London but lived with his mum and dad.

'Well I'm really impressed,' she said, while at the same time feeling just a touch uneasy. Something definitely wasn't right and still she couldn't put her finger on what it was that was causing those little warning bells to go off. She swept any hint of dark thoughts from her mind as she watched Kenny plump up the faded red and gold cushions of a two-seater sofa. He then invited her to sit down and make herself comfortable while he went and put the kettle on so as to make them both a nice cup of tea. A touch easier, the girl slipped off her shoes and pulled her legs under her, making herself comfortable on the old-fashioned sofa. She was beginning to relax more by the minute and when her host returned carrying two glasses and a half bottle of Scotch whisky she sparkled. He was managing to warm her parts before he had even touched her.

'You've got a choice,' he said. 'Scotch and water first or a cup of tea?'

'Scotch,' she said, smiling at him.

Looking at her all cosy and comfortable on the sofa like that he felt chuffed with himself for having drawn her in. And then, as she made herself even more snug on his couch as if she owned it, he felt a seed of anger and knew that this one might have to be added to his shortlist of women who had brought the worst out in him. It wouldn't be the first time that he hadn't been excited enough by a tart to want to screw her. And it wasn't because he didn't fancy her – he did. Now he was wondering if she had been singled out for him by the powers that be. Singled out in the same way that others in the old smoke near Aldgate and Brick Lane had been. Girls with whom to have sex had just not been on the cards. He had needed something far more exciting and dangerous.

The old lust for risk that came and went was back again . . . and he had with him, in his pad, the right girl for the cause. This new-sprung urge that was like a driving force had been coming and going over the past month or so, and it was back. He didn't want her for intercourse – he wanted to kill her. The persuasive voice that had snaked its way back inside his head was telling him over and over to do just this. To kill the prostitute. To kill the slag. To strangle the last putrid breath out of her filthy mouth.

'You all right, sweetheart?' said Rosie the uneasiness returning. 'You've gone a bit pale and serious.'

'Have I? Well it must be you that's doing it. Seeing you in the orange glow of that table lamp . . .' He smiled.

'You're sweet.' She pulled her knees up and then said, 'Come on. Pour us both a drink and then massage my poor aching feet.' Searching his face and seeing the look in his eyes Rosie felt that his mood had changed. The warmth had gone, as had the cheeky smile. And there was no sign of charm in his eyes any more. 'Smile for me then,' she said, trying to lighten the sudden dark atmosphere. But it was too late. She had not been as canny as she should have been when accepting the invitation into his home.

Kenny was filling with resentment and loathing towards the girl lounging on *his* settee. Lounging as if she *belonged*. And to make matters worse she had slipped her shoes off without asking if she could. He placed one of the empty glasses onto the coffee table and poured himself a measure of whisky straight, which he drank in one. Narrowing his eyes he peered at her and as he did he felt a kind of a smile creep in. She was talking to him but he wasn't really listening.

'Get you,' he heard her say. And then, 'My turn now. I'll give it a try. Whisky straight please.'

He placed his glass and the bottle onto the coffee table and sat down next to her, slowly shaking his head as if deeply disappointed. He then released a profound sigh as he poured her a drink that she would not be taking. He was a touch disappointed that she had spoken of alcohol and not love or romance since these were going to be her last words. He turned to face her so that he could look into her eyes, into her very soul. She had beautiful hazel eyes. Almond shaped and lovely, but sadly, he felt that they had drunk in too many faces of lusting men who she had given herself to. 'You're very beautiful,' he said as he gently stroked her soft wavy hair. He then ran a finger down the side of her face and touched her full lips, whispering, 'Is it all right if I kiss you?'

The expression of unease as she nervously smiled filled him with a kind of love and compassion. 'You really are an old-fashioned gentleman on the quiet ain't yer,' was her answer. 'I've never met anyone like *you* before.' She smiled.

'No, I don't suppose you have.' He grinned and then softly chuckled as he searched her thoughts. Looking more serious and going quiet he whispered gently, 'Sweet dreams and sleep forever peaceful.' He then gently clasped her lily-white neck with one hand to push his thumb into the hollow and brought up his other hand so as to strangle her with his eyes shut tight. He preferred to bring about a quick death rather than an agonising slow end that he felt might possibly lodge in his mind and darken his conscience. He didn't want to see the look of terror in this girl's eyes the way he had needed to with the first of the London whores whom he had delivered from a degrading lifestyle . . .

The flat seemed awesomely silent now that the body of the girl lay limp and lifeless. Kenny had talked to her during the void between her struggle for life and acceptance of death because he didn't want her to think too badly of him. He had said that he had her interest at heart. That she was a slut who was sliding further and further into the depth of the gutter. Then, having brushed long strands of hair off her face, he had carefully lifted her legs so as to lay her comfortably on the sofa before crossing her arms. He knew exactly where he was going to put this sweet young corpse to rest. But he needed a quiet time now and he needed another drink. He also needed it to be as dark as possible outside, with the town sleeping, so that he could carry her unseen to the bottom of the overgrown and somewhat secluded back garden. His plan was to simply drop her down into the ancient disused wishing well that was deeper than deep. When he had first arrived in his little rented flat he had dropped a penny in and made a wish, and had heard no sound of it hitting water or anything else.

Out of interest he had then dropped down a dilapidated watering can that he had seen in the undergrowth and still he had heard nothing. From this he gleaned that the base of this particular old wishing well was way down below ground level and in the pit of hell itself. Now, of course, it would be the perfect private last resting place for the whore – with a few old coins for luck.

Resting back in his armchair and gazing at the girl's peaceful body that looked quite angelic with its arms crossed, Kenny couldn't help thinking that, given different circumstances, she might have made something of herself. Shaking his head and talking under his breath, he berated her for telling him silly lies. A model for an artist? He very much doubted it. No. The only brush that she was ever near as far as he was concerned was the one that she used to tease and torment men so as to earn a living, or at least some cash on the side. The bitch had no self-respect whatsoever. With his breathing and heart beat more or less back to normal, he decided that he would wrap the corpse in an old grey motheaten army blanket, one that he had found in a cupboard when he first came into this furnished pad.

He thought that this was far more humane than simply dropping her down into the depths in only the clothes she had on. He would keep her shoes though, and add them to the others in the battered suitcase that he stored under his bed. Come the day when he would leave this flat, the collection of shoes that were part of his trophies would also be sent tumbling down the well. But not yet. They were, after all, the only mementos that he had to remind him of the girls rescued by himself from the dark side of life and the back alleyways of Wapping.

Sipping his drink, he was overcome by a strong desire to close his eyes and give his brain a rest. He was tired and it was time for a doze in the armchair. Rosie was fine. Rosie was sleeping. Once it was dark enough he would lay her to rest. Entomb her in her final resting place where people in years gone by had dropped spare coppers and made hopeful, desperate wishes. This, of course, was after it had been used as one of the town's watering holes that had become redundant, and was now part of the land that was little more than a sprawling overgrown back garden.

Going into his makeshift kitchen in the passageway Kenny poured himself a cup of boiled water to help wash away the taste of alcohol and took it into the sitting room and to his armchair. He thought that the girl on the sofa looked like an angel lying there. At peace and no longer worrying about anything. He was pleased. He had done well by her. Saved her from a life of degradation. Prostitutes had been part of his life ever since he could remember. His own mother and her sister used to go out arm in arm in the evenings, dressed up to the nines and sometimes heading for the West End to wealthier clients than could be found locally in the East End. He smiled at the irony. His mother and aunt had been the queens of whores once upon a time, whores who were paid handsomely for their services, and his dad had pretended not to have a clue as to what was going on or where the extra cash came from. So far, Kenny had only ever been able to afford the slags that worked in Brick Lane and Shoreditch. But that had, in its own way, been a light to show him the pathway that he felt he had been born to tread. The way of cleansing a corner of God's earth of women who sold their souls as well as their bodies to dirty old men.

To his mind, now that he thought himself a mature young

man, he knew that life was all about the survival of the fittest, about selection. A bit like the chickens at the local farms that were kept for the laying of eggs and were not slaughtered and dished up for Sunday dinner. He thought about his dad, whom he had always believed to be too honest and innocent for his own good until he learned that he had turned a blind eye to what his mother got up to. The money that she had earned as a professional prostitute had, after all, put rump steak on their plates instead of cheap mincemeat. His dad, also hard-working, had never missed a day's work if he could help it. And he had always made sure that Kenny went out in the mornings with two soft-boiled eggs inside him.

He looked at Rosie's white face and wondered if anyone ever did pass away with a smile on their lips the way people said they did. Not that it made any difference. She wouldn't be missed as far as he could tell. This is what pained him more than anything. The poor wretch of a girl would not be missed.

He had put to sleep others of her kind during the past month or so. The first hadn't been premeditated. In fact, it had shocked him to the core once he'd done the deed. But then after a few days he fancied that this was why he had been put on this earth: to cleanse it from the evil that was like a spreading disease. The harmless women who had sold their souls within the East End of London, just so as to have a roof over their heads, had not even been missed. There had been no word of their disappearance in the newspapers or broadcast on the news. The wretched prostitutes working in London's Aldgate and Whitechapel were dead and gone and had not been missed. He had taken them in his dad's van and given each of them a brief but moving service from the bank of the river Thames, in a quiet dark spot close to the Prospect of Whitby in Wapping. Here in Bridgeford, of course, he could not let the river be the last resting place for Rosie because too many people either fished or swam in it. But he had found the girl a nicer place, whether she deserved it or not. She would sleep for ever in peace at the bottom of the long and narrow overgrown wild garden. A little paradise that was often filled with the sound of birdsong and the buzzing of the bees.

Once the trial of laying to rest the girl whose name he had now wiped from his mind was over, Kenny stood in his little bathroom with his shirtsleeves rolled up and the collar of his light blue cotton shirt tucked in. He was ready for a refreshing sluice before he headed for the pub in search of a Dunhill lighter that he hadn't actually lost. This was to be his excuse for going back, to give himself an alibi later on if the tart's friend reported her missing. After all, Kenny was the last one to have been seen with her when they left the pub together.

Ready to go out again, he glanced around the room to make certain there was absolutely no sign of the girl having been there. He then strolled out of his pad as if nothing untoward had happened. As far as he was concerned, the old saying 'no point in crying over spilt milk' was a sound one; he had had it drummed into him since he was a boy. The girl was gone, and to his way of thinking she was better off for it if all she had to look forward to was letting strangers abuse her. He had in a way been her salvation and it felt good. Better in fact than when he had sent the whores back in the East End from the gutter to the depths of the river.

Quietly closing his front door behind him, Kenny whistled a little tune as he strolled out towards the pub, past the old workhouse and prison. He was wondering if it was time for him to return to his roots, and as the vision of the council estate where he had been brought up came to mind so did Charlie, the girl from his childhood whom he'd seen in the pub earlier on. He had heard that she and her parents had moved to Norfolk a few years back but no more than that. Thinking of her and those old days brought the fat Jew boy to mind again, and he wondered if Nathan still lived in the same place. Kenny's own family had moved from their flat three years since to live on the Brine council estate close to Stepney Green underground station. He mused on the fact that the lovely Charlotte and he now lived in the same small Norfolk town. He quietly laughed to himself at the thought of snogging her, the way he had once dreamed of doing when he was a kid. But those fantasies had long since dissipated. He didn't know why nor did he care. He knew that Charlotte had to be all of eighteen by now, so to his mind there must have been a few cornets dipped into her ice-cream and she was probably no more decent than all of the other sluts he came across. It did seem a coincidence, though, that they should be living in the same little orb again. He wondered if fate was having a game with him. Teasing and testing. Given the right circumstances, would he kiss the girl or kill her? Quietly chuckling at the irony, he laughed freely as he pushed open the door into the busy pub as if he had just remembered a joke that someone had told him.

Going up to the bar, which was still fairly busy, he ordered a pint and then casually asked if he had left his make-believe Dunhill lighter there. The barman was too busy to get into conversation at that point so speedily checked under the bar and nearby the till and then shrugged and shook his head. 'Can't see it anywhere, mate.'

'Don't worry about it,' said Kenny. 'It'll turn up. I've got fed up with looking for it now. It was a present from my mum and dad.' More lies. He then grinned and winked and said, 'Any excuse to come back for another pint, eh?'

Taking payment from a customer the barman then pulled a pint for himself and turned back to Kenny, smiling. 'Was she good?'

'Who?'

'The girl.'

'Do me a favour. Not my type, mate. Anyway, we hadn't gone twenty yards or so and someone else caught 'er attention. My own fucking mate who I was drinking wiv earlier nicked 'er from under my nose. I didn't fancy 'er in any case. Too common.'

'You're telling me. If I had my way I would ban that sort of a girl. I've got a reputation to think about.'

Kenny grinned and then chuckled knowingly. 'Me thinks you do protest too much,' he said. 'You've not been giving 'er one on the quiet 'ave yer? While your old woman's not looking?'

'Pigs might fly,' the barman said. 'And not so much of the old woman. We're only in our forties thank you.'

'Are you? Blimey, I had you both down for pensioners.' He laughed and then said, 'Only kidding, mate. And I agree with you as it happens. You don't want slags in a nice family pub like this one.'

'I don't know about family pub, but I s'pose we are getting more married couples coming in and less spivs from London with their swearing and wheeling and dealing.'

'Oh don't mention London,' Kenny said, sporting an actor's pained expression. 'I'm gonna 'ave to pack my bags and go back home before the week's out. The old man's not well. He's had another little heart attack,' he lied. 'The next one will make three and that could be it. He's been warned, but will the stubborn bastard take notice of the heart specialist? Of course not.'

The bartender shook his head gravely. 'It's not wanting to believe it, son. That's what it'll be. Your dad most likely hates the fact that it 'appened to him. What work does he do?'

'Carpet fitter, just like me. He taught me everything I know. We've got our own business. We do all right at it down there in London town.'

'There you go, then. Can you imagine? A hard working East Ender like myself having to sit in a chair all day long so as not to put strain on the ticker. No way. I'm sorry to hear it, son. You must feel terrible.'

'I do, mate. I do. I'm gutted to be honest. But I've tried not to show it, I prefer to cry alone – if you know what I mean.' Kenny finished his pint, proud of his ability to lie with conviction. 'And we've all got to stand by our parents after all they've done for us, haven't we? Yep. You're right. I think he does hate being ill. I might go back sooner rather than later.'

'Well, don't you just sod off without coming in and saying cheerio, will yer?'

'Course not. You're a mate, even if you do charge over the top for my beer.'

'Well, you can charge a little over the top for that carpet fitting in our bedroom up there that you keep on promising to do.'

'As soon as I'm back. And that's a promise. I'll come in the company van and fetch a bit of good quality thick pile that fell off the back of a lorry.' He gave the barman a wink and left the pub. Once outside he pulled his handkerchief from his pocket and wiped the beads of sweat from his forehead. He had pulled off his bucket of lies, but it hadn't been as easy as he thought it would be. Not only had he started to tremble just before he left but had felt a surge of burning heat sweep through his entire body.

'You're not as hard as you're made out to be, Kenny boy,' he murmured as he leaned against an old flint wall for support. 'But you did well in the pub.' He sighed. 'You did good. Mister barman'd stand up in any court of law and be your alibi if it goes pear-shaped. Which it won't.'

He smiled inwardly as he pushed his handkerchief back into his pocket and then took out his door key. Without a body there couldn't be a murder trial, he told himself. Arriving at his front door he pushed the key in the lock and realised just how tired he was on this somewhat strange evening. He needed a bit of shut-eye, that was for sure. Getting rid of another whore had taken it out of him. He was in want of his pillow and a decent night's sleep.

With no more thoughts of the girl in the well, Kenny, in his little makeshift kitchen, spread butter onto a piece of sliced bread ready to make himself a corned beef sandwich. His mind was still ticking over. He had all but come to the conclusion that there was nothing in this part of the world for him any more other than some fencing of stolen goods. And besides which, he missed his mum and her lovely home-made steak and kidney pies and apple crumble and custard.

Back in his armchair with his sandwich supper on a cracked plate, he thought about all the good things that he liked about Bethnal Green and Stepney. The list outweighed what Norfolk had to offer, no question. At least he had a choice though. He wondered if he should give it a couple of weeks or so before he made a move, or do a moonlight and leave early in the morning with his bags packed. He decided to sleep on it. Making snap decisions gave him a headache in any case and he had already had to take two painkillers before he had gone back to the pub. None of it really mattered in any case. Home was wherever he laid his hat. And the next day was his most favourite day of the week. Saturday. Saturdays had always felt special ever since he could remember. And all because of the ABC picture palace on the Cambridge Heath Road, which had once opened up especially so as to show films and cartoons for children. He had loved going to the Saturday morning pictures more than anything in the world when he was a little boy. The mere thoughts of those days gone by brought a flow of tears trickling down his face. Then he heard himself sobbing. And it was strangely comforting.

Six

The next evening Rita and Eddie were keeping company with their small group of friends who had formed a bridge club. Charlotte, once again, was at home watching television alone. This was the Swinging Sixties and yet she had nothing to do and no one to share her time with. She was watching *Top of the Pops*, where Sandy Shaw was singing without shoes while girls danced around her wearing fabulous clothes in the latest style designed by Mary Quant and others of her ilk. She imagined herself wandering along the river in a psychedelic mini-skirt like the dancers on the show were wearing, and with a Vidal Sassoon razor-sharp haircut to show off to people like the old boy Eric or the women at the place where she worked.

And all the while her birthplace and home town of London was smack bang in the middle of a fantastic era and was being heralded as the Swinging City. Beatlemania was going strong and the Rolling Stones were hitting the big time. There was a new revolution pushing forward in the capital on all levels and Charlotte was sad not to be part of it. It didn't seem right since she was a true-blue born and bred Londoner, and the desire to go back home was almost overwhelming. Leaving in 1959 at thirteen going on fourteen was the worst thing that could have happened to a young teenager – and it had happened to her. She switched off the television set, ready to go and have a long soak in the bath with plenty of bubbles.

But then, just as she told herself that she had to accept the lonely life that she could do little about, the sound of the doorbell pierced through the silence. She instinctively looked at the clock to see that it had just turned seven, a bit on the late side for a travelling salesman.

Going to the street door she put on the safety chain and then turned the catch to see a tall, good-looking young man around her own age standing on the doorstep. He was wearing a lightweight summer suit and open necked shirt and didn't have the air of a salesman; possibly a Jehovah's Witness, she thought, and slipped the bolt from the safety chain. She opened the door properly, intrigued by her visitor at first, and then stunned when he spoke in a quiet and familiar voice while smiling at her. 'How long are you going to leave me standing on your doorstep, Charlie?' he said. She could hardly believe her eyes or the way her heart was rapidly beating. Had her old friend really come to her rescue just when she needed him most?

'Nathan? It *can't* be you?' Was all she managed to say.

'Charlotte? I *know* it's you.' Was his joker response.

'My God, it is you. I can't believe it.' Her face lit up and she started to laugh.

'Why wouldn't it be me? You phoned home and here I am. I don't know if you gave my dad your new address or whether he got it from Directory Inquiries, but it was in my hand the minute I walked in from work on the day that you called him. So? Are you going to let me in?'

Opening the door wide she stood aside and waved a slow but welcoming hand, inviting him into her home. Once he was in the passage she closed the door behind him and as she turned around her childhood friend just stood there, looking at her until Charlotte finally said, 'I still can't believe it's you.'

'Well it is. And you look just as beautiful as I imagined you would be after all this time.'

She looked beautiful? What about him? He had turned into

a Prince Charming! 'Well, that's a lovely compliment . . . but my God . . . look at *you*!' She grinned, and shook her head in amazement. He was six feet tall, slim, broad and incredibly handsome. 'Where's my short fat friend gone?' she said.

'Nowhere. He's still right here, inside.' He patted his heart. 'Now are you going to offer me a cup of coffee? Or something stronger?'

'A cup of coffee for now, because I need one. That and a cigarette.' She stood to one side and waved a theatrical hand in the direction of the sitting room, but he was having none of it. He stood looking at her, a gentle smile on his face and a touch tearful. 'Don't I at least deserve a hug?' he said.

'Of course you do. Let's break a habit of a lifetime. We never hugged, Nathan, but perhaps we should have done. We were good friends. We were there for each other but we never hugged – I don't know why.'

'Nor me,' he said, taking her into his arms and kissing her lightly on her soft white neck. His heart was beating faster and he felt the tears coming. Only just managing to subdue his emotions, he said, 'It wasn't that I didn't want to hold you close. I was shy and I didn't think for one minute that you felt the same about me as I felt about you.'

Cupping his face, Charlotte swallowed against the lump in her throat. 'I didn't know what either of us felt. All I know is that I missed you badly when we left. And when you stopped writing to me I felt as if I was in mourning for a lost love. Then I told myself off for being stupid. That helped.'

'Well, I apologise, I really do. I thought that I had to let you lead your life and that I might not be part of it any more. So I threw myself into the world of theatre.' He smiled and then shrugged. 'It helped, but it wasn't a cure.' He then stepped away from her and turned his head so that he could wipe an escaping tear from his eye. He went into the front room, followed by Charlotte.

'I love this house,' he said, attempting to be matter-of-fact. 'I thought you would be living on a council estate up here.'

'We were at first,' said Charlotte, falling in line with his conversational gambit. 'But the work just kept on coming for Dad. Good electricians are not exactly two a penny up here, and what with all the new houses and flats being built . . .'

'Good. He did the right thing then?'

Charlotte slowly nodded. 'For him and Mum, yes . . . I suppose so.'

'But not for you?'

'No. But don't tell them that I said that.'

'How can I if they're not at home?'

Charlotte laughed. 'I'll make the coffee and you make yourself comfortable. Turn the telly on if you want to.'

'No, it's fine. I love the quiet.' Flopping down into a feather-cushioned armchair, Nathan let out a sigh of relief. He was here. He had found the girl that he had missed so badly when she left London. He was under the same roof as his Charlotte at last, content just to relax and not think about anything. He leaned his head back and closed his eyes. It had been a long and arduous journey, one way and another.

Coming back into the room, Charlotte asked if he wanted something to eat. He said he didn't. She asked if he had already eaten on the train. He said he hadn't. 'Well then, after we've had a cup of coffee we'll go for a walk and I'll treat you to the best fish and chips in the world. How does that sound?'

'Heavenly,' he said as he looked into her beautiful face. 'I can't tell you how this feels, Charlie,' he said. 'I just can't find the words.' He let out a long sigh of relief. 'After all this time. And all I had to do was get on a bloody train and then trek from the station to here.'

'Trek? But we're only five minutes' walk from the station, Nathan.'

'I know. But I turned right instead of left and nigh on

circled this bloody town. But I've found you now, so that's all right.' He closed his eyes and sighed contentedly.

'You can have a doze if you want to,' she said.

'Don't be mad. I'm just relaxing after the *schlep* up here for God's sake. Leave me be. Go and fetch our coffee.'

Smiling to herself at the way Nathan had changed and yet at the same time was still his same old self, she felt happy. And happiness was an emotion that hadn't been around for a while. An hour or so later, after they had caught up with each other's lives and talked non-stop, Charlotte then asked if he felt like a short walk to the local pub to say hello to her parents and their friends. He had no problem with this and was up and ready to leave before she had had time to swipe on some fresh lipstick. On the way to the pub they talked more about their lives. All kinds of things to do with all that had happened in the world since they last saw each other, which seemed at least twice as long as it had actually been.

Charlotte had had to use every bit of willpower not to cry when he said, 'At one time I thought that my dad would die of a broken heart once Mum had gone. He took her death very badly. They were so close. From what I can gather she stumbled a little and then keeled over. At least it was quick for my beautiful mother.'

'But when she was alive, she was a really happy person, Nathan. I remember her smiling face.'

'I know. But it was so hard for our parents in the old days. In the early days my mother had to take in dry washing to press. And during the day, on and off, she would look at another pile of clean laundry waiting to be ironed and roll her shoulders back and forth to ease the burning pain before she began again. And that would be after a ten-minute tea break.'

'But she was happy for most of her life.' Charlotte reached out and squeezed his hand. 'You know that she was.'

Smiling warmly at the girl that he was still in love with,

Nathan took her hand and kissed it. 'You always were my light in the dark,' he said.

Arriving at the pub, Nathan, feeling as if he was walking on air, opened the door for Charlotte and followed her through the public bar to the room out the back where a game of bridge was in play. Nathan waited while she opened the door marked private and courteously gave her dad a nod to say she wanted to have a quiet word. Turning around she saw her friend chatting to the guy behind the bar who was pouring another customer a drink. She couldn't believe just how tall, broad and handsome Nathan had turned out. Beyond him and the barman she could see someone staring at her and couldn't think why. She turned her face away letting him know that she wasn't interested, should this be the reason why he was giving her the evil eye.

Coming out of the back room, the serious expression on Eddie's face melted into a smile as he saw Nathan. He smiled broadly as he joined him and studied the eighteen-year-old's face and then started to laugh. 'Well I never,' he said. 'Look what the wind's blown in. Look at you. You're broader than I am, son!'

He offered his hand and Nathan took it gladly. 'It's good to see you. How you got here I'll never know. But I'm in the middle of a game so I'll see the pair of you later on. But I'm really pleased. Chuffed. You wait until I tell Rita you've moved up 'ere. She'll be over the moon.'

Nathan didn't have time, nor the inclination, to tell Eddie that he was on a chance visit but Charlotte was in straight away. 'He hasn't moved up, Dad. He's come to visit us.'

Eddie slowly nodded, pleased as punch. 'There's a guest room in our house for you any time you want to use it, son.' He gave him a fatherly wink. 'We'll 'ave a nice chat later on, back at home, before we all go to bed.' With that, Eddie left them to it.

'Well,' said Nathan. 'This really is fantastic. I walk in out of the blue and get invited into the fold.' He was genuinely moved. 'Once we've had a drink here shall we go for a nice stroll along the river?'

'Fine by me. Or we can leave now and have a drink in a different pub a bit further along.'

'I think I would prefer that, actually,' said Nathan. 'I need to be out in the fresh air and walk a bit after travelling all day.' He then took her hand and escorted her out of the pub – a true gentleman.

'Looks like the girl you just had your eye on has got a boyfriend,' said the bartender to Kenny, who had watched them go.

'Does, don't it? Ah, well. You can't win 'em all. Anyway, I've gotta go back to London to take care of Dad.' He shrugged.

'Ne'mind son. You're putting your dad before pleasure and that's no bad thing. You're a good kid.'

'Thanks for that,' said Kenny, a touch on the sentimental side. 'I'll be back though. In a year or so.'

'Course you will, son. Course you will.'

Walking away from the pub with Nathan and through the back streets on the way to the river, Charlotte kicked off the conversation to cover the darker side of their childhood so as to get it over with. She said, 'I wonder what those bullies are doing now. The ones who tormented the life out of the both of us, one way or another? I bet they're mostly married with families and are as dull as ditch water.'

'I don't care where they are, Charlie. I had to force myself to let it go. I had to will myself not to think about those bastards. I focused on my career and made it happen. I didn't want to be a tailor like my dad and I didn't want to run a delicatessen the way my grandpa did for all of his working life.

'Dad keeps himself busy with the list of private customers

that he managed to build while working as a tailor which is great, because he works from home now and he prefers that. He makes a respectable living from his trade these days. They say he's a master tailor. He wanted me to follow in his footsteps but tradition or not I wasn't going to have that.

'I didn't want a shop with a cutting and stitching room out the back. My grandpa insists that I should let my dad show me the way to cut a decent suit, though, so that I've got a second string to my bow.' Thinking about his grandpa he chuckled.

'He still smells of Lifebuoy soap – and he still has plans for the kind of house I will buy for my own family one day and where it will be. At the moment he thinks Golders Green is the place to focus on. He drives my dad mad but he also makes him laugh. They're more like brothers with a twenty-year age difference, and the bond between them is really helping now that Mum's gone.' He paused for a moment and then looked into Charlotte's face, saying, 'You know, Mum's funeral was the only one I had ever been to.'

Still holding his hand she guided him through a narrow courtyard with flint stone walls on either side of them. 'It must have been horrible, Nathan. I wish you had let me know.'

'I didn't want to talk about it or tell you, my closest ever friend, because it would have made it real. I just hoped that I might wake up one morning to find that it had all been a horrible dream.'

'I can't imagine what it must have been like. Your mum was so alive and full of spirit. She was too young to die. She can only have been in her late forties.'

'No, she was in her mid-fifties, but she had been taking tablets for high blood pressure for two years before the attack without telling any of us. Dad was angry with our GP at first but then saw that the man was right to respect Mum's wishes. She didn't want anyone to know that something had gone wrong with her heart. She had been advised to take it easy, but can you imagine her not helping out at the delicatessen when they were busy and my grandparents needed her? She left the umbrella factory to work there because it got so busy. She thought of the delicatessen as a second home.'

Touched by the way he was trying to salvage something from his mother's life, Charlotte slipped her arm into his. 'I'm really proud of you, Nathan.'

'What for? What great thing in life have I accomplished? I'm a trainee junior accountant, for God's sake. But I hope to work for myself one day.' He stopped in his tracks and looked into her face. 'I really wanted to see you again but didn't know if you wanted to see me. I swear on my mother's life I've never loved anyone the way I loved you when I was thirteen. I thought you had moved on and forgotten all about me.'

This made her laugh. He hadn't changed at all. 'How could I forget you! And why do you think I made the phone call?'

Blushing, he changed the subject, saying, 'Anyway . . . I'm okay in the two-bedroom flat that I share with my dad. It will do until we get a brand new council maisonette with a garden. Until I can afford to get a mortgage and buy something.'

They continued on their walk. 'So you and your dad will stay together forever?'

'Of course we will. Until my sister comes back from America in any case. Her marriage isn't working out, so she's going to move in with my grandparents close by to where Dad and I are living until she decides what she wants to do. My grandparents' Victorian terraced house is in a quiet tree-lined street not too far away from Ravenscourt buildings where we live. The wily old couple bought it off the landlord years ago for a song – a quarter of what it's worth now.'

'It sounds like there's been a few changes since you last wrote.'

'Yes. And I'm sorry I never let you know about Mum going, but it affected me badly. I didn't want to go out, I didn't want to go to work, I didn't want to wake up in the mornings. I knew I had to think about something horrible and I couldn't bear it. But I'm okay now, I've got used to it. You know, to the fact that life is fragile. I can bring Mum's smiling face to mind, so that's something. I couldn't at first but I can now. I can also see the cross look that she used to give me when I wouldn't hit back.'

'Her being cross with you was only her way of trying to get you to have more confidence in yourself.'

'I know.'

'And now you live with your dad close by to your grandparents. That must be better than living on our estate, surely?'

'Much. But the flat doesn't have an inside lavatory and that's not brilliant if Dad needs to pee in the night. He goes in a bucket. But I like being there. I'm content living with him. He's funny. And he still keeps a paraffin heater in the corner of the room as a back-up in case there's an electricity cut worldwide. And he keeps busy with his sewing machine. He wanted to be closer to my grandparents but not live in and I felt the same. Now that Mum is dead my dad needs me.'

'So things are a lot different for you as well as me, and everyone else I expect,' Charlotte murmured as they paused by a little old wooden bridge that crossed an inlet into the river. 'Hundreds of East End families wanted a better way of living. Hundreds have moved out, from what I can gather from my nan and granddad. We all seem to be spread around all over the place. Not them though. They would never leave the East End.'

Taking hold of her hand again, Nathan said, 'Well, I can't blame them. But for you? This is a much better lifestyle, surely? You're surrounded by forests and rivers as well as historic buildings.' He drew her to a wooden bench on the bank of the river and they sat down.

'It is beautiful in this part, Nathan, but the shops and some of the houses of old Bridgeford haven't changed much since time immemorial. We could do with a decent supermarket.

It's all very well having fantastic ruins but we do need a bit of twentieth century as well. A bit of modern living.'

'I'm not so sure. I let myself into our flat just after my mother passed away and my dad hadn't heard me come in. He was in the kitchen, sitting at the old walnut table for two wiping his plate with a piece of dried bread. He had fried himself some kippers. I just stood there staring at him and realised that old habits and old ways were helping him through his loneliness.'

'Oh Nathan . . . I'm sorry . . .'

'No, don't be. It happens. We're okay, we're fine. I've got more responsibility than I've ever had in my life but I don't mind. I like being there for him. And he can cook a decent meal any day of the week, so it works both ways.'

Charlotte broke into a comfortable smile. Her childhood friend hadn't changed one bit, except of course that he was now six feet tall and handsome. He still wore glasses but they were horn rimmed and up to the minute in their design. So much water had passed under the bridge and five years had been struck off thc calendar. She wasn't in the least bit awkward in his company. 'Come on,' she said. 'Let's walk further along by the river. We might see a kingfisher. I've only seen it half a dozen times in all the years I've been here along this part but you never know . . . this could be our lucky evening.'

Without saying a word, Nathan took hold of her hand again and in the most natural way they left the bench together and continued to stroll along, happy and content. When they came to a spot where the bank of the river was far too over-grown to battle with, they paused and looked around them-selves. With the sun on his face, Nathan smiled. 'This really is a beautiful place, Charlie. I had no idea.'

They stood watching the water flowing gently and he couldn't resist picking up a smooth pebble and skimming it across the surface of the old river. He had done this many times before when they had mucked about down by the river in Wapping. They quietly laughed, and both of them felt as if they had slipped back in time to when they were messing around on the banks of the old Cut. The boyish look on his face in that moment was exactly as it had been then. Studying his relaxed expression, Charlotte was again taken by the change in him. His shoulders looked so much broader now that muscle had replaced fat.

Tilting his head so as to look at her, Nathan smiled and then gently sighed, a touch overwhelmed. The dream he had dreamt for all of his childhood and early teens had at last come true. He wanted so much to hold her close and kiss her but didn't know if this was what she wanted. He felt that she still saw him as a brother figure. Looking away and focusing on a swan passing by he said, 'Do you know something, Charlie? You're even more beautiful now than when we were scruffy kids and I worshipped the ground you walked on.'

'No, you didn't worship me.' She smiled. 'I was your mate. Your tomboy friend.'

'And now you're a beautiful young woman,' he said, in complete awe of her. 'And I'll tell you something else.'

'Go on then,' she said, as she looked around for a clearing where they could sit by the river again.

He turned to face her and reached out for her hand to lead her through to the idyllic spot that he had seen. He took off his jacket and folded it inside out, then laid it on the grassy bank as a cushion for her. Once she was settled he sat next to her and reached for her hand again to hold it the way he did when they were no more than five years old. 'The something else that I want to tell you is that it took me a long time to get over you leaving. I missed you so much, Charlie, that it hurt. But then—'

'Time being the great healer,' she cut in, 'you met someone else to love.'

'Not exactly. I didn't have a girlfriend until two years ago –

86

when I was sixteen and had shot up and lost weight in the process.'

'And are you still with the same girlfriend? Or did you have a string of them once you got going?'

'No.' Still holding her hand he locked fingers and then looked into her lovely face and those beautiful soft green eyes that he still adored. To be sitting in this spot by the river was almost too good to be true. 'The girl I'm going out with wasn't the first, but there wasn't a string of girlfriends. Only three in fact. The first was from the office block where I work and I only took her out a few times.

'We liked each other but the spark wasn't there for either of us. Then the second one came along right out of the blue. She was a college student doing study work at our library and I met her, of all places if you can believe it, while I was sitting in the park-keeper's hut and sharing a bottle of beer with him. I kept on going to see him once you'd gone and we became really close.'

'Oh Nathan . . . if you go on like this I'll cry, I swear it. Just the thought of you and our park-keeper sitting there . . . he was such a lovely man.'

'He still is. Did I say he was dead?' He smiled at her and then softly chuckled. 'He might be a bit of our past but he's not past it yet. And he still goes on about the old days and when there was no coal to shovel into the grate of the fireplace.'

'Good. He hasn't changed then. I'll go back and see him one day. So what about number three girlfriend then? How long did she last?'

'I think it must be almost a year now. She's from an orthodox family. I had seen her before at the synagogue when we were kids but I don't think we ever actually said anything to each other.'

She didn't know why, but this news that Nathan was serious with a girl made her heart sink. She quickly brought herself to heel, though. 'We were all too young and busy surviving to think about all that love stuff, I suppose.' Looking across the river again, this time at a man who was sitting on the bank in a world of his own while fishing, she just couldn't leave it there. She had to know. 'And what about now, Nathan? Are you and number three planning to get engaged? Or have you already slipped the diamond ring on her finger? Are congratulations in order?'

'It's number four whose finger I would love to slip a ring onto, actually. Number four who used to be number one.'

Charlotte laughed. 'You bloody flirt! So what's she like then? The new girl who you're head over with.'

He drew breath and looked thoughtful. 'Well . . . she's a Christian and I've loved her for quite a while. Love's lost dream I suppose you could say.'

'So it wasn't mutual then?' Part of her hoped not.

'I don't know. I don't think so.' Shaking himself out of this confessional mood he had talked himself into, he laughed. 'Love's young dream is what it was. On my part that is. I had already made up my mind that I would marry her when I was ten years old, can you believe? From the age of five when I first saw her in class at the infant school I wanted to marry her. I loved the smell of her. I think it was Camay soap. Not perfume, just a nice soap smell that she used to wash with every day.'

'Nathan? Do you have a penchant for soap? You asked me during a geography lesson about my soap, then during history the next week and then when we were walking home from school together . . .'

'Did I?'

'Yes.'

'Well, there we are then. It must have been you that I loved so much I couldn't sleep at night.'

'Oh stop it. You'll have me in tears in a minute . . . let's forget about memory lane and make the most of now.'

'Memory lane,' he whispered. 'Yes, I suppose that's what it is. Just a memory.' He turned his head a little to look at her face. 'But this isn't a memory, is it? This is the here and now.'

'That's true, but it will be by tomorrow once you've gone back to London. It will all be another recollection to bring up in a few more years time when we might just find each other again.'

'Who knows?' he drew a slow breath and then looked sideways at her. At her beautiful face and her beautiful natural blonde hair. 'I like the new hairstyle. You look like Sandy Shaw except that you're prettier and blonde. It suits you. It's very fashionable.'

'And that's surprising, is it? Me having an up to date style even though I've turned into a carrot cruncher. A country bumpkin.'

Nathan giggled. 'Country bumpkin? I don't think so. You can take the girl out of the East End but you can't take the East End out of the girl. You're still a Londoner.'

'Good. I'm glad you think so too. I know where my roots are.'

'And I'll tell you something else.'

'If you must, Nathan,' she sighed and then looked into his warm brown eyes. 'Well go on then. No holds barred.'

'Really? I can really say whatever I want?'

'Well, you always did. Why stop now? Go on, I can take it. Criticise me if you must.'

'Criticise?' Again he laughed, and loved the way she was now blushing pink. 'No. I wasn't going to do that. I was going to say . . . what I am saying . . . is that I would love it if you were to consider moving back to London. I missed you so much when you left that I got a pain in my chest that wouldn't go away. There was nothing medically wrong. I just kept wishing you hadn't gone. I suppose I was suffering from what they call puppy love?' He grinned, more from embarrassment than joy. 'We were too busy surviving and too young to even consider what love meant at that time.'

Not quite sure what lay behind this confession, Charlotte leaned towards him and brushed a kiss across his cheek. 'You're just as lovely a person as you ever were. And I still love you and your funny ways.'

Seizing the moment of a lifetime he placed an arm around her so that she could not escape. 'Am I allowed to kiss an old friend on the lips then?' he said.

'I don't see why not.' Charlie blushed a little and smiled.

His voice was soft and husky now and the sky was a lovely light blue and the sun was just beginning to set. 'Is that a yes, then?'

'It think it must be. I've missed you, Nathan.' She smiled affectionately, and then lowered her eyes, a touch shy all of a sudden. 'This is insane,' she murmured. 'I can't believe this is happening.'

'You sound like my dad now. That's one of his expressions that you must have picked up years ago.'

The silence and warmth between them said it all. Her funny fat childhood friend had gone from an insecure boy to a confident, tall and handsome young man. Placing her hands on his shoulders Charlotte realised just how much she had missed those warm brown eyes. 'I love you in the same way as I always did. Even though you've changed. Even though my fat and funny nervous friend has turned into a bit of a Romeo.'

'I've never been anything else where you were concerned.' He placed his hands around her slim waist and gently pulled her close. 'I loved you so much, Charlie, that it hurt. And I still love you. And I can hardly believe that I'm here and with you again. I've been kidding myself for years that I'd got over you, but I don't want to do that any more.'

Looking into his eyes as if they were the only two people around, Charlotte gently pressed her lips against his. Locked in each other's arms as if they were never going to let go, Nathan whispered in Charlotte's ear – 'I think I've never stopped loving you.'

'Stop it, Nathan, or I'll be in a flood of tears,' she whispered back.

'I don't care if you do cry. I want you to cry . . . on my shoulder. You don't know how I've longed to kiss those lips ever since I was five years old.' His voice was filled with emotion and love. 'I never stopped thinking about you. I *couldn't* stop thinking about you. I was so lonely after you'd gone I thought I would die. I haven't stopped wishing that you would come back home since the day you left.'

Gazing into his solemn handsome face again, Charlotte used the tip of her thumb to wipe away a little smudged lipstick from his face and he used his thumb to wipe away an escaping tear that was trickling down her cheek. 'Who would have thought that you would have grown into Prince Charming,' she said.

A touch embarrassed he eased himself away and drew breath. He then slipped his hand inside his jacket pocket to pull out a packet of cigarettes and the Zippo lighter given to him by his granddad. Once he had lit his cigarette, he slowly shook his head. 'My grandpa gave this to me when I confessed that I had had a few drags of a cigarette from a packet of five Woodbines that I bought two days after you left for Norfolk. I wonder what he would say if he could see me now? Here with you like this? He always said that you were a very special girl.'

'And I always thought that he was a lovely person. What about your dad? Did he know that you had the smoke?'

Nathan chuckled and they walked slowly onwards. 'Probably. He's never mentioned it and he doesn't criticise me now for having taken up the habit. He doesn't smoke. I don't think he ever did. But he doesn't interfere with what I do.' He drew on his cigarette and then blew a smoke ring. 'Thank God we left the old house in the courtyard and moved onto that council estate, else I might never have met you. But it doesn't matter now. Now that we've found each other again.'

'And it doesn't matter that I was dragged out into the back of beyond to Norfolk . . . now that you're here.' Charlotte slipped her hand into his.

'Our estate was lovely though, wasn't it? We had all those grassy areas; a proper football pitch that doubled up for cricket.'

'And there were lovely cottages with front and back gardens as well as the four-storey blocks of flats everywhere. I loved living there.'

Taking a last drag of his cigarette he then flicked it into the river. 'Would you like us to go for a meal this evening? I saw what looked like a very nice Chinese restaurant along by the main bridge on my way into town.'

'I'd prefer fish and chips.'

'Good. So would I.' He smiled and asked, 'Do you think that your parents are really fine with me sleeping over?'

'Of course they are. They wouldn't dream of you going into a bed and breakfast. We've got a spare room. It's small but cosy and Mum and Dad would be hurt if you didn't stay. You're our neighbour from the past, don't forget. They'd love to catch up.'

Nathan looked into her face again. 'Really? Well, I can't ask for more than that, can I. After all this time of not seeing each other and I'm welcomed back into the fold.'

'Of course. Why wouldn't you be? You were my best friend, Nathan. And we hardly see anyone from our old neck of the woods nowadays. They'd welcome your dad and your grandparents if you ever wanted to fetch them up here. They always got on well with your family. You know that.'

'Yes they did, didn't they. I'll phone Dad later on and tell him I won't be back home tonight.'

'Good.' She brushed a few fallen leaves off the shoulders of his jacket. 'You know . . . just before you turned up out of the blue like this I was feeling miserable and down. I felt like Nora-no-friends.'

'You haven't made friends in all the time you've been here? I can't believe that, Charlie.'

'Well, it's true. I knew I didn't like it here soon after we moved in. The new housing estate we were on at first was great, brand spanking new and we had a lovely back garden. But there was nothing to do. Nowhere to go.'

'And now?'

'Nothing much has changed. It is a lovely old historic town, but people of our age need more. It's great for kids, what with the rivers and new footpaths everywhere, but I've been bored out of my brains and lonely. I can't tell you what it was like. I hated it at first.'

'Nothing for your age group to do then, and now, isn't healthy,' said Nathan, slowly nodding his head and reminding Charlotte of his dad. 'I do see what you mean. What about work for the men? Or have they had to go on the dole?'

'No, of course they haven't. There's plenty of work because of the new firms and factories that keep coming into the town.'

'New firms coming in? Well then, I suppose that's because the rates are low and old factories or pre-pack buildings can be bought on the cheap.'

Charlotte laughed at him. 'A true blue accountant then?' she said.

'Absolutely.' He looked sideways at her. 'I can't believe that we're here together like this by the river and talking. Will I wake up and find it's all a dream, Charlie?'

'No. It's real. This is me and you again – just like old times. Almost.' She smiled. 'All right, we're not sitting in the park-keeper's open shed looking forward, but on the river's edge looking back, with a five-year gap between and a lovely country pub just ahead of us. I think we should drink to that, don't you?'

'Yes,' said Nathan, a little more choked than he would like to be.

Later on, as they strolled back to Charlotte's house, having enjoyed fish and chips and a drink in the quaint old pub by the river, they linked arms and Nathan talked non-stop about what he had been doing with his life. But when it came to Charlotte, she had nothing much to tell him about hers because in truth there was nothing interesting to say. She had filled him in on the little that there was in her world. Nathan was full of enthusiasm.

'So come on,' he said. 'Enough about me. You must have one or two boyfriends?'

'No.' She smiled coyly and shrugged. 'The girls and women at work are really nice but they're mostly older than me with young families. I just don't seem to have been able to make friends up here the way I could down in London. I don't know why.'

'Well, maybe that's because you don't really belong up here. Maybe your roots are calling you back home?'

'I don't know, Nathan. I don't know anything anymore. What I want from life, or where I want to live. I just get on with things like everyone else has to. You've been luckier than me.'

'No. Luck's got nothing to do with it. We have to make things happen. You know that. Come on, Charlie! Where's the girl that used to lead the way? What's happened to you?'

Charlotte smiled warmly. Yes, he was the old Nathan that she knew so well. Before she could answer he was off again. 'You like working at the council offices, and you've made a few friends there – even if they're not your age.'

'Nathan! Stop trying to make my little world sound interesting. It's not. Okay?'

'Well, at least you're admitting it, so I suppose that's something.' He shrugged in his lovely old familiar Yiddish way. 'Everyone has to have a passion,' he said, 'especially someone like you.'

'So what do you suggest?'

He stopped in his tracks and turned to face her. 'Come back, Charlotte. Come back to where you belong. Where you were born and grew up. Where your roots are. You said earlier on that you miss your grandparents – well, why not stay with them? Look for an office job and then maybe a bedsit. It's not impossible. Lots of young people are doing that now. You could come with me to the Fringe theatre group. It's a great world to be part of, I promise you.'

Charlotte felt her heart sink. 'It's not that easy.'

'Yes it is! You'll shrivel up and die if you stay up here with nothing to do and no one to do it with.'

Charlotte forced herself to laugh so that she wouldn't cry. 'You're still mad.'

'Maybe – but at least I'm happy. Come home, Charlie . . . please?'

'You don't need me. You've been having a great life without me by the sound of it. You don't have to pretend otherwise just to make me feel better about not having done anything to improve mine.'

'Okay. But let me say it just once more. Come home. Stay at your grandparents' house. Be in London and be part of a buzzing world that's going on there right now. You can help me with the theatre group's bookkeeping and backstage management at weekends. You could even fill in as a bit part actor now and then.'

'Talk sense. I can't act.'

'It doesn't matter! None of us can bloody well act. But who gives a shit? We enjoy ourselves and the audience loves it.'

'It does sound like fun,' she murmured. Deep down she was beginning to feel excited by the possibility of turning her life around.

'You would love it. We hardly make a profit.' Nathan

smiled. 'But nobody cares. The entire company is happy to be involved. They love it.'

'And so do you by the sound of it.'

'Me?' He shrugged. 'Of course I do. Haven't I been banging on about it?'

Charlotte could hardly believe how his life had turned around. 'I'm really glad that I made that phone call, Nathan. I'm glad you came. I've missed you.'

'And I've missed you. We might be five years older but we can't have changed that much. I don't ask God that I should marry you one day, it's true, but . . .'

'You silly daft thing.' Charlotte smiled as she looked into his handsome face and those big soft brown eyes. She then took his hand again to walk slowly on.

'Seriously now – aren't we still best friends? Look at us. Strolling along as if the five years hasn't passed. You can't ask for much more than that. And you know what my dad always says? That people, whether they like to believe it or not, even though they change as they grow, they stay the same inside.'

Charlotte considered this and then slowly nodded. She felt just as close to him as she used to when they were kids. She wanted him to put his arms around her and hold her tight. Then just as if he was reading her mind he placed one hand on her shoulder and cupped her chin with the other. 'My mother used to say what goes round comes round. I could have ended up bitter and twisted, you know. From all the bullying and then losing you. But luckily my religion helped me to wave it away and leave it where it belonged – in the past. The little green devils sit on the shoulders of the intimidators. Not on ours.' He then leaned forward and kissed her lightly on those beautiful soft shapely lips that he had loved since the day he had set eyes on her in the infant school.

She looked at him and sighed contentedly. 'And you really think that I would be able to settle in the East End again after living in a world that's surrounded by rivers, forests and fields?'

'You know very well that you would. And you don't need me to tell you that, Charlie. You know you'll slip right back into the way of life and you also know that it's what you want.'

'I'll think about it. Think about whether you're right or wrong.'

'It was only five years ago that you left, and you've got a lifetime in front of you. You don't want to spend your life regretting that you didn't take the chance while you were still young.'

She swallowed against a lump in her throat and tremulously smiled back at him. Feeling a little awkward and needing time to think about both his feelings and hers, she glanced at him to see that he was finding the conversation difficult so changed the subject. Trying to sound casual, she said, 'There used to be a theatre here in Bridgeford. Years ago.'

'You already told me.' Nathan turned his face to look at hers. He knew her so well. She was not only forcing back tears but also trying to find something in common and was using the theatre to do it. And it wasn't necessary. As far as he was concerned nothing had changed between them. 'It's a pity that it's not still going. A small theatre for panto at Christmas would be good. It brings families together for a bit of fun. It could make a big difference to a small town like this.' He looked sideways at her, at his lovely Charlotte. He adored her as much as ever. 'It must have been a lively little town in the old days, Charlie.'

'It was, according to my friend Eric. There used to be an old fashioned baker, a blacksmith, cobbler, grocer, muffin maker, stay maker and straw hat-maker.'

'Your friend Eric?'

Charlotte smiled. 'He's an old boy. But he remembers all the old traders, or so he says.'

Relief swept through Nathan and replaced the fear of someone younger being close to her. But he was soon back on track. 'Most of those old trades are defunct now,' he said. 'More's the pity.'

'There *is* an old fashioned cinema . . . it reminds me of the one in Bethnal Green but not so run-down. Do you remember that place?'

'How could I forget. It was a bug hole.'

Drawing closer to the street where she lived Charlotte tried not to think about the next day when he would be gone. He was lovely company and the thought of him going away again made her heart sink, but she smiled at the sound of a black-bird's song drifting through the air close by. They reached Charlotte's house. 'Well, here we are then. Back home after a tour of the place where I live.' When she turned the key in the lock she knew in her heart what was going to happen once they were both inside with the door closed behind them.

Putting his arms around her Nathan gently brushed some loose strands of her blonde hair off her face and looked into those lovely blue eyes. His voice low and charged with emotion, he said, 'I can't believe I'm standing here with you like this.'

'Well, you are. This is us and this is real.'

He gently pressed his mouth against hers and then, after all the years of knowing each other, they shared their first real kiss and both wanted more. Much more . . . But they were going to have to wait. Charlotte was young and Charlotte was a virgin. But they kissed lovingly and they held on to each other and this made up for everything.

The following morning before saying goodbye to Nathan, Charlotte was sure of what she wanted. She wanted to see more of her long lost best friend, who she was falling in love with all over again – a different kind of love this time, though. During the years of their living miles away from each other, each of them had grown in their own way, of course they had, but, more importantly, they hadn't grown apart. Now, more than ever, she knew that she had to move back to London. Her first priority, of course, was to look for a position back in London and somewhere to live in the East End. She felt that her parents would be against it, but she was determined to turn her life around. She was going to have to find herself a furnished flat and she was going to have to see if she could transfer from the Thetford office to a branch in London. And in the East End if possible.

Having learned quite a bit while working in the local Town Hall, as well as going to evening classes locally much earlier on to learn touch typing, she felt quite confident that she could cope in a London office. Her typing speed now was sixty words per minute. Apart from all of this, she knew that her grandparents, Nell and Johnny, would put her up if necessary, and that her parents would help her out financially if she was stuck for cash – once they accepted that she really didn't want to live in a small country town any more. She knew that her gran couldn't wait to have her back in her realm where she could keep an eye on her. And in any case, Charlotte wanted to see more of the funny old couple who had always managed to make her laugh no matter what. It was the banter of her grandparents that she loved – never mind the easy flow of swearing that came naturally to both of them.

Yes, she *was* looking forward to a more cheerful way of life. She could hardly wait.

Seven

Once Charlotte had said farewell to Nathan and promised to meet him in London to view rooms to let, she felt more positive. And was excited about a few days' break away from home and from her parents and Bridgeford. Getting it past Rita and Eddie that she was going down to London to look for a place of her own, was not going to be easy . . . but she had always known that would be the case. She was, after all, their only child, but without realising it they had been overly protective and a little bit self-centred. And now she was ready to sit down with them and talk openly about plans that she had been secretly making for quite a while. In fact, ever since the first year they came to Bridgeford she had, in the quiet of her bedroom, thought about going to live with her grandparents in Bow one day. Nathan's visit out of the blue had been exactly the kick-start she needed to spur her into action, and she silently thanked him for it. And now, taking a leaf out of her gran's book, she was determined not to put off until tomorrow what could be said today.

So, that evening, just as the family of three were settling down and ready to switch on the television, she braced herself for a battle of words. On her favourite armchair and in her pyjamas and dressing gown, her legs curled under her, she looked across to her mum and dad, together on the sofa, and quietly said, 'I need to talk to you.'

Eddie looked sideways at her, a touch amused by her adult

tone. He sported a warm smile. 'Can it wait till after *Corona-tion Street*? You know your mother won't want any interruptions.'

'Nor will you,' said Rita. 'You don't 'ave to pretend to us that you don't like it, watching the goings-on in the Street. We won't tell your mates in the pub.' She looked across to Charlotte and winked at her.

'They wouldn't take any notice of you in any case, Rita. They, just like me, 'ave to give way to the woman of the house.'

'I'll come straight to the point then,' said Charlotte, determined to say what she had to. 'I want to go back to London. To find work in an office and rent a flat.' Eddie smiled and then looked at Rita. 'Over to you, sweetheart.'

'She can do what she likes. She's not a kid any more.' Her eyes were still fixed on her programme. Taken aback by this casual response, Charlotte could think of little else to do other than look at her mother's face and try to read from her expression whether she meant what she said or not. 'I thought that I would take a furnished flat nearby to Gran and Grand-dad . . .' She murmured.

'Whatever you think best,' was Rita's next easy reply. 'Do what you want. You're only young once.' In truth she didn't think for one minute that her daughter, her only child, would have the gumption to get up and go and find herself some-where to live as well as somewhere to work. But, as far as Charlotte was concerned, she had just been given the okay and without any arguments. There had been no condes-cending smirks and no remarks as to how she would not last a week on her own in the capital. And so, while the going was good, she decided there and then to set it in stone.

Her eyes lowered to the floor, she spoke in a quiet voice. 'The thing is . . . I feel as if I missed out on my teens so far by living up here and not being in the East End.'

'Missed out on what?' Rita smiled as she turned to look into Charlotte's face. 'What was there to miss out *on*?'

'Going out on a Friday and Saturday night with my mates. Most of the girls in the third and fourth year of senior school went to our local youth clubs and dance halls when they were fourteen and fifteen. They wore make-up and nail varnish and clothes that were in fashion. That's what I would have done if we had stayed put.'

'What are you talking about? You were only thirteen when we left Bethnal Green. You were still a girl.'

'I know. But thirteen-year-olds who were at my school were beginning to go to local dance halls along with fourteen, fifteen and sixteen-year-olds. They were all jiving and twisting to the latest records, which I would have loved to have done, but you said that I was too young for all of that and then you dragged me up here where there was nothing happening. I missed out on everything. On all of the fun that my mates at senior school were having. I didn't even have a transistor radio to listen to pop records in my bedroom.'

'Well, if you'd 'ave asked we would 'ave given you one for Christmas or your birthday. You never mentioned it. Anyway, you were still wearing socks at that time. I let you have some of those terrible luminous green, yellow or pink ones, if you remember.'

'Course I remember – and I liked them. But eleven-year-olds were wearing them. Thirteen-year-olds were getting used to stockings and pretty suspender belts.'

'Rubbish. And any girl that did wear stockings at that age would 'ave been seen as a Lolita.'

'Charlotte has got a point, Reet,' said Eddie, as ever the pacifier in this small family of three. 'She did spend her early teens up here. And it's true, there wasn't anything for her age group. It never occurred to me at the time.' He glanced at Charlotte and smiled. 'Sorry, babe. I think we might 'ave behaved a little bit on the selfish side without realising it.' He was now thinking about his youth and how he had enjoyed being a spiv in London when swing and jazz was all the rage.

'No. I don't agree,' said Rita. 'Hundreds of girls from the East End would 'ave given an arm and a leg to 'ave been able to live in a house like this with rivers all around us. You couldn't wait to get out of Bethnal Green, Charlotte! You wanted to move up here.'

'Out of Bethnal Green, maybe, but not out of the East End. You always said that one day we would live in one of those lovely Victorian houses overlooking Victoria Park and the boating lake, and then you changed your mind. And in any case, I thought from what you'd said about Bridgeford there was gonna be people of my age around. That's what you said at the time. That couples with young families who were teenagers were moving up here.'

'And . . . some did.'

'Not many. Not in Bridgeford and there wasn't one youth club or dance hall for people of my age to meet up in.'

'What is this?' said Rita. 'I didn't think you meant it when you mentioned it before. You don't think that we're gonna pull up roots and go back to the East End, do you? Is this what it's all about?' Rita was getting redder in the face. 'Because if it is, you're wrong. Me and your dad love it up here. And anyway, being eighteen is a lot different from thirteen. You're old enough now to make up your own mind. Do what you want. Go and rebel against life and have a taste of the youth freedom that the papers keep printing. Take purple hearts. Smoke marijuana. And when you've done all there is to do, you can come back home and appreciate what we've set up for you.'

Charlotte broke into soft laughter and avoided looking at her dad, who was also trapping laughter. 'Forget I even mentioned it,' she said. She knew that there was no point in having a conversation to do with her moving out. But as far as Charlotte was concerned, her mother had, whether in jest or not, given her free rein to leave home and she was going to grab it with both hands and go back to look for somewhere to live and somewhere to work. She would arrange to have time off from work, which would then be deducted from the holiday leave that was due her. She knew that if she were to continue with this conversation now, her parents would take it more seriously and talk her out of it. So she held her tongue.

'It's all this business of the Swinging Sixties that's going to your head,' murmured Rita. 'You wouldn't last six months in London. But go if you must. Have it your way. Find out for yourself. Make your own mistakes. But don't come back here if you get hooked on drugs.'

This was more than Eddie could take. He started to laugh and then got out of the room before Rita gave him an ear-bashing as well. 'I'm glad your father thinks it's funny,' she said, her eyes still focused on the television and Ena Sharples going on and on to Annie Walker about the price of a half pint of stout.

Pleased that she had started the ball rolling, Charlotte could hardly stop herself from smiling. 'You won't have to worry over me, Mum. I won't take drugs and I'll be safe and sound living close by, if not with, Gran and Granddad. And you like Nathan, don't you? He'll see I'm okay.'

'Whatever you say,' said Rita fixing on her soap so as not to have to think about it.

Charlotte could hardly believe that it would be so easy. She had managed to get it across that she was going to go ahead with what her mother saw as madcap plans and she wasn't going to try and stop her. And if Rita was right and she found that she had made a mistake and wanted to come back after six months or so, it wouldn't matter. Nothing gained, nothing lost. She was so carried away with the thought of moving on, she hadn't noticed Eddie coming back into the room. He strolled over to the window and gazed out, miles away. The truth of the matter was that he knew how his daughter felt.

He remembered when they had first arrived in Bridgeford how he had had the rural blues. He had smiled his way through it for the sake of his wife and daughter, but his romantic vision of a friendly community of rustic villagers turned out to be pie in the sky. He, just like other incomers, had found a touch of resentment from the locals at first because they believed that all of the Londoners would soon buy their own houses and push up property prices beyond the reach of their own born and bred young families. It was different now, of course, because most Londoners still lived in council houses.

Apart from this, Eddie had always kept up with the news about his neck of the woods in London. He knew that from as far back as 1952, East Enders who were moving away were being replaced by a huge influx of people from the West Indies for a start. Hard-working people who would no doubt also want to own their own homes one day. And within the space of just a few years it was being reported in the press that over a hundred thousand people from not only the West Indies but also Pakistan were living in and around the capital. So his fear had been similar to the locals in Norfolk and had turned out to be inconsequential. He had always wondered that, should he and his family want to move back later on, for instance, would he be able to. Would there be any council properties available? And would the cost of private housing rise above what the likes of people like himself could afford? But he was over all of this worry now because he was settled into his new way of life and reasonably happy. But his daughter wasn't, and he couldn't find it in his heart to blame her for wanting to be back in London. She was young and single with her life before her.

Eddie also knew that Rita was more than content with her lot. She had a washing machine and tumble dryer, a refrigerator, a deep-freeze and a new cooker. In London she had always had to use the bagwash or the launderette and had kept butter and cheese in a cool larder cabinet. Now, she had even achieved her dream of having wall-to-wall carpets. Not only were things cheaper to buy in Bridgeford, but there were no charges made for the fitting and fixing of things such as carpets and plumbing. It was all part and parcel of the service. And food was fresher and cheaper. Dairy produce, eggs, poultry, meat and fresh vegetables came into the local market from the local farms on a regular basis. And there was always a homemade cake stall run by the WI and the Red Cross so there was no need for Rita to bend over a hot oven any more. She simply adored her new life. But it wasn't too exciting for a teenager and Eddie was fully aware of this.

A week later, after thinking things through and having made arrangements to go to London, Charlotte was boarding a train from Bridgeford to King's Cross with Eddie seeing her off from the station platform. If truth be known, he felt proud of his daughter for taking this big step. He watched her walk away from him carrying her small suitcase and felt a lump the size of a fist in his throat. Once she was on the train, waving from an open doorway and then giving him the thumbs-up sign to say that all was well, he felt like bursting into tears. His daughter was taking a first big step out into the world of independence and he admired her guts and her confidence for standing up for her rights. Deep down, though, he still didn't quite believe that she would actually give up her position at the council offices, never mind her lovely bedroom in their lovely house. Rented rooms in London, from what he had heard, were seedy and less than desirable. But he knew that his daughter was going to have to find this out for herself. And if he were honest with himself, he would have to admit that he was hoping that this little trip that she was embarking upon would put the lid on her dream because he didn't want to lose her.

He didn't believe for one minute that Charlotte was simply rebelling, but nor did he believe that she truly wanted to be part of the so-called Swinging Capital and youth freedom. She had been wearing mini-skirts for a while so hadn't exactly turned into a country bumpkin. What he couldn't accept was that she was the sort of girl who was cut out for high fashion, boutiques, discos and live concerts. He couldn't imagine her in a crowd, watching the Beatles on stage performing to hysterical girls screaming so loudly en masse that it was impossible to hear the voices of John, Paul, George and Ringo. She just wasn't that kind of a person. At least he didn't think she was.

Walking slowly along the platform towards the exit and feeling a touch emotional, Eddie spotted Kenny Wood strolling towards the train. The thought of asking him to go and sit next to Charlotte to give her some company flashed into his mind and then flashed out again. The lad who had been known as Ginger had been a little bastard when young, and even though he seemed quiet and placid now, Eddie didn't think that his daughter would appreciate being stuck with him for the duration of the journey. In fact, he knew that she would be furious if he interfered in this newfound independence that she had discovered, and which had at least boosted her morale from what he could tell. So he let go of the idea.

Kenny, having done his homework, now knew that Charlotte's dad was one of the most respected men about town. And since they shared the same local and not being one to miss an opportunity, smiled broadly at Eddie and showed a hand, saying, 'All right, mate? See Charlotte off okay?'

This stopped Eddie in his tracks. How come he knew that Charlotte was on the train? He looked sideways at the teenager and then broke into a warm smile. 'Yeah. She's settled with a window seat, Kenny. I take it that you are that same little fucker with the ginger hair that couldn't be tamed when a kid?'

'Not any more, mate. I've grown up.' Kenny smiled. 'Still,

better to be bad when a boy than later on when a man. I know I was a right little bastard. Dad didn't know what to do about me so let it be. He don't think I've turned out too bad. I thought it was you seeing Charlotte onto the train. Anyway, I'm off back home for a bit. Back to my roots and my mum and dad. It's nice up 'ere but I miss all my aunts and uncles and cousins and that.'

'I know what you mean, son. It can be a bit of a wrench moving from your roots. How is your dad? Still in the carpet trade?'

'Yeah. It's a successful little family business now. Keeps me busy and out of mischief. Let me know if you want your place fitted out. I can do you a special price.'

Eddie laughed warmly. 'You're a bit too late, son, we're all fixed up. But if I can put any business your way I will. I'm glad to see that you're following in your dad's footsteps.

'Thanks. I tried to talk Mum and Dad into coming to live up here but they didn't much fancy the idea. I suggested a move to Haverhill as well, where loads of other East Enders are going, but they weren't up for that either.' He shrugged. 'Bridgeford's a lovely old town, don't get me wrong, but my mum and dad and my old gran would feel like fish out of water in this place.'

'And what about you?' said Eddie, hoping he had bought a one-way ticket to London. He felt sure that he had just been told a load of mumbo-jumbo.

'Oh, I reckon it's a lovely little town in the country! But it's not for me on a permanent basis, mate. But there you go. Maybe once I'm married wiv a family and that. Who knows? Anyway . . . it was good to see your familiar face in the pub the other night. Cheered me up that did.'

'Good. And as for your parents not wanting to live up here, each to their own, boy, each to their own. Take it easy.' With that Eddie winked at him and continued on his way.

He hadn't got far when he found himself wondering if he

should have a little chat with Rita and touch on the subject of Charlotte and birth control, and then checked himself for even thinking it. But then he remembered that it hadn't been more than a couple of months of courting Rita back in the old days before they were making love. And now, in the mid-Sixties, from what he had heard, birth control clinics had been set up not only for married couples, but single girls too. He decided to sleep on it, and made a mental note for when he next went into the library to return his books. He thought that he might just pick up a guide to safe sex and leave it around for Charlotte to see when she came back from her London trip. He felt sure that there had to be books on the subject. After all, the contraceptive pill was now available on the National Health, from what he had heard.

Hardly able to believe that he was thinking about his daughter being old enough to be made love to, Eddie blew air as he turned the key in the lock of his car. He blamed the beatnik students of the Fifties, who had proclaimed the right of young people to have sex freely, and with more than one partner, before marriage. He got into his motor and tried not to think about it. It was a fast-changing world and there was nothing that was going to slow it down. He smiled as he recalled when bohemian demonstrators first started to hit the news. They had waved their banners and chanted that nuclear war would soon bring the world to an end so everyone should live for the day. And this was exactly what the young from all walks of life had done and were still doing. Enjoying life to the full regardless of old established standards. They were jiving the nights away at all-night sessions at such places as the Albert Hall, and some had made love on the dance floor with no shame attached. The age of recreational sex for young single women was now seeing a heyday. And his daughter was about to walk smack bang into the centre of it. Nathan had talked quite a bit about his fringe theatre world and the 'arty' friends he mixed with. Whether or not they smoked marijuana he couldn't say. He could only hope not, and this was what he was now doing. Hoping his daughter wouldn't be drawn into a set that took drugs and believed in free love.

'Fucking cheek,' murmured Kenny. *'Each to their own?* Smart-arse bastard.' He then climbed aboard the train via the same doorway as Charlotte and as he approached her while choosing somewhere to sit, he winked and smiled all friendly. Pushing his luck he stopped in his tracks and said, 'Look, I hope you don't mind me talking to you like this, Charlie, but . . . I just wanna say I'm sorry for being an evil little sod when I was a kid. And I really do mean that. You might not recognise me now – but I was that little ginger-headed bastard with the crew-cut.'

Taken by surprise, Charlotte was momentarily lost for words. Then, once she found her voice she said, 'I know who you are. I recognise your face. And it's okay, all done and dusted.'

'Can I buy you a drink at the other end? Just to show a bit of good will?'

'No, that's all right, thanks. Say hello to your parents for me.' Charlotte smiled faintly at him. She couldn't believe that he was on the same train as herself but she wasn't going to let it get to her. She could leave all that had happened and been said in the past where it belonged, no problem.

'I will say hello for yer,' he said, 'I will. And may God bless you for being an angel, Charlie.' He nodded farewell and walked through to the end of the carriage with the air of a Jehovah's Witness and only just able to contain his laughter. He could hardly believe what a brilliant actor he could be when the need arose.

Once seated in his chosen place by himself, Kenny had to release a bit of pent up laughter, albeit quietly. He liked his seat by the window and thought he might sleep on the train until it pulled into King's Cross. As he settled down for the long and boring journey away from what he considered to be a boring town he wondered what the tart, Charlie, was up to. Maybe she had had enough of Bridgeford too? She had been carrying a small suitcase, so was she staying with her relatives or the tall good-looking dark-haired guy he saw her with in the pub? He thought that it might be fun to discreetly follow her from King's Cross, or even walk boldly beside her along the platform and ask where she was going. He chuckled and then murmured to himself, 'Don't forget what killed the cat, Kenny. Don't forget what curiosity did. Well, fuck the cat and fuck the saying. I'll find out what the slag's up to. For all 'er airs and graces, she's no better than a whore, except that she dresses as if she wasn't born and bred in the same mould as them. Toffee-nosed bitch.'

During her journey, Charlotte had plenty of time to think while she watched the changing scenery from the window as the train made its way to the capital. Most of her time was spent on thoughts of her evening with Nathan, whom she couldn't wait to see again. She smiled at the way his father had talked to her on the phone in the first place – the call that had kick-started Nathan into action. It felt as if it was only yesterday that she was living in the same block of flats as his family on the same council estate. And her recollection of those times summed it all up. Country people were kind and obliging but East Enders were this and more. The old-fashioned community spirit that she had been brought up within could not be bottled. And now she couldn't wait to walk on the busy pavements of Whitechapel, Mile End and Bethnal Green again. She was looking forward most of all to being part of the London buzz, living amidst people of mixed religion and race. It wasn't until Nathan had mentioned a Jamaican lad with a great sense of humour who had been in their class at school that she realised she had not seen one black face in Norfolk. Not one. Thinking about this, and

III

other meaningful things about her childhood, she slipped into a lovely sleep and didn't wake up until the train pulled into King's Cross.

Eight

Once Charlotte had got off the train and was outside the station, she was comforted by the fact that little had changed and everything seemed just as familiar as ever, even though there seemed to be a lot more people about. Five years on, and still it all felt so wonderfully easy to slip back into the hub of things. Instead of feeling like a girl up from the country, which was her worry when she had boarded the train from Bridgeford, she was immediately into the swing of things as if she had never left in the first place. On the underground train heading for the Angel Islington, with the addresses of two flats that she had acquired from the *Evening Standard* scribbled onto a piece of paper held in her hand, she felt her old confidence flowing back. From the station she made her way towards the High Road as if this was an ordinary everyday occurrence.

When she got to Camden Passage, where the antique market was in full swing with shops and stalls selling furniture, old silver or bric-a-brac, she felt a rush of adrenaline. It was lively and it was colourful and she was ecstatic at being back home, albeit in a different part of the city. Peering at her handwritten directions to the street where she was to meet the landlady of a four-storey house who had advertised a furnished flat to let, she knew that she hadn't far to go.

It had been her granddad who had sent her the property to let page from the *Evening Standard* and she was quietly thanking him for it. The *Standard* was a newspaper that he took regularly and he had lost no time in mailing her that copy. Ever since her grandparents had picked up the tiniest hint that she wanted to try her hand at living by herself in London they had been on the case – they couldn't wait to have her back on home ground. They knew her budget and felt that she could not afford to pay more than three pounds ten shillings, or at the most four pounds a week for lodgings. They had done as she asked and marked any in the paper that they thought suitable, but Charlotte had chosen just one of them. This one in North London she herself had marked with a red pen. The few that her granddad had underlined were, naturally, smack bang in the middle of East London and just a short bus ride away from where they lived. Quite naturally too, her grandparents hoped that she would choose to return to her roots, not too far away from Bromley by Bow – their own little patch of heaven. Deep down, though, Nell and Johnny felt that Charlotte wouldn't last long in furnished digs wherever they were, and certainly not in a part of the capital where she knew no one and would most likely feel like a fish out of water rather than London born and bred. It had been five years since she had lived there, after all. This aside, they had agreed between themselves to hold their tongues when it came to talking too much about her moving in with them. It was what they wanted but they weren't going to push it. So, in their wisdom, they were going to keep shtum, leave things be and wait to see how it all went. And in any case, they didn't know whether she would still love London after all this time or hate it. Only time would tell.

Rita and Eddie were no different. Both of them had eaves-dropped on the evening when Charlotte had spoken on the telephone to the owners of each of the two furnished flats that she had fancied of those she had seen advertised. From what they could make out from listening behind the open door, it seemed that both flats were part of large houses that had, at one time or another, been converted. This had made Rita pale and despairing as she whispered to Eddie, 'My God, it sounds like she's going to be living in a commune.' This vision had struck both of them with horror but they managed to allay each other's fears by saying that Charlotte wouldn't last five minutes in that kind of a place and would either move in with her grandparents or soon be home with her tail between her legs.

Now, in the buzzing atmosphere of north London, Charlotte was feeling less and less a girl up from the country. Her stomach was churning a little and her thoughts had been all over the place ever since her parents had tried to brainwash her into believing that she didn't belong in London any more . . . but all her doubts were now draining away. They had been wrong. London was busier than she remembered but then, during the past five years, thousands had come from overseas to live in England, so the numbers of people and the mix of races was to be expected. The sight of the familiar red buses warmed her, as did the black taxis everywhere. Resisting the urge to stroll through Camden Passage and look at the stalls selling everything from old-fashioned kitchen sinks to ornate chandeliers, she pushed on towards her destination, eager to view the first flat.

Before she knew it, she was in the quiet back turning that she had been heading for, having asked directions from a passer-by. She found herself standing outside a large period terraced house, in a street lined with a few trees and with similar houses on both sides. The reality of stepping out on her own like this was suddenly no longer daunting but wonderful. She checked that she was on the right side of the road for uneven numbers and walked slowly along, looking at each of the houses and trying to imagine the kind of people that might live in them.

Arriving outside number forty-one Bethel Place, Charlotte was reassured to see that the small area behind the waist-high brick wall wasn't as pristine as the others in the turning, and neither were the curtains at the windows as posh and expensive looking. Checking the piece of paper in her hand to be certain that she was where she should be, she went through the small open gateway and up to a dark-green painted front door that had an old-fashioned brass knocker and letterbox that was in need of a bit of Brasso and a good rub. Pressing her finger on the old black and white china bell she looked around her and was surprised at how clean the road and the pavements on either side were. There was no litter on the ground, which had been part and parcel of the back and beyond of Stepney and Bethnal Green when she had lived there, and the road sweepers arrived with their huge brooms and push carts.

Standing on the doorstep and listening for a noise from inside the house, she heard the sound of quick footsteps on floorboards and could hardly believe that there would be no wall-to-wall carpet in a house that had been described as splendid. She started to have doubts about the advert, which had painted a very nice picture of the property to let. When the door opened, however, she was immediately at ease because the hallway with its stripped and waxed floorboards and long narrow patterned rug was more than just warm and welcoming – it was lovely. And so too was the gentlewoman who opened the door to her and who looked to be in her mid-thirties.

Looking a touch seriously at Charlotte she said, 'Are you the girl who telephoned yesterday?'

'Yes, I am.' Charlotte smiled inwardly because she realised that the woman had forgotten her name. 'I'm Charlotte, and I'm sorry if I'm a bit late.' She glanced at her wristwatch to see that she was actually fifteen minutes late. 'I should have kept an eye on my watch. I'm really sorry. I hope I've not inconvenienced you.'

Moving aside the good-natured woman waved a hand and

smiled at her. She then spoke in a whispering kind of a voice saying, 'It doesn't matter. But I am expecting some friends so we might have to be a little quicker than you would like.' She then closed the door behind her, saying, 'Please do call me Petusha.'

'Thank you. I will. And I'm Charlotte,' she said returning the smile and realising that she was repeating herself.

'Yes, of course you are,' said Petusha, who was doing her best to put her at ease. 'I remember now. I was in the garden when you rang, just seeing off the dog from next door who decided to jump over my lovely new low brick wall and pee on the back step for the fun of it.'

'Oh dear,' said Charlotte. 'Was that the first time he's done it?'

'It's a she and no, it isn't the first time. But it's only been happening since we had the builder in and got rid of the old dilapidated fence. It's such a naughty dog and it chases my three cats for the fun of it, knowing that it makes me cross. But her owner is a lovely man, if a bit careless when it comes to the duties of a pet owner. But then he's a journalist and always busy so we must make allowances.'

The woman looked directly at Charlotte and broke into a warm and friendly smile. 'I am so sorry for going on like this. You must think me quite mad. Shall we start at the top where the rooms to let are?'

'Why not?' said Charlotte. 'I like your house. It's got a homely feel to it.'

'Has it? How sweet of you to say so.' Petusha, who had dark hair cut into a kind of scruffy version of the urchin style, said, 'You're a natural blonde, aren't you?'

'Yes,' said Charlotte, wondering why she would ask such a thing. 'I used to hate it when I was small. Mum used to say that the angels forgot to add a bit of colour when they were making me. But I like it now.'

'I should think you do. I've friends who pay a fortune to

arrive at what you were born with. How funny that you should have hated it as a child. So many would die to have hair like yours. White blonde is very much in vogue.' Floating up the staircase and leading the way, Petusha gave a running commentary on the area as if time could not be wasted with silences. Following her, Charlotte couldn't help smiling. She had taken an instant liking to this off-the-wall lady, who was wearing a dark red and inky blue striped mini-dress and thick black tights, with slingback shoes that had lavatory pan heels. Even though she was from a totally different class, Charlotte felt at ease in her house and in her company. She wasn't in the least bit snooty or snobbish.

When they reached the attic flat at the top of the three-storeyed house, they paused for breath then entered a very spacious room with a high ceiling, that was divided by a large framed and beautiful antique silk screen. In the sitting area was an old fashioned red and gold damask sofa with two matching armchairs either side, set around a coffee table and facing a carved pine fireplace inset with patterned tiles and a small but ornate black grate. Behind the silk screen, which ran the full width of the room, was an old-fashioned double brass bed and a large Victorian pine wardrobe. Off the sitting room there was a short narrow passageway with just enough space to swing a cat. This area led to a small kitchen. The bathroom, Charlotte learned, was off the landing and was to be shared by herself and another tenant, a South African called Mary.

Once they had done the lightning tour the landlady discreetly studied Charlotte's expression and then said, 'What do you think?' She tipped her head to one side and smiled while she waited. 'Is it the sort of place that you were looking for? I've only let it once before and that was to a cousin who was here for several years. He's just bought himself a flat in Battersea close to where he works, which is why you're here of course.' She smiled.

'I think it's lovely,' said Charlotte, pausing to take it all in. Then, just as she was about to ask about house rules and whether or not her parents could stay for a weekend now and then, or whether she was allowed to have a friend stay overnight, the sound of the doorbell could be heard.

'Oh dear . . . I think we are going to be descended upon,' murmured Petusha, looking at her pretty gold wristwatch. 'I'm expecting some friends, but I thought I had at least half an hour to spare. Of course it might not be them.' She waited to see if whomever it was that had rung the bell was going to go away or try again. When the sound rang through the house again she chuckled. 'It *is* my friends, and one of them is clearly enjoying the finger on the bell bit. Please do excuse me while I rush down to let them in.'

'Of course,' said Charlotte. 'I'm fine.'

Turning away gracefully, Petusha was out of the room and on her way down to the ground floor while calling out in a kind of sing-song voice, 'I'm coming! I'm coming!'

Pleased to have the opportunity to be by herself and quietly check out the kitchen, and the bathroom on the landing, Charlotte felt a wave of excitement at the thought of having a place of her own like this. She quite fancied herself living in this private place at the top of the house where she could look out on the world and all of its people that passed by. She glanced out of the window and down at the pavement to see a gaggle of folk in their late twenties or early thirties talking and laughing together. They, similar to the lady who owned the house, were dressed differently from the people that Charlotte mixed with or knew. A completely different set altogether, quite trendy and a touch arty. She had in fact walked into the realm of someone who had fashionable friends.

Having seen as much as she needed of the attic flat she wandered downstairs and met Petusha halfway. She could see that the woman was a touch flustered. 'I'm awfully sorry to have left you by yourself,' she said. 'You must think me terribly rude, but some of my chums have arrived and—'

'It's all right,' said Charlotte. 'I've seen all I needed to see. And I love the rooms.'

'Do you really? Oh well, isn't that marvellous. Do come and meet my chums – we're having a little soirée in the kitchen. They're mostly actors, I fear, so they do tend to be a little flamboyant, which can be taken the wrong way. But they're all very nice beneath the guise.'

'That's okay,' said Charlotte. 'I might be up from the country but I was born and bred in the East End so I'm used to oddballs.'

'Oh.' Petusha broke in her lovely smile again. 'What a marvellous description. I shall use that myself from now on. Oddballs.' She giggled with delight. 'It sounds quite rude and yet flatteringly eccentric. Depending, of course, on one's wicked mind. I shall tell them what you said.'

'I'd rather you didn't,' said Charlotte. 'At least not while I'm here. Say what you want once I've gone.'

'Oh, darling girl, I was *teasing* you. Of course I wouldn't repeat it. Please do come and say hello.'

'Oh no, thank you, but I won't intrude.' Charlotte was now beginning to feel as if she was being drawn into a cradle of humanity where she didn't belong. She did like the flat though.

Trailing behind Petusha she said, 'If it's all right with you, I could phone from my grandparents' house later on, once I've talked it over with them. That's where I'll be staying tonight. At their house in Bromley by Bow.'

'Yes, of course you may phone,' said Petusha, waving an elegant hand as she went. 'Whatever you think is right and proper. We don't want to offend your grandparents.'

Once they reached the ground floor Petusha turned to Charlotte, slipped an arm around her slim waist and, smiling, said, 'Oh, come on – come and meet everyone.'

Having little choice other than to go with the flow, Charlotte drifted into the entrance of the kitchen-cum-dining room, with double doors that opened out to the walled garden. It was clear that this woman, who was Charlotte's potential landlady, was oblivious to what she had been trying to get across: that she had seen enough and wanted to go, because Petusha was calling her friends in from the back garden to come in and say hello. Feeling embarrassed, her cheeks burning, Charlotte wished that she had stood her ground and left once she had reached the bottom of the stairs.

The guests who were now coming into the kitchen consisted of three very attractive men, dressed expensive-casual, and two women who were looking at her and smiling graciously – no doubt wondering where she was from. Coming towards her with a smile on his lips and a kind of expression of mutual understanding as if she were one of them, a young man in his mid-twenties asked if she would like a cold drink or a cup of tea. This *almost* put Charlotte at ease. She told him that she would prefer a cold drink, which she had spotted on the big old-fashioned pine table. There stood a beautiful large cut-glass jug filled with freshly squeezed orange juice, melting ice cubes and bits of sliced lemon and cut up strawberries.

'I feel as if I might have seen you somewhere before,' said the young, attractive guy, who was wearing a psychedelic cravat, white shirt, grey slacks and navy blazer. 'Or is that too much of a cliché these days?' He held out a limp hand. 'The name's David.'

'I doubt you will have seen my face before,' Charlotte replied, 'but I think I might have seen you on the box?'

'And?'

'And what?'

'Did you enjoy my show?'

'I can't remember.' She shrugged apologetically.

'Oh.' He scratched the back of his neck. 'Fair enough, I suppose. My own fault for being so bloody vain as to ask.'

Before she had a chance to answer him another good-looking young man came up to join them. 'Well, *hello* . . . and *who* have we here?'

'The name's Charlotte,' she said.

'Well *hello*, Charlotte. I'm Bertie the bit-part actor. Not famous like one or two of the others here that I could mention, but who gives a monkey's toss?' He gave her the once-over and showed his approval with a raise of an eyebrow. 'So, sweet child, might I have seen you before today . . . and if not, might I see you tomorrow? I take it that you've come to look at the room with a view?'

'I've come to look at the *apartment*, yes, and no, you won't see me tomorrow. I'll be on the train back to Bridgeford,' said Charlotte cutting to the chase. 'I'm born and bred East End and my family moved to Norfolk in 1959 when I was thirteen, so I don't think that our paths would have crossed.'

'Really? How interesting. And how long have you been living in the outback of dreary Norfolk?'

'Five years.' Charlotte wanted to tell him to mind his own business but kept her cool.

'Which makes you . . . *eighteen*. So tell me: before you turned into a beautiful swan did you visit Norwich or Bury St Edmunds as a child, to see pantomimes at Christmas?'

'No. I was thirteen when we went to East Anglia. That's a little bit old to be taken to see a panto with the parents.'

'Is it *really*?' he said, shaking his head. 'How times do change.'

'Were you in the pantos in the Theatre Royal then?' Charlotte felt sure that he must have been or he wouldn't have mentioned it.

'Oh, one or two . . .' he said, floating a hand. 'Lovely little theatre. Quaint little towns. I was put on the stage as a boy, you know. It's what Mother wanted, and I have been on it ever since. Well, on and off. How I *longed* to serve in a shop for all of those years and now of course it's too late. I shall be forty next birthday, alas.' He looked slyly at her, inviting her to express surprise at his age.

But Charlotte, not used to actors, didn't take the bite. Really and truly, all that she wanted to do now was to drink her drink and take a look at the garden that she would be sharing – if she decided to live in the house. She also wanted to stroll around the area to see if it suited her before she headed for the next flat in Lavender Square, Stepney Green – her old home ground in the East End.

Finishing her drink, she excused herself and then went out to inspect the garden, politely chatting back to those who chatted to her. They all seemed to want to know when she was going to move in with Petusha. Ready to leave, she told the woman who might end up being her landlady that she had another flat to see before she returned to Bridgeford. She then thanked her for her hospitality and left them to it. She wanted to be out of the place and back in her roots with her own kind. People who didn't tend to go on about Mary Quant clothes, and fashionable boutiques like Biba in posh Kensington. She was an ordinary girl who had no wish to link arms with the famous, even though some shared her working class roots. Both Twiggy and Jean Shrimpton had been name-dropped by another of her potential landlady's chums who was clearly one of the small group of highly successful photographers. He was also someone who had subtly dropped in that he often worked with rock stars as well as aristocrats. All in all it had been an eye-opener, and one that Charlotte would not forget.

Nine

Charlotte stepped out of Stepney Green underground station, happy to be back on home ground again. She could almost smell the old days as she recalled herself back in her childhood – a time from which she had never quite been able to cut herself free. She was a little early for her second flat viewing, so could afford to take a nice easy stroll with no rush, and this was what she wanted. She soaked up the atmosphere of familiar surroundings, that hadn't changed even though there were far more people about now than when she had lived a stone's throw away. She made her way through the narrow back streets towards Lavender Square and the grand towering terraced house that faced a beautiful Arts and Crafts building. She felt a surge of nostalgia for the days when she had played in this area, and immediately knew that this was where she wanted to live – where she belonged.

She found the house that could possibly become her home and studied it from the opposite side of the open-gated green. This was a spot where she and Nathan had often gone together as children, and later on when almost into their teens. They had sat there together now and then, discussing the ways of the world, guessing at what might be their future and whether they would be living in this neck of the woods or elsewhere. The old-fashioned square was enclosed on all four sides by ornate black railings, and hedged with established trees. The smoothly worn slate paving stones still had the same wild flowers and weeds growing through the cracks and, to her joy, the four wooden benches were still there. Secured to the old paving stones with heavy bolts, and now weathered and bent with age, they were a sight for sore eyes. Charlotte felt thoroughly at home. She *was* at home. She was back in a world that was familiar to her in every way.

This lovely corner of London also served as an enchanting home for the lady who owned the house with the flat to let. Isabelle Braintree, an agile and elegant woman in her early sixties, lived on the second floor in her large apartment, and on pleasant days such as this would sometimes sit for an hour or so on one of the benches in the garden square. It was an oasis to her, as it was to many others, even though she had her own spacious private gardens to the rear of her property. In the main, Isabelle liked the square because she always seemed to find someone there who was interesting to talk to. This well-bred intelligent woman was in fact writing her diaries to include the recent history of the local people and the area. She intended to self-publish a dozen copies as a record for her family.

The woman had seen many changes taking place over the years and, as far as she was concerned, it wouldn't take a genius to see that by the turn of the next century, the millennium, this little section of old London would look quite different. The East End was close to the City when all was said and done. Charlotte's potential landlady had felt for quite some time that the community would have a different atmosphere by then, even though the historic houses would remain. In her opinion, old London town had for decades been, and still was, spreading outwards to the very edges of suburbia. Small oases such as gardens fenced in by old-fashioned railings might one day be a thing of the past.

Of course, she had no idea that the girl who was coming to view the flat had also once sat in this square, enjoying a bag of piping hot chips purchased from a nearby fish and chip shop.

This little tucked away place had always been a favourite of the local people, and the sad thing for Charlotte was that the fish and chip shop was now boarded up with a sign informing customers that it would soon be another of a chain of betting shops. This section of the old East End had, a century or so ago, been a mix of the downtrodden and the affluent. A place where the well-heeled had private town houses that they came to from their country residences during the fashionable party seasons. Charlotte had not been that interested in local history when she was at school, but now the idea of living in one of the elegant period terraced houses sent a thrill down her spine and brought a smile to her face. It all seemed like a glorious dream. She wondered what the woman whom she had spoken to on the telephone looked like. Her only concern was that she sounded quite posh, posh but friendly. Knowing that she was ten minutes early, she slipped in through the open gate of this little piece of paradise and sat on a bench to soak all of this in before she went to view the flat, unaware that she was being observed by a tenant at the top of the house.

Sitting by her window in the house, her thick black hair highlighted by a few natural silver-grey streaks, the forty-five-year-old woman with lovely dark blue penetrating eyes was indeed observing Charlotte, who, she felt sure, must be the potential new tenant who was due to view. Normally Wendy would have tried to work out what sort of a girl she was by her demeanour, but her mind was filled with the past, recalling times when she had caught the attention of handsome young men who she would have once thoroughly enjoyed having chase her. This was before she had married the man of her dreams who had once loved her deeply, but had left her to run away with his lover and broken her heart. Even now, Wendy believed that he would come in search of her one day. Which was why she would sit by her long sash window and watch out for him every so often. Today, having taken time off work, she was sipping hot lemon juice and waiting for the

Aspros that she had swallowed to take effect. She had a bad cold and another of her headaches, but was trying to stay alert because she didn't want to fall asleep for hours on end and possibly miss *Crossroads*, the new television programme that she loved. Comfortable in her self-contained one-bedroom flat up at the top of the house, Wendy was quite content to live alone in what she saw as a serene environment, and had been living this way for almost seven years.

Glancing down at Charlotte, she felt sure this was indeed the girl her landlady was expecting. She hoped so. She liked the look of her and would convey this to her landlady once the viewing was over – should she be correct in guessing who she was, of course.

On the surface, Wendy appeared to be a bit of a loner, and gave little away as to her past life. It amused her to think that her landlady imagined her to be the sort of person who might sleep with a gun under her pillow in case a masked burglar found his way into her flat one dark night. She knew that she was seen as a bit of a recluse, but the truth of the matter was that she had got into the habit of being by herself for most of the time and quite liked it.

Employed at a rather nice book shop in Whitechapel, where she was known as friendly and helpful, this woman wished for little else other than a particular person to re-enter her life. She liked routine, and part of hers was to sit by her window and watch the world go by as well as keeping a lookout for the husband who she hoped would come in search of her. To anyone else, hers would appear a sad and sorry life but Wendy had her memories of happier times – times before her husband had packed all of his clothes into their matching leather suitcases while she had been out shopping for presents one white Christmas. On her return she found that he had gone without a trace. At that point in her life, the handsome couple had been living in Palmers Green, in a lovely, self-contained spacious apartment with a small balcony that overlooked a children's park.

All that her husband had left behind were serious debts. She had hated him with a vengeance at first but then, after a time, began to forgive and forget his bad behaviour. She had let their families know where she was now living, with instructions to give him the address should he ever deign to show his face. Whether she would take him back or not should he come in search of her she couldn't say, but she did want to see him again. She wanted an explanation and an apology. After all, she had now forfeited seven years of her life waiting for him.

From her viewing place Wendy could still see Charlotte, who was now standing on the pavement on the opposite side of the hedged-in green, looking up at this slightly faded grand house. Wendy now felt sure that this was the person who had come to view the vacant flat on the floor below her own – the girl who, the landlady had told her, was coming down from Bridgeford in Norfolk. She thought that the girl looked as if she would fit in. She reminded her of a little lamb wandering around nervously as if a fox was about to pounce. Even from the distance of her window Wendy thought that she could detect apprehension and joy rolled into one. The poor soul also looked a touch on the vulnerable side, which to her mind was no bad thing. She thought that those who appeared vulnerable were actually those who, beneath the surface, were stable; it was the cocksure who were insecure. Whatever the case, she felt that her landlady would like this girl. She had been worried about the medical students from the London hospital that had been coming and going for two or three weeks, all of whom had looked as if they had been smoking marijuana. None of this mattered in any case because none of the students had ticked the boxes that her landlady had set out on a piece of paper, and given a copy to Wendy, which she kept taped to the inside of a kitchen cupboard door. The list was short: *Single person; Full time employment; If at college then contracts to be signed by parent or guardian.*

She continued to study Charlotte who was now slowly walking around the outside of the fenced green to the wide steps leading up to the entrance of this house. Once she was out of view, the sound of the old fashioned bell-pull resounded through the building and could be heard by all, except for the tenant in the basement flat, which had a bell of its own. Getting up from her chair by the window, Wendy stole to her front door and opened it just enough to ease herself out and creep onto the landing where she could eavesdrop unnoticed. She had to be mindful of the creaking hinges of her door, hinges that had never been replaced because they weren't broken. This wasn't ideal because, of course, a creaking door goes on for ever . . . but at least the landlady's son, Donald, did oil the hinges now and then.

Wendy was a little hard of hearing, so when her landlady raised her voice to her son when calling from her flat to his, she only heard it as someone speaking normally. The same went for when Donald shouted down to his mother. And the hindrance of her slight deafness was also a help when it came to little annoyances that would drive those with excellent hearing quite mad. But the old louvred shutters on her windows that rattled in the draught she could just hear. Apart from such minor irritations, Wendy was quite content and liked to be in touch with all that was going on in the house so as to keep her mind tick-tocking.

The most important thing was for her to know what was happening at the heart of her realm . . . Which was why she tended to eavesdrop now and then. When she first moved in to this house she had little inclination to go out unless she had to. But now, after dinner, she would rest a while and after supper walk almost a mile. She liked to fill her free time as best she could, and listening in the passageway now and then to the mix of people who came and went had become a rather interesting pastime. Her policy was to believe little of what she heard and only half of what she saw – and in her elevated position at the top of the house, she considered herself to be a bit of an eagle. Proud and still, listening to every sound within and watching every move without.

The eagle had always fascinated her ever since she had seen one in a film that her father took her to when she was a child – many decades past. She could remember what her daddy had said when she asked if the bird with the big claws would ever pick up a kitten and fly away with it. His reply had been simple but poignant, and had left her in awe of the feathered friend until she was old enough to know better. He had told her that eagles didn't bother with pint-size, and from this she had understood that he meant they took something more worthwhile to eat – such as a little girl. This fantasy had caused her to have childish wonderland dreams on and off until she grew up.

Now, discreetly hidden on the landing and listening by the stairwell, Wendy felt no guilt at eavesdropping because, since she was going to have to share the common parts with whoever came to live in the house, she felt that she had every right to pass judgement. Or at least be part of the jury, even if she couldn't be the judge as to who should move in to the vacant flat below and who shouldn't. This didn't mean that she didn't trust her landlady's opinion when it came to character – the woman had her own good name and welfare to think of, and had said to her on more than one occasion that she felt it better to live alongside a good kind of a person than a person of good kind. Wendy thought this was very admirable.

Opening the door to Charlotte, Isabelle Braintree was pleased at what she saw. A nice ordinary girl with an intelligent face. 'You must be Charlotte,' she said and smiled. 'Do please come in.'

'Thank you,' said Charlotte. 'You must be Mrs Braintree.'

'Yes, I am.'

Immediately at ease as she stepped into the elegant, generously proportioned entrance hall, Charlotte felt a warm glow inside and knew that her cheeks were going pink. 'This is a lovely house,' she said.

'Yes,' said the gracious Isabelle, 'it is. I've always thought so. I've always loved it. Now then, you've come such a long way . . . would you like to take off your coat and have a nice cup of tea before you view the flat? Or coffee if you would prefer it?'

'No, I'm fine thank you. I stopped in a café and had some lunch soon after I had seen the first flat to let. In Islington.' Charlotte was feeling more comfortable by the minute.

'Goodness, you have been busy.' Isabelle closed the door behind her guest and led the way up the wide staircase to the second floor. 'I trust you're not going back to Norfolk today? That would be quite a lot to fit in.'

'No,' said Charlotte. 'I'm staying with my grandparents overnight. They live in Bromley by Bow.'

'Oh well, that's just a bus stop or two away.' Stopping at a cream-painted panelled door bearing the polished brass number three, Mrs Braintree pushed the key into the lock and then turned the lovely Georgian brass handle. 'I did open the windows an hour or so ago so the rooms should be nicely aired.' She then stood aside and gestured gracefully. 'Please do go in and feel free to look around by yourself. I always think it unnecessary to have everything pointed out.'

Taken aback by this, Charlotte said, 'I'd rather you did show me around. It wouldn't feel right. This is your flat, after all.'

Mrs Braintree smiled warmly. 'What a lovely thing to say. I do hope you're going to like it.' She then led the way, clearly proud of the room they had entered, a spacious sitting room with a high ceiling, pretty cornices, and a lovely pine fireplace set with coal and with a brass poker on a hook next to it.

The room was almost floodlit by the early afternoon sun coming in through the long sash windows and Charlotte had to pinch her lips together and force herself not to shed a tear of joy. She looked around the room and then at Mrs Braintree. 'I love it,' she said. 'It feels so homely and yet it's so elegant. I really, really love it.'

'Oh I am pleased!' The landlady clasped her hands together, a radiant smile on her face. 'Now then . . . if you would like to open that door you will find the bedroom, and off the bedroom you will find a shower cubicle. And that other door opens to a little kitchen. And if you were to take the flat, but prefer to soak in the tub you will find a door into a small bathroom for your sole use is just outside on the landing.'

There really was no more to be said. Charlotte was by the window now and looking down at the square that had been such an important part of her childhood. 'I presume that the rent is a month in advance,' she said. 'And I think that my granddad said that there will be a deposit to pay?'

'One month's rent in advance will be absolutely fine, if you feel that you can run to it. I expect you'll be arranging interviews for a position during your first week here so you won't be having any salary to kick off with so—'

'No, I wouldn't take the flat unless I've already been accepted for the position in the council offices. The interview is lined up for tomorrow morning. I'll fit that in before I catch my train back home.'

'My word, you are organised for someone so young.'

'I'm eighteen,' said Charlotte. 'I thought that was quite adult.'

'Well, of course it is, but to someone of my age it seems young to be setting out on your own and paying your way.'

'My parents are going to let me have the month's rent in

advance to give me a clean start. I'm an only child so they do worry about me.'

'I'm sure they must. And luckily we do have a spare room in this house for guests. So if all goes to plan and they wanted to come and visit you now and again I'm sure we could accommodate them.'

'It gets better and better,' said Charlotte, laughing delightedly. 'Although, between you and me, I am really trying to be independent so I won't encourage them. They could stay at my grandparents' house. It's what they usually do when we come down to visit our old home ground.'

'Well . . . am I to take it then that you would like to think seriously about living in this house?' Isabelle smiled.

'Definitely. I don't even have to think about it. I just know I would be very happy here. It's exactly what I could have wished for.'

'Marvellous, I am pleased. Very happy. Now why don't we go into my apartment and have a nice refreshing hot or cold drink. I'm sure you must be ready for one?'

'I am now, thank you. Then I must be on my way to tell my grandparents the good news. I'm really happy about this. I couldn't have wished for a better place to live that's part of my roots.'

The ladies of different generations and walks of life went down the stairs as if they had known each other for years. Following the warm and graceful lady of the house into her own apartment, Charlotte gasped at what she saw. It was stunning. It was both spacious and homely, jam-packed with antique furniture that was being used and not just for show. Drifting towards the wide open French doors that led out into the back gardens she could hardly believe her eyes. She felt as if she were in another world, far from the East End.

'On warm sunny days you might enjoy sitting in the back garden,' said Isabelle, waving a graceful hand. 'It's very pretty in all four seasons. Of course neither I nor my tenant Wendy, who lives at top of the house, ever remove any of our top clothing to sunbathe. I've always thought that swimming costumes or two-piece sunsuits are best kept for the beach.' She looked sideways at Charlotte, hoping to get an important message across. 'We have, after all, to consider the two men who live under the same roof as we ladies. There is one gentleman, a tenant, in the basement, and my son Donald lives on the first floor.'

'It wouldn't be right in any case. Not in this setting.' Charlotte sighed. 'It's so special . . . it's beautiful.'

'Oh, I'm so pleased you agree,' said Isabelle.

Through the French doors, Charlotte saw a raised patio where there was a table with an old-fashioned sun shade over it and four garden chairs. Beyond this was the spacious garden that stretched back to an old and high red-brick wall. 'It must be lovely sitting out there in the quiet and reading,' said Charlotte, totally captivated. 'Especially when the sun's setting. It must beautiful then.'

'It is, and since it's a shared garden you shall have every right to sit out there whenever you choose. I leave the back door in the hall unlocked during the daytime so that my tenants may go down the steps and into the garden. And I lock it at nine in the evenings unless something special is happening out there. We sometimes have a house barbecue evening when Donald takes over the cooking, which is rather nice. Of course we all chip in to a kitty for the meat and salad and so on.'

Charlotte looked from the grounds to her prospective landlady and smiled. 'It sounds to me as if living in this house is like being in paradise.'

'Well, that's very sweet of you to say so . . . and in a way you're right. We all seem to rub along together quite nicely. Not in and out of each other's lives, but not cool and distant either.'

'It is such a beautiful garden,' said Charlotte, gazing out.

'Perfect for a barbecue. I would love to join in that kind of a thing.'

'Good. And you know you could always come and go if you felt that you wanted to sit by yourself out there to read a book and so on. I should hate to think of you inside the apartment all of the time. So – there we are then. You've seen all there is to see. Can you see yourself living here?'

'I can. It feels right. As if it was meant to be.'

'Good.' The woman beamed. 'I *am* pleased. And you may move in whenever you wish and the sooner the better. I think that rooms left empty for too long tend to get a sad and lonely feel about them.'

Her face now glowing Charlotte said, 'Thank you again. I've made my decision. And I would love to live here.'

'Oh I *am* pleased,' said Isabelle again. 'Now, would you like to meet Wendy before you go? She'll be your neighbour. She lives at the top of the house, in the flat above the one that's vacant. She's at home today, nursing a dreadful cold, so we would have to keep at arm's length. I can't introduce you to my son who lives on the first floor because he's out at the moment. And the young man in the basement flat, although he is perfectly charming, isn't the sort who would want to meet a potential neighbour. He's quite a loner but does join us for drinks on the terrace very occasionally.'

'To be honest with you? I think I would prefer not to meet anyone yet. It's all been a bit much for me.' Charlotte smiled. 'I think I need to get to my grandparents' house and tell them about it. Get it off my chest before it bursts.'

'Well, of course you must. But do just let me write down my telephone number.'

'But I've already got it . . .'

'Oh, of course you have. How silly of me.' Isabelle relaxed her shoulders and smiled warmly at Charlotte. 'Do please forgive me. I promise that I shan't mother-hen you once you move in. I really do.'

'Oh, what a shame.' Charlotte giggled. 'I think I'll need every bit of mother henning once I've made the break from my parents. And you've got your son living under the same roof so you never know, a big brother figure might be here for me as well.'

'Oh, I'm not so sure about that. Donald is a bit of a loner too. A touch of an oddity, in fact. But then that's more interesting in a way than run-of-the-mill.' With that, Isabelle walked with Charlotte to the front door of what was to be her new home and they said their farewells, each of them sensing that they could be close friends even though the difference in their ages would easily place them as mother and daughter.

Five minutes later, with her head in the clouds and feeling as if she was in her seventh heaven, Charlotte boarded a red bus for the first time in ages. Once in a seat by the window she felt more and more at home – almost as if she had never left the East End in the first place. She watched the comings and goings that had once been a major part of her world and couldn't wait to tell her Gran and Granddad about the flat.

Ten

'Stone the crows, look at the state of your face!' Charlotte's granddad Johnny leaned his skinny body back and roared with laughter. 'It's got success written all over it!'

'Oh, shut up, Granddad, and let me in. I'm dog tired.'

'I should fink you would be, mutt,' he said, standing to one side. 'What wiv all the travelling. You must feel like a stray that's bin out all of the day and all of the night.'

Passing him, she sniffed discreetly and, as expected, the fumes from his breath matched the redness of his cheeks and the glassy look in his warm hazel eyes. 'Been on the beer already, Granddad?' she said a touch teasingly.

'Beer? At this time of late afternoon? Course not! I've been swigging straight from a bottle of rum.'

'Many a true word spoken in jest,' she said, as she strode through the passage to the kitchen-diner. This was at the back of the house and where her gran was sitting in her tall-backed chair with the *Daily Mirror* open in front of her. She was doing the crossword puzzle. Glancing up over her bifocals that were held together with a sticking plaster on one side, she gave Charlotte an all-knowing scolding look for mentioning Johnny's drinking habit. It wasn't the first time.

'So what's brought this cockiness about then?' said Nell, doing her best not to smile just yet. 'You look like someone who lost a penny and found a pound. And your granddad 'ad a pint with 'is bubble and squeak. So no more of your sauce.'

'I was only joking, Nan. And as for me being happy . . . I've found a flat.'

'Oh, 'ave you now? And where's your boyfriend? Or are you too ashamed of our humble home to 'ave fetched 'im with yer?'

'Boyfriend, Gran?' said Charlotte as she flopped down into another of the kitchen chairs. 'Now let me see . . . who could you possibly mean? Not Nathan, that's for sure, or you would have spoken his name. You did after all grow up living beside 'is granny in the back and beyond of Whitechapel in slum dwellings once upon a time. Or did I *dream* that you told me all of that?'

'Saucy cow.' Nell then lifted her eyes to her husband who had come into the kitchen, having just nipped into the best room at the front of the house for a spoonful of rum from the bottle. Why he did this in secret was still a mystery to his wife and family because it was as clear as a cucumber to them that he was almost always merrily half cut. No one minded in the least because he was always so cheerful with it. If asked, he would openly say that he loved his drink and the way it made him feel; that it was a habit he wasn't going to give up while he still earned a wage at the market sweating blood and tears.

'What's she said now then for you to have cause to call 'er saucy?' Johnny winked at his wife and grinned. 'She'd better not 'ave cheeked you, sweetheart. We can't have that.'

Nell raised her eyes and then shook her head slowly. 'Why don't you go out for a nice walk along the Cut? Find one of your mates to talk to.'

'What, and not spend time with my granddaughter who I hardly get to see any more? I don't fink so! I've been looking forward to this day all week.' He looked at Charlotte and smiled. 'I've got a little surprise for you upstairs. I've been busy. I think you are gonna be very pleased. I always said—'

'Oh, for fuck's sake tell 'er what you've done.' Nell raised

138

her eyes to heaven again and shook her head. 'I wouldn't mind it's not yet evening and 'e's tipsy.'

'I am not tipsy, if you don't mind! Not yet I'm not. I've had a celebratory drink that's all. My granddaughter's come *all* the way from *Bridgeford* to see me. Any miserable old sod would drink to that, never mind *me* . . . her flesh and blood.'

'Well, put the kettle on and make your flesh and blood a nice cup of coffee.'

'That would be lovely,' said Charlotte, settled in her chair and easing off her stiletto-heeled shoes.

'Oh. So you're not interested in what your bedroom looks like then? What sort of wallpaper I've put up?'

'Of course I am, but you did send me a square of the wallpaper with a sample of the paint on the back of it. And I did phone you and say it was lovely.'

Johnny narrowed his eyes, as he looked at her a touch suspiciously. 'No you never.'

'Yes I did.'

'When?'

'The day after it arrived. I can't remember which day it was exactly . . .'

'Ah ha!' Johnny grinned broadly. 'So it's not me who forgets then, is it? It's you, your mother and your gran. I was born with a good memory, me.' He shook his head slowly and then nodded. 'I always came top in class when it was question time.'

Not wishing to get into an argy-bargy over Johnny's terrible memory Charlotte said, 'Well, don't you want to know about the flats I've looked at then, Grandad?'

'Course not!' said Johnny. 'Flats? Who do you think you are? One of them West End girls? You don't wanna live in a flat. Not when you've got that lovely room up there all freshly wallpapered and painted and wiv all mod cons. A lovely little lamp and a gas fire and a two-bar electric fire and all at the flick of a switch or two. And anyway you can't afford to pay rent.'

'Salaries have gone up to match rising prices, Granddad. You should read your Sunday paper more thoroughly. And anyway . . . we've never 'ad it so good is what you've told me more than once.'

'Yeah, but I was talking about the Welfare State and the National Health Service, wasn't I? We all had our doubts in 1948 when it was first established, but now? Now it's *really* kicking in. We're all better off now than what we were. But that's got nuffing to do wiv greedy landlords charging a bomb for flea-pit rooms to live in.'

'Take no notice of him love,' said Nell. 'What was the flat like, sweetheart?'

'Oh hark at it. All lovey and sweethearts. What are *you* after?'

'Go out for a walk, Johnny, or make a cup of coffee.'

Sighing reluctantly Johnny set about his chore and switched off from the women's talk and sulked with what he considered to be good reason. It had taken him days, if not weeks, to do that little room up for his granddaughter and she hadn't even wanted to run up there to see it. And his wife had gone on about his drinking in front of her in her own artful way, and now, even though he was making a hot drink for Charlotte, they were acting as if he was invisible. Talk talk talking about bloody flats and landladies. And posh land-ladies at that if all he was hearing was correct. 'I wouldn't mind,' he mumbled, 'but she 'ain't even got a job yet and she's talking about flats. Where's the money gonna come from, that's what I'd like to know. She's got a free room up there and I won't charge a penny for a full breakfast.'

Letting his rambling that he meant them to hear go above their heads, grandmother and grandchild were not only talk-ing about where Charlotte was going to live but also about where her gran had once worked for a couple of months as a scullery maid – in one of the other houses on Lavender Square. Charlotte had not heard this piece of Nell's past before and was fascinated by it. 'So why didn't you stay longer, Gran? It must 'ave been even lovelier when you was young all those years ago.'

'I'm only sixty-four, Charlotte. Same as your granddad. That's not old. Anyway . . . I never liked being bossed about and bullied.'

'Bullied? You're not saying that they knocked you about, Nan, are you?'

'With words, Charlotte, not wiv their fists. Had they 'ave done, I would 'ave punched back, make no mistake. They needed to smell their own backsides that lot. Shit is the same no matter how it's shaped.'

'Oh Nan . . . please.'

'Anyway I did 'ave a bit of a lark there wiv one of the boot boys.' Her eyes now sparkling, a big grin spread across her face. 'We did have some fun in them days. One lad in particular fancied me rotten and he was very popular wiv the other young parlour maids working in the square. Us girls below stairs used to make sandwiches and homemade lemonade and go fishing wiv the lads down the Cut. I did like that lad – who was in love with me as it happened. I liked him a lot.

'We went to the pictures and then nestled up in the stables that used to be close by. There was always a few bales of fresh hay or straw in there. I'd never enjoyed anything so much in my life. Romance? You younger generation don't know what the word means. I go all tingly just finking about it.' She leaned back in her chair, smiling wistfully as she reminisced, and then murmured to herself, 'It was just as well I wasn't a virgin.'

'See what I mean?' said Johnny. 'See what kind of talk I 'ave to put up wiv? Now if you were to live wiv us you could set your gran a good example.'

Charlotte laughed. 'Granddad, I am not living here. All right? I'll visit you often but I'm not moving in. Got it?'

'Well . . . you never were one for mincing your words. It suits me, I don't care. Do what you want. I was only trying to 'elp. It took me two weekends non-stop to do that bedroom. Still, there you are. That's life. I did it for a good reason—'

'You did it because I've been nagging you for more than a fucking year to sort out the damp in that spare room and replace the old-fashioned peeling wallpaper. Lazy sod. You should 'ave done it years ago,' said Nell.

Johnny slowly shook his head. 'See what I mean, sweetheart? See how she treats me? It's no wonder I need a little drink now and then.' He went and fetched his bottle of rum from the room and poured a drop out before topping up with warm water.

'So . . . who's gonna go out and get the fish and chips from the best fish and chip shop in the world then?' Charlotte asked.

'Me, of course, said Johnny. 'You don't fink that your gran would put 'erself out, do yer? Not while she's got a skivvy like me around. Never mind that I've done a hard morning's work when most people are having fun shopping down the Saturday market.'

'My heart bleeds for you, sweetheart,' said Nell. 'It fucking well pours with blood at times. Sitting on your backside all Saturday afternoon watching the wrestling and boxing on the telly and cheering on your favourites as if you're there in the hall wiv 'em. They'll be calling you Square Eyes Johnny next.'

'See what I mean, Charlotte? She's grown bitter with time. Don't ask me why. I do whatever I can to make 'er 'appy but all I get back is moan, moan, moan.'

'Yeah and pigs fly at night. It's you who do all the groaning when there's nobody around but me to listen to it. It's your fault she don't wanna live with us.'

'Ah . . .' Johnny smiled and his blue eyes lit up. 'That's

what this mood's about is it? Why didn't you come out with it in the first place? Tell Charlotte that she should move in wiv us and it's what you've been looking forward to all this time.' He turned to his granddaughter with a pained and worried look. 'It'll break 'er heart you know if you go and move into lodgings instead of—'

'Not lodgings, Granddad. A proper self-contained flat in a fabulous converted period house.'

'I'm sure it's very nice, but how much is it gonna cost you?'

'Four pounds a week plus electricity and gas.'

'Oh. Well, that's not too bad . . . depending on 'ow much you reckon you can pick up a week working in the council offices.'

'Twelve pounds a week if I'm prepared to go in every other Saturday morning, which I am. But I've not even been for the interview yet so let's not get too excited.'

'*How* much?' Johnny could hardly believe it.

'You heard,' said Nell. 'And I think that's very fair money.'

'Fair money? It's a bloody fortune! Stone me blind! Well, they did say that you postwar children would benefit from our sufferings, and now a girl of your age can earn twelve pounds a week. What we 'ad to get by on don't bear finking about.' He looked across to Charlotte and there was a hint of a tear in his eye as well as pride in his expression. 'Our little grand-daughter earning all that money. Well, I might just buy you a bottle of cider to go with your fish and chips to celebrate, Charlotte love. Well done. And I mean that. Hand on heart.'

'She hasn't got the job yet you silly old sod. But you can still buy the cider. And once you're in the fish and chip shop ask the fryer straightaway to put in a bit of fresh haddock each for the three of us. I don't want any of that drained and dried up muck.'

'You've never ever had anyfing other than fresh out of the fryer.'

'Exactly. So don't break the habit so that you can be there

143

and back sooner rather than later so as not to miss the wresting on the telly. I saw you looking at the *Radio Times*.'

Clearing his throat and rolling his eyes, Johnny left the room grumbling under his breath.'

'You're getting worse, Nan. Always picking on Granddad.'

'He loves it, sweetheart. It's when I give him the silent act that he gets all sorry for 'imself. I know 'ow to play the silly old sod, don't you worry.'

Charlotte chuckled as she tried to imagine herself living with her grandparents, and wondered if it would be more fun than living in the grand house in a flat all by herself. A touch confused, she strolled out of the room telling Nell that she was going to have a look at her granddad's handiwork. Once alone, her Nan smiled and then winked to herself. She had deliberately got the banter going between her and her husband because she knew how to amuse her Charlotte. She wasn't certain that she wouldn't try out the flat, but she reckoned that she wouldn't last more than three months coping by herself. And if not, at least she was only a bus ride away. Nell was more than happy.

A little later on that evening, Isabelle was listening to her favourite Johann Strauss record, 'The Blue Danube', while looking through her family photograph album as she often liked to do. On this occasion though, she had Charlotte on her mind and knew instantly that they were going to become good friends. She had immediately warmed to the girl the moment that she had looked into that lovely honest face. She knew that Charlotte, as her tenant, was going to be part of her world. And not only that, but she had been reminded of herself when she had been the same age. When she had also stepped out into the wide world of independence.

She hadn't been quite so brave as to go out looking for a flat in London for herself at Charlotte's age, but she had gone on a trip to Europe – Paris, Rome and Berlin, with her parents just after her eighteenth birthday and, instead of coming back to England after three weeks, had stayed on to study French in Paris for some months. Once back in Britain, Isabelle, young slim and beautiful, had adored living in this, her family's town house, while they were at home in Suffolk. She loved the house so much that when she married Donald's father, when she was twenty-five, her parents signed it over as a wedding gift. Sadly, her beloved husband, a commanding officer in His Majesty's army, who had been stationed abroad during the war, was killed in action, leaving her to bring up their son alone. Donald had once been her torch in the dark and now she felt that she was his. Her son was not ill or lacking intelligence, but he wasn't an ordinary average young man who wanted to settle down with a family of his own. He had never had a girlfriend, neither had he been attracted to his own sex. He simply didn't seem to need a comforting partner. He had his work as assistant librarian at the local library and he had his hobbies. It was enough. He was content and so was Isabelle.

Both of them loved this part of London, with its interesting mix of people. They were more than happy to stay put forever overlooking the lovely square, provided that there weren't too many changes on the horizon, knocking down old characterful buildings and houses to replace them with skyscrapers, as was being predicted in some of the newspapers. Isabelle's old family residence in the heart of the Suffolk countryside, close to the town of Newmarket and the race courses, had provided her with wonderful happy weekends and short holidays in the past with her husband and their son, and that had been enough. Now the house in the country was let out to a wealthy American family who needed a base in England.

Isabella had no idea why Charlotte had had such an impact on her other than that, for some strange reason, she reminded her of her younger self. She had come from a wealthier background of course, and she had inherited properties along the way. She was a successful landlady with a handsome income from the house in the country and enough coming in from her tenants here in the Square. This suited her very nicely and she felt comfortable with it. But more importantly, she liked this new tenant called Charlotte. She liked her a lot.

Eleven

That night, having been out with Nathan for a candlelit dinner at the Steak House in Aldgate, which had been wonderfully romantic, Charlotte lay in the single bed in the spare bedroom of her grandparents' two up, two down. Now, realising that the feelings she had for her childhood friend were stronger than she imagined they ever could be, she was worried that she might have let herself get carried away with the romance of it all. Her old friend had been very close to her when they were young it was true, but later on he had led a completely different life in London and had met lots of people of his own age with whom he had things in common. She was now troubled by the possibility that, once he had seen her a few times, he would find her dull compared with the set he now mixed with.

With more and more of these thoughts filling her mind as she tried to imagine the girls he worked with at the theatre, she suddenly smiled as she remembered what Nathan had said to her: *'You'll probably meet and possibly fall in love with more than one man once you're living in London.'* She had been flattered by the remark and, especially, the worried tone in his voice that he had tried to cover. She loved him all the more for it.

And she loved this little terraced house in the quiet street in Bow, where the fragrance of fresh paint and wallpaper still hung in the air. It was the perfect place and she was in the perfect cosy room to re-live everything, from the time that Nathan turned up on her doorstep in Bridgeford out of the blue, to this very moment. She had seen as much of London as she could take in one day and had loved every minute of it. Now she was more than ready for a good night's sleep, but her thoughts were all over the place and she couldn't wait to see Nathan again. Once back in Bridgeford she was going to have to make do with talking to him over the phone until she returned for good.

She recalled the house and the people in Islington. She would have had Petusha there, but this was not enough. She knew that she didn't belong there and that she would not fit in with the bohemian set of people who were, from what she had gathered, very much part and parcel of that little pocket of the world. A world that she too would have had to be part of should she have taken the flat.

The lovely lady who owned the house that had been converted into four apartments in Stepney, however, she had felt at one with. Even though they were from different backgrounds it hadn't seemed to matter one iota. And to live in a flat that overlooked her favourite square, that held some of her most precious childhood memories, was more than she could have wished for. She had felt a genuine and immediate bond with Isabelle Braintree, and she did love the flat. The woman had a natural mothering persona, and Charlotte knew from gut instinct that Isabelle had taken to her too. She could easily picture herself living in the house, coming and going, and not being drawn into anyone else's world in the way that she might have had to if she'd chosen the flat in North London. So much had happened in such a short space of time that she was already seeing Bridgeford as a retreat rather than a place to live and work. Living in London and having weekend breaks by the river with her parents would be a perfect lifestyle.

Her thoughts flying from one thing to another, the

tormentor of old, Kenny, drifted into her mind. She pictured the way he had looked at her when they had been on the train . . . as if they were old buddies. But she was older now and so was he, and the fear that she had once held when it came to him had dissipated. She didn't care if she bumped into him while living in the same area. She was no longer scared of someone who she saw as a coward who picked on those weaker than he was. She no longer loathed him – she simply didn't care.

He had come across as a reformed character on the train and looked like an ordinary guy, but she had wondered if this was partly because his once bright ginger hair had turned into a soft brownish auburn and softened his features. He had seemed capable of all things evil in the early days and had been a bastard when it came to Nathan . . . but that was all in the past. Nathan had turned into someone who could stand up for himself and would throw a good punch if the need were to arise. Snug and warm in her bed, thinking of Nathan, she couldn't believe that her lonely life was turning around almost overnight. As long as she came up to scratch during her interview at the council offices the next day, she would be home and dry.

Feeling hopeful about everything, she turned on her side and curled up ready for a peaceful night's sleep – she was in her grandparent's home and this in itself gave her a warm glow inside. She was happy. And she *was* doing the right thing.

The following morning, after a breakfast of fried eggs, bacon and tomatoes, cooked by her granddad, Charlotte set off, looking very smart in her black and white dogtooth-patterned jacket and skirt. As she made her way to the interview for the post of copy typist and clerk's assistant, she knew that she was going to have to prove that she could live up to the letter she had sent. She had written to say that she had a touch typing speed of sixty words per minute and a good aptitude for mental arithmetic. As she walked in the warm sunshine towards the bus stop, the butterflies in her tummy began to settle down and she felt less frightened of failure – it was now all in the lap of the gods.

Now that she had had this little taste of being back in her old world, she knew for certain that living in Bridgeford was never going to suit her the way it did her parents. For her that life was over, and Eddie and Rita were going to have to accept it whether they liked it or not. She was not only ready to spread her wings, she was desperate to do so. She couldn't wait to move into the fabulous flat in Lavender Square, or stroll through all of the back turnings that were so familiar and still felt like home. Apart from her own feelings, she knew that her grandparents were overjoyed to have her back in the fold again and living just a bus ride away.

While all of these thoughts were going through Charlotte's mind, Nell and Johnny were sitting around the pale primrose, Formica-topped table in their kitchen. They were enjoying a fresh pot of tea and coming to terms with the disappointment of not having her under their roof permanently and making a fuss of her.

'We've gotta learn to let 'er go, Nell,' said Johnny, himself not totally convinced that he could stand by and see Charlotte live in a flat by herself. 'She's not a kid any more. And she's got more sense than you 'ad at 'er age.'

'No she bloody well 'ain't. Going for an interview in that black and white suit and looking like a model! That's not what they wanna see. She should 'ave toned it all down a bit. Wore grey and white with a little bit of red popped in. A neckerchief and a pair of summer gloves.'

'Like in the early nineteen-thirties you mean? When you was a beautiful young woman and working as a secretary at the Houndsditch Warehouse?'

'If you like,' said Nell, a touch sniffy. 'But I don't think I was beautiful so much as very smart with my appearance.' Nell gazed out at nothing as she sank deeper into her memories, smiling and nodding as she remembered one or two of her lovers before she met Charlotte's granddad . . . but she kept these thoughts to herself.

'It will be nice to see a bit more of 'er, though, won't it,' said Johnny. 'She can come round for Sunday dinner and we can take a bus to Stepney Green and visit 'er.' He leaned back in his chair and chuckled. 'Our little Charlotte, all independent and living in 'er own place? I bet she don't last a month before she realises where best her bread is buttered. She loves the way I've done that room up, don't she?'

Nell arched one eyebrow and slowly shook her head. 'Yes, Johnny, she does. But don't keep on going on about it. You'll only take the joy away and bore me to death.'

'I don't know why she can't stop for a few days. What difference would it make? She could take a sick note back to work once she's in Bridgeford.'

'She wouldn't do a thing like that. How many more times must I tell yer? That's three times now that you've said that. Not in so many words but you've repeated it one way or another. And in any case, from what I can make out, she'll be back for good in a couple of weeks' time. Two weeks' notice is what she said she had to give at the council offices, and now that she's found 'erself a flat there'll be no stopping 'er.' Nell gazed at the floor and then smiled. 'She's so much like me that girl. Makes up 'er mind to do something and not even wild horses will stop 'er.'

Johnny didn't think so. To his mind Charlotte was a chip off the old block all right, but from his block and not Nell's. 'Course she's like you,' he said so as to keep her happy. He liked a nice calm atmosphere. 'I swear on my life that you're like two peas in a pod the pair of you.'

Leaning back in her chair and sipping her tea, Nell was dead chuffed to hear him of all people saying this. She thought that he was mostly too argumentative to agree with anything she came out with. 'I'm really looking forward to 'er stopping overnight now and then – just for a change from 'er rented rooms.'

'So am I.' Johnny slowly nodded. 'I hope she comes straight back here after the interview. I don't wanna be on tenterhooks all day long.'

'Course she will. You promised you'd pop out and get pies and mash didn't you? She won't wanna miss that.'

'Did I? Oh well . . . that'll be a good stomach liner for that train journey to the back and beyond. If she wants pie and mash that is. She might not do, she might want to eat at our table and enjoy a bit of your lovely home cooking.'

'We'll see,' said Nell, fed up with him going on and on. 'Leave it be for now. You've given me a fucking headache.'

The job interview took less time than she had imagined and Charlotte, in a kind of a daze, was making her way through the backstreets towards the square where she hoped that she would soon be living. She wanted to make sure that her landlady really would keep the flat vacant for a fortnight until she was able to leave her old life behind her. She was so happy that she could hardly stop herself from smiling. She had got through the interview and the typing test with flying colours and was told that the position was hers if she wanted it. The employment contract was going to be put in the post that same day. Now, she was almost bursting with joy as she realised just how happy she felt being back in this neck of the woods, among people that she had grown up with.

Strolling through the back streets, she imagined herself in the Lavender Square flat, with some of her own special bits and pieces from home around her – things such as the table lamp that she always read by at night, a best-liked bedroom chair, and posters of her favourite pop singers the Beatles, the Kinks and the Rolling Stones. She was longing to get settled into the apartment that she already thought of as her own. Arriving at a red telephone kiosk she felt like phoning her grandparents straight away to tell them her good news but decided against it. They would have appreciated the call but she was eighteen years old, no longer a child that couldn't wait to tell them about the gift – which is how she saw the outcome of the interview. That she had been given a gift.

Deep in thought, she found herself at an Italian café before she realised it. This café, close by Stepney Green underground station, had not been open more than six months and it was the aroma of percolating coffee that had drawn in the East End folk as well as the Italians who lived in the area. Going inside, she was pleasantly surprised at how warm and friendly it seemed and didn't feel sorry any more that the old-fashioned shoe menders that it had once been had gone forever. The place was decorated in warm colours and there were cheerful red, green and orange cloths on each of the tables.

Sitting down by the window so that she could watch people going by, Charlotte remembered a model-motion shoe mender, tapping at the heel of a tiny boot in his wooden hand. She wondered what had become of the little attraction that had once been in the window and was adored by all children. She brushed sentimental thoughts aside. She was ready for a hot drink and one of the cigarettes that she liked to have occasionally when her parents weren't around. Once she had given her order to a young and good looking Italian waiter, she brought back to mind all that had happened at the Stepney council offices. The woman who had showed her around had been so nice to her and the people who were employed there seemed happy in their work. Their smiling faces had meant more to her than anything else. Content in her little world of recollections, it was a jolt when the last person that she expected to see walked through the door. Kenny the bully.

For a moment she wondered if he was shadowing her, but

shook off the thought and told herself not to be stupid. The East End was a small place, after all, and he had come down from Norfolk on the same train as her. Of course he would have been heading for this area where he was born and bred. They were in the same pocket of London at the same time, that was all there was to it. She opened the pages of a *Daily Mirror* that someone had left behind and pretended not to have noticed him as she artfully inched her chair by the window around so as to have her back to him. She didn't think he had spotted her, but he had – way before Charlotte had even stepped over the threshold of the café.

Kenny had seen her walking along the Mile End Road and had followed her. He had wanted to know what she was up to, and now he was settling himself down at a small round table for two in a corner of the café. Once in his chosen seat he gazed out at nothing as if he were deep in thought and behaved as if he hadn't seen Charlotte. He looked every bit the contented harmless young man, not someone who was playing a rather sick game of shadowing her to extract a little revenge for the way she had teased him when they were thirteen-year-olds. And he certainly didn't look as if he would harm a fly, let alone that he could be a serial killer . . .

To his mind, Charlotte still had the air of a snob and behaved as if the likes of him were beneath her . . . never mind that she had been the one to hang out with a Jew years back. And Jews, as far as he was concerned, were still the low understrappers. He hadn't forgotten the time when she had sent him on a wild goose chase. The day when he had been made to look stupid in front of his friends when the bitch had told him lies about the Roman Road gang knocking on his mother's front door. He hadn't found this amusing at the time and he couldn't see a funny side to it now. So, as far as he was concerned, he owed her one for having degraded him in front of the lads in his gang. Lads who had respected him. To Kenny, all of this coming together again, first in Bridgeford and now in his own neck of the woods, meant only one thing: fate was dealing him an interesting card to play in his game of to kill or not to kill.

He hadn't been that surprised to see her walking along the Mile End Road like a stuck up cow because he knew that she had relatives in the area. He hadn't fully intended to follow her in to the café but neither had he intended to trail her for a short while when he disembarked at King's Cross the day before. It just seemed to have happened, but now that he had, it was as if he was in a scene from an Alfred Hitchcock film. He didn't really know, nor did he care, why he had shadowed the silly bitch all the way to the house that she went to view in Islington. He couldn't say that he hadn't been intrigued to know what she was up to. And he couldn't understand why she would want to come back and live in the East End again when her parents were doing all right living by rivers and forests. It didn't sit right with him. And Kenny wanted to know more. He *had* to know more.

Pretending to study the racing pages in his newspaper, he slyly glanced towards Charlotte every now and then, wondering if he should rattle her cage by going politely to her table to ask if he could join her. She could hardly say no, he thought. But then, as he looked around him, he didn't think it such a good idea for him to be seen with her by those in the café since he didn't know how things were going to turn out with this one. Not that it mattered. He hadn't much on today and he liked the thrill of the stalk. He wondered if Charlotte would lead him to her childhood sweetheart. Nathan the Jew. He wondered what he looked like now. The same as before but older, and with a bigger nose? He smiled at the thought of it.

Once he had ordered himself a cup of frothy coffee from the young Italian waiter he sat back, every bit the relaxed young man, but kept on peering at Charlotte every so often. He was interested to know where she was going next. It would be an extra bonus if she led him to the Jew, the drip who had lived in the same block before his own family moved from one council estate to another just around the corner from where he now sat. He knew that Charlotte had been thick with Nathan from the first year at the junior school when he had come top in the class at spelling, arithmetic and geometry. Kenny's granddad, who had been a Blackshirt before the Second World War, had told his son more than once to keep an eye on all Jews because they were set on running and owning most of the East End, if not the City itself. He told him that in order to do this, Jews would sit huddled over candlelight through the night just so as to work every God given hour and save every brass farthing.

Uncomfortable to be in the same place as Kenny, and feeling that she was being slyly watched by him, Charlotte wondered if the bastard who she had once hated was going to be a pain in the neck again. Deciding to take the bull by the horns and face him full on, she took a deep breath, picked up her cup of coffee and went over nice and casual and sat at his table. 'So what brings you back into the East End then, Kenny?' she brazenly asked.

Pulling his head back Kenny pretended surprise. He sniffed as he peered at her, and then broke into a sly smile. 'Are you following me, Charlie?'

'I was just gonna ask you the same thing, Kenny.' She returned his smile.

'Was yer? And why would I want to do that? You're surely not still carrying all that shit from when we was kids are yer? It *was* five years ago.'

'And you've turned over a new leaf have you?' She raised an eyebrow and then sipped her coffee, waiting to see if he could keep up this chummy stance.

'I don't know about that, Charlie, but neither of us are school kids any more, are we? So where do you live and work now? In Bridgeford or back here? Not that I'm overly interested, but we're adults and making conversation comes with age.' He grinned.

'Oh, right . . . well, as for me, I'm the girl that lives nowhere and works there as well.' She wasn't going to give anything away. 'My parents live in Bridgeford, as you must know because I saw you talking to Dad at the station. But the rest of our family lives here in the East End. I'm always popping down by train to see them.'

'Yeah? And there I was finking you'd turned into a country bumpkin. So what are your plans? Are you gonna go back today or stop a bit longer? We could go for a drink tonight in one of the old local pubs if you've got nuffing planned. I feel like I owe you a drink or two because of all the tormenting I did when I was a little bastard back there in the old days.'

She *was* staying over another night and she was going to meet Nathan that evening but she wasn't going to tell him. 'I'm going to spend time with my grandparents and then go back by train first thing tomorrow,' she said, ending it there.

'Ah, that's a shame. Still, maybe another time, eh?' He pulled a business card from his pocket, one of the original fifty that he had got a mate who worked in a stationery store to print up for him. A mate who was an amateur small time thief as good as he was.

Taking the card that was offered to her, Charlotte read the print beneath his name: Member of the Charity Trust Society. 'Which charity trust would that be, Kenny?'

'Oh, I cover about ten, but in the main I work for Oxfam, the NSPCC, the Aged and the Jewish poor,' he lied.

Silently laughing at him Charlotte slowly shook her head. 'The Jewish poor? You hated the Jews, Kenny. What kind of a scam is this?'

'It's not a scam. My gran got me into it when my granddad was in the hospice up by Stratford. I spent a lot of time visiting 'im and it went from there, really. I do a lot of charity work as it 'appens. Serve in the Oxfam shops around London

157

that 'ave cropped up 'ere there and everywhere. We 'ave a rota system going.' He looked into her face and showed compassion to cover his lying eyes.

'And what about paid work? What are you doing for a living these days?'

'I can't work, Charlotte. I'm on the Panel. I 'ad an accident when I was carrying a heavy roll of carpet on my shoulder.' More lies. 'I ended up flat on my back with two crushed discs for six months. It was murder, but at least it gave me time to reflect. I nearly died, you know.'

'And Bridgeford?' said Charlotte not believing one word of it. 'Have you got relatives there?'

'Nah.' He grinned at her and slowly shook his head again. 'You've gotta be joking. None of my lot would live in that dump. I was there to arrange for one of our charity shops to open up in the town. The Red Cross is interested.'

Now he was beginning to sound as if he just might have turned over a new leaf. 'So you'll be backwards and forwards then?'

'Do me a favour. No. My business there is done and dusted. I did what I could to set things up but the Council passed it over to Diss, a quiet little town in—'

'Yeah, I know where it is, I've been there a few times on the local bus.' Charlotte checked her wristwatch. 'I'd best be going soon. Got to fit a lot in before I go back in the morning. I'm staying at my grandparents.'

'I know you are.'

'Do you? How come?'

Kenny looked affectionately at her and then slowly shook his head. 'Because you said so no more than a few minutes ago.'

'Did I?' She couldn't remember whether she had or not and this worried her.

'Listen . . . we all get stressed out now and then. Don't worry about it, Charlie. And look after yerself.' He swallowed the remains of his coffee and stood up to leave. 'Take care of yerself, Charlie, and look after your grandparents. Old people need more loving than most people realise.'

'I'm sure they do,' said Charlotte, fazed by his certainty that she had mentioned staying with Nell and Johnny. Once he had left the table and paid his bill at the till she told herself to slow down a bit and get a grip. She was a bit young to be losing her memory. The truth of it was of course that he had got to her again the same way as he always had done – and she didn't like it. Glancing up, she watched as he left and was puzzled by his smile and the show of a hand once he was outside and had a view in via the window. Could he really have turned over a new leaf? She didn't think so. She checked her wristwatch again, drank the remains of her coffee and once at the till smiled back at the friendly Italian woman as she handed over a two shilling bit. Giving her the change the woman said, 'Know him do you, darling?'

'Who? Kenny?'

'Mmm.'

'We used to live in the same block of flats when we were kids. Why do you ask?'

'Why? Because I don't think that he's quite right in the head, if you know what I mean. And if it were up to me I would ban him from coming in here. But who am I? I am only the paid worker.'

'What's he done to rattle your cage?' asked Charlotte, a touch puzzled. He had come across to her as quite tame compared to what he was like when young.

'He always was a little bastard when a kid and I don't think he's changed. Call it a woman's intuition. Call it what you like. But keep an arm's length. I think he's an evil little sod in a false guise.'

'Oh don't worry.' Charlotte smiled. 'I know him from old too. I was surprised to see him come in here though. Where does he live these days?'

'Just up the road on the new council estate. I'm telling you, sweetheart, he's an evil little toe-rag. And it's not just my sixth sense that tells me so. I know his mother. The poor woman has been beside herself at times, wondering what he's been up to when he gets home in the wee hours and then sleeps right through the next day. But don't tell her I said so . . . should you meet up.'

'Of course not,' said Charlotte. 'And thanks for the warning. I appreciate it. See you again.' With that she smiled and left the warm and friendly place with a horrible nagging worry deep down inside her. 'Forget it, Charlotte,' she murmured as she made her way to the place where she hoped she would soon be living. 'He can't harm you. And besides which, gossips are part and parcel of the way of life in this part of the world, you should know that.' Pushing all that the woman had said from her mind, she walked through the back turnings to the square, with the warm glow slowly coming back into her heart. She so wanted to see the beautiful house that had been converted into lovely apartments again. The place that would soon be her new home.

Twelve

Standing in the shadows of the ground floor of a two-storey block of modern maisonettes with shops below, Kenny had every intention to wait and then follow Charlotte. He knew that she had been holding back the real reason for her being in this little corner of the East End. He didn't know what the reason was but he intended to find out. He had always made it his business to know his patch inside out and she had not been in this particular part for years. So what was she hiding, he wanted to know? And what was he was about to find out? He felt sure that just like most slags she had been lying to him through her back teeth. Yes, she had definitely been holding something back from him, of this he felt certain. And he didn't like it.

He watched her stroll along and commended himself for scrambling her brain a little bit. It was an old trick that he had learned along the way. One of several that he had used when he needed to fuck up someone's thinking the way life had tried to mess up his. He followed in her footsteps once she had turned a corner. Soon he would know what the little bitch was about. He half hoped she was on the game. This would have been the biggest bonus he could have wished for. She would be just another piece of shit that he could rid the world of. Another name that he could add to his list of women that he had now put an end to.

Precisely nine minutes later, according to his wristwatch, he was at the lovely green that was enclosed by the old-fashioned black railings and open gateway. The girl who had tried to intimidate him those years back had returned to the place that she had gone to the day before. Knowing this area like the back of his hand, he slipped in and sat on one of the benches and watched through the gaps in the thick shrubs. The sky was a light blue, the sun was warm, and he was more than content to watch as Charlotte rang the bell of the posh-looking house. To his delight but to Charlotte's obvious disappointment it seemed that there was no one in. After a few minutes of waiting and hoping that someone would appear from inside, Kenny smiled to himself as the girl he once fancied rotten turned to leave but was waylaid by a tall and gaunt guy who had just arrived at the house. Leaning back in his seat, Kenny was quite content to watch as some-one who he considered to resemble a weirdo chatted to Charlotte.

Watching them talking all nice and friendly Kenny won-dered if his earlier thoughts about her were right – that she had turned into a call girl and that the drip was one of her punters. Smiling, he cupped his chin and observed as the tall and lanky young man pushed the key into the lock of the front door and then stood aside to let Charlotte go in before him. He couldn't believe that someone like this could possibly be a boyfriend that she was shacking up with. Slowly shaking his head, he wondered if she was no better than any other trollop who sold herself for a hot dinner. But then, just as he was about to leave the square and take a slow walk so as to think things through, he saw another woman come along. She too went up the steps to the front door of the very same house.

Recognising her from somewhere, Kenny wracked his brain until the penny dropped. Of course he knew her. She worked in the second-hand bookshop on the Mile End Road where he bought thrillers and dark horror paperbacks for next to nothing because they had been read and thumbed so much.

He was intrigued. This was almost like a chapter from one of the books to do with the local serial killer from the nineteenth century that he had read up on. The man who, just like himself, had a loathing for prostitutes. Jack the Ripper. The man who was never caught for his crimes but had been made famous and gone down in the history books. Someone he admired.

He pondered whether he should make friends with the women when he next went into the bookshop so as to perhaps get inside the front door of the imposing building and see if it was being run as a whorehouse. Thinking back, he felt sure that this woman had given him the come-on more than once when he had been studying the books on the shelves in the bookshop. It would seem that this was his lucky day. He had possibly caught two fucking-birds with one stone. He laughed at the thought of it. He liked the idea of kissing one and killing the other. Depending how each of them treated him – with respect or derision. Then, for some reason that he could not put his finger on, he was reminded of something that his dad had said to him that morning. He pushed his hands into his pockets and stayed right where he was on the bench in the tree-lined square, tucked away from people coming and going. His dad, before he had left for work had popped his head around Kenny's bedroom door where he had been curled up and said, quite sincerely, 'Why haven't you got any mates any more, Kenny boy?'

He had pretended that he hadn't heard, that he had fallen back to sleep after the cup of tea that his mum had brought up to him first thing. It wasn't as if this question hadn't crossed his own mind, it had. But he preferred to be by himself in any case, answering to no one. It was as simple as that. Most people irritated him, and the amusement had gone out of kicking the shit out of someone who got on his nerves. He had never had a girlfriend and nor had he wanted one for that matter. But neither was he a pansy. He quite liked the company of older people who he sometimes sat and had a chat with in one pub or another. He liked hearing about the old days from those who had lived in them rather than reading it from a history book. He didn't know if he was lonely or not because he had nothing to compare his run-of-the-mill life with. But he did have a mission. A mission to continue the good work of Jack.

Given a choice, he thought that his ideal occupation would be to sit on the ship in the North Sea and take the place of Tony Blackburn as DJ on the pirate station Radio Caroline. This kind of work would suit him down to the ground. He could imagine himself tucked away from the world, and away from women who constantly lured him in for the kill. But this was all right. If this was his predestination, then so be it. Who was he to argue?

Having invited Charlotte into the house, Donald, the land-lady's son, felt not only obliged to show her around for a second time but also was more than happy to do so. He was delighted to have the opportunity to let her view the flat that she was going to rent so that she could familiarise herself with it once again. Enjoying his sense of importance, the tall and lean twenty-eight-year-old, with dark blond hair cut neatly into a short back and sides, led her into his mother's kitchen first and poured each of them a glass of Lucozade. Doing his best to make conversation so as to have her feeling at ease, he tried to keep a warm smile on his face. She looked very much more at home than he imagined she would and seemed quite comfortable listening to him explain the way of things in the house. It was good to have a bit of company in his mother's big friendly kitchen, with the gentle ticking sound of the old fashioned wall-mounted clock.

'My own personal apartment was sparsely furnished once upon a time.' He spoke in a quiet voice as he grew more relaxed at the old pine table. Nudging his loose horn-rimmed

164

glasses on to the bridge of his nose, he said, 'My sitting room had an old fashioned patterned rug over the dark red lino at one time, but I removed it and carried it to a skip that was parked further along the road. I wasn't keen on it. There were all kinds of things in the skip and I think that this was what started me off into being a collector. I think that people living in these houses must be quite rich because they throw away perfectly good pieces of furniture as well as other bits and bobs.'

'Good for you,' said Charlotte warming to him. She liked this innocent oddball and felt sorry for him without really knowing why. 'I'm sure you won't be the only one who dives into skips for bits and pieces one day and then slips in a bit of your own rubbish the next.' She smiled. 'We all love something for nothing don't we? And we all love to have a clear-out now and then as well.'

'Yes, I think you might be right. I did check that it was fine by my mother for me to get rid of the old mat. And she didn't mind at all and thought that somebody else would be glad of it. This is why I rolled it upside out so that people could see the pile that hadn't flattened and the pattern that hadn't faded. I replaced that one a couple of days later with a rug that I found, which is much brighter. It was in a rag and bone shop in Whitechapel. They let me have it for five shillings in the end. I washed and polished the lino before I put the mat down. It came up a treat. I quite like the idea of polish but I don't think I shall do it again. I couldn't get used to the strong smell of lavender. It woke me in the night and I would sooner sleep when it's dark.'

Charlotte tried not to laugh at him. He was quite funny in his own sweet way and he was also a bit of a conundrum. He seemed a bit on the simple side and yet intelligent. 'I'm sure you *would* rather sleep at night,' she said. 'There's nothing worse, is there, than to be all alone and wide awake when the world is snoring.'

'I suppose not. I don't hear the woman upstairs walking about when I'm asleep in my room of course, but the flat that you'll be taking is directly below hers and she does tend to pace the floor. I did sleep in the flat below hers for a week or so when it was uninhabited, just for a change, and I did hear the floorboards creaking. Hers is not fitted carpet because Mother thinks that kind of a thing encourages dust mites and all sorts of germs. What do you think? I'm not so sure myself.'

Charlotte wasn't quite sure what to say so as not to offend him, or cross his mother should he be the type to report a conversation such as this one. 'I don't know,' she finally said. 'I've never really thought about it.' She then glanced at her wristwatch ready to bring this little chat to an end. 'God . . . I can't believe how quickly the time's gone today. My grandparents will be wondering where I am. I had better scarper.' She smiled.

Seeming as if he hadn't heard what she had said, Donald became thoughtful, rubbing his chin as he spoke. 'I think that you will find that the woman above the flat that you'll be taking really does have a bit of trouble getting to sleep. I think I'll get my mother to have a word with her about the opening and shutting of drawers. This was something else that I heard when I slept below her. It was as if she was always searching for something or other. And then, at other times it sounded as if she was turning out her wardrobe because I could hear the rattle of the hangers. At least, that is what it sounded like. I could have been wrong, of course.'

'You should try shoving slightly dampened cotton wool in your ears,' said Charlotte light-heartedly. 'That works. That blocks all noises out. I did it when we first moved to Norfolk because of the early morning cockerels and the sound of the birds calling to each other in the woods close by. And I'll do it tonight, because in my grandparents' house the walls are thin and I don't want to hear either of them snoring.'

Thoughtful and serious, Donald slowly nodded. 'Yes, I

suppose I could try that. But of course I have my own rooms now. Below yours.'

'I love the flat by the way,' said Charlotte, returning his smile. 'And I can't wait to move in.' There was a small pause, then she said, 'I'm sorry that I missed your mother. Perhaps you could tell her that I came back to say that I definitely want to live here and that I have been offered and have accepted the position at the council offices.'

'Yes, I will tell her. And congratulations on the appointment.' He searched his brain for another conversational angle and said, 'Incidentally . . . do you have use for an ironing board? If so I've got one in the garden shed that you can have.'

'I haven't used one up until now because Mum does all of my ironing back home. But I suppose I'm going to have to do it myself once I move in.'

'Well, I don't want you to waste your shillings. I'll get the one out of the shed for you. This was something else that I found leaning against the skip. It's perfectly all right. Personally, I never press or iron anything. When I take these slacks off, for instance, I lay them flat on the base of my bed and then carefully replace the mattress on top. I do this with most of my clothes so they never need ironing. It's quite a thin mattress but very firm. I mostly wear one of my four Fred Perry shirts during my leisure time, which drip-dry without creases. I'm not certain if this green and white Fred Perry goes with these slacks that I bought yesterday from the Red Cross shop. What do you think?'

'Absolutely fine,' said Charlotte, beginning to feel as if she were talking to a brother. A brother who was a bit simple and somebody that she liked. She did like him, possibly because he wasn't run of the mill. She glanced at her wristwatch again and then raised an eyebrow. 'I could sit here all day and chat to you in this room at this table but needs must. My grandparents will be dying to know whether I got the job so I'd best get going. You don't have to show me my rooms. I just wanted to come into the house again. That's all.'

'Oh, well then, I mustn't keep you.' Her host got up from his chair, and like a true gentleman went round to her chair and gently eased it back for her once she was on her feet. He then walked with her out of the room, into the passage and then the spacious hall that led to the front door. 'I should think that yesterday was probably the best day I've had in a while with regard to my purchases,' he said, crossing his arms as he stood by the rather grand front door. 'I went down to the scrap yard and came back with change from a ten-shilling note, and yet I got quite a lot of useful things. I know I'll be able to make use of every single item. Even the oily bicycle chain once I've soaked it in hot water and suds. I also bought a beautiful pure cut-glass vase. I scrubbed it clean and now I've got it soaking in raw potato water. This will get rid of the old watermark. I've got a very good book on household tips should you ever wish to borrow it.'

'You sound like my granddad,' she smiled. 'The pair of you would really get on. He's always pulling bits and bobs out of skips that he thinks he can make use of and he's got one of the old type of books that you mention.'

'Oh well, then you must let him know about another skip that's just been set down in this road this week.' He stopped talking and cupped his chin thoughtfully and said, 'Look, I don't want you to get the wrong impression. I've no complaints about Wendy . . . the woman who paces the floor. She pays her rent on time and this keeps my mother in good spirits.'

'Well, that's no bad thing and it's one way of looking at it,' she said, opening the main door that led back out to the street and the real world. 'But you don't have to worry about me. I'm a heavy sleeper, and I've always got the homemade earplugs. Thanks for the Lucozade and good luck with the hunting. You seem very good at it.'

'Hunting?' he looked mystified. 'I don't agree with the hunt. I never have done. My cousins in the country have only just accepted that I won't ever join in. What made you think I was one of them?'

'I was talking about the things you find in second-hand shops and in the skips,' said Charlotte.

'Oh . . . yes . . . I see what you mean. How slow of me.' His self-conscious smile touched her, but enough was enough. She bade him farewell, said that she would be seeing him soon and left.

Walking slowly away along the tree-lined pavement and past the enclosed public garden where Kenny still sat, Charlotte felt so happy she almost cried. Not only was she thrilled to be back, but she was also in her favourite place in a quiet spot in Stepney Green that she had always seen as heavenly. She could hardly believe that she was going to be living here. Her thoughts were flying from one thing to another as she walked through the back streets on her way to the bus stop where she would ride to Bow and her grandparents' house. She was ready to have a little rest before Nathan called to see her.

Hidden behind the foliage in the small square, Kenny lit himself another cigarette with a satisfied smirk. If Charlotte was planning to live in the house on the square he couldn't have asked for anything easier. This place was a spitting distance from the council flat where he lived with his mum and dad so he could keep an eye on her. See what she was up to. If she turned out to be someone who simply fancied herself as being independent and living in her own furnished flat that was all right by him. He was just going to have to see how things panned out. He was more taken with having seen the woman who wore too much lipstick and powder going into the house than he had been at seeing Charlotte. The woman who he felt sure he had heard being referred to as Wendy by one of the other assistants in the bookshop.

If she *was* living in that house he felt he could have a bit of fun by playing one woman off against the other. He could pass a little bit of false gossip to Wendy when he was next in the shop – perhaps that Charlotte had been a little whore on the quiet when she had lived in the town of Bridgeford in Norfolk. Then, when he might accidentally on purpose bump into Charlotte, he could tell her that the woman called Wendy, who was like mutton dressed as lamb, was an Aldgate whore after dark.

Laughing to himself, his hands in his pockets and his head lowered, he walked out through the open gateway of the Victorian square to saunter back home. He couldn't believe how his life had livened up during the past four weeks or so. He momentarily thought about the girl who was at the bottom of the wishing well in the overgrown garden in Bridgeford. But then he told himself that even though it was a sad way to end a life of misery, at least she was better off dead than to live the rest of her life soiling her body with randy old men who got off on paid sex. He was more certain than ever that she had been a prostitute on the quiet.

To Kenny's mind he had done that Rosie the biggest favour that anyone could have done, and he felt a rush of self-pride from top to toe. After all, he had given the girl a quick end and a nice resting-place in the dark, away from the stinking underbelly world that she had been dragged into.

What he didn't know, and what he hadn't even considered as a possibility, was that back in the small Norfolk town of Bridgeford, questions were being asked about the disappearance of the young woman. The girl's best friend, who she had spent most of her time with, after making several phone calls to the old ramshackle mansion house where Rosie had lived, had called in at the Bridgeford police station and reported her friend missing without a trace. And she hadn't been alone in her worries because other people, with whom the young girl had shared the same roof, had also been concerned about her sudden disappearance. The giveaway was that there was no sign of her having packed up any of her personal possessions, and her clothes had been left around her room in an ordinary scattered way. And not only this: her best friend, who had been the last of her friends to have seen her alive in the pub, had seen her go off with a young man – one that she saw as a bit of an outsider who had not been staying in the town for that long, and who had *also* disappeared.

Thirteen

After spending a nice cosy evening with her grandparents and Nathan and then enjoying a good night's sleep, Charlotte was back home in Bridgeford after a tiring journey from London. She was telling Rita and Eddie how pleased she was that she had not only been offered the position at the local council offices, but that she had also found a lovely flat. A flat in the East End that she loved. Taking her by surprise, there were no flowing tears from her parents, but a big hug from both of them. They, having had time to think about it, were in their own way admitting that it was time for them to let go. Their little girl was now a young woman after all, and clearly a young woman with a mind of her own.

Charlotte slept well again that night, but the very next morning as she was getting ready to go to work, she picked up on the fact that there was a sombre mood in the air. Not knowing whether to leave things be and allow a cooling off period, she carried on as if nothing was amiss so as to give her parents a chance to have their say and get it over and done with. But she was pleasantly surprised that nothing came in the way of admonishment, and neither were either of them causing her to feel guilty for wanting to fly the nest that they had built for all three of them. In a relaxed mood, she sipped her tea and looked from her mum to her dad, and said, 'Nan and Granddad were really pleased to see Nathan again. He came to pick me up and we went out for dinner to the Steak

House in Aldgate. It was lovely. Really nice. Candles and everything.'

'We know,' said Eddie, as cool as a cucumber. 'Your granddad phoned to tell us.'

'He's a lovely lad,' added Rita, 'and from what I gather he's got a good job.'

'And he's a lifelong friend,' continued Eddie. 'You can't ask for more than that.'

'I'm not saying that we're making plans, other than to go courting, but who knows? His family being Jewish, though . . . I wasn't sure how you'd feel about that.' Now she really was testing the water.

'About what? You're not engaged to be married, for God's sake,' said Rita.

'No . . . but we love each other just as much as we did in the old days—'

'Don't talk daft,' Rita laughed. 'In the old days as you call them, you were children who were good friends. Love?' She broke into soft laughter again. 'You wouldn't 'ave known the meaning of the word.'

'Whatever,' said Charlotte, shrugging. 'But we do now.'

The room went quiet. Then, shrugging and drawing breath Eddie said, 'If you're thinking of marriage, Charlotte, you're gonna have to give us time to take this in. We're Church of England and . . .'

Charlotte slowly shook her head. 'So all the old hang-ups of the past are still with us. I might 'ave known.'

'Your dad never said anything about anti-Semitism,' Rita said, a touch coldly.

'Anti-Semitism?' Charlotte smiled. 'Who ate the dictionary for breakfast then?'

'And who was it who once told me that sarcasm was the lowest form of wit?'

'I wasn't being sarcastic, Mum. All I'm saying is that I love

Nathan and that he loves me. So try and get used to the idea of it. That's all.'

'But we're not talking about wedding bells, surely?' said Eddie. 'Not yet anyway?'

'No . . . not yet. But who knows? His dad seems overjoyed that we've met up again by all accounts, so I don't think he'll have any problems if we decide to be together forever.' Charlotte smiled. Then just to change the subject, she asked about the headline in the local paper to do with a missing girl. She focused on Eddie because she knew that Rita was pre-occupied with all that she had just told them.

'It's come as a bit of a shock to tell the truth, sweetheart,' said Eddie. 'I know neither me nor your mother knew the girl . . . but it don't make you feel all that easy with something like this on the doorstep. She could be laying strangled somewhere for all we know.'

'Or, she could be lying beside her lover in a bed in a cosy little cottage. Don't forget our local doesn't 'ave much in the way of a headline to report.'

'That's true.' Eddie leaned back in his chair with a faint smile. 'I suppose that me and your mum was getting a bit carried away. The thought of you going missing made our blood run cold. I don't think she was more than a year older than you, sweetheart.'

'Was? Come on, Dad. She's not gonna be murdered, dead and buried. She's probably having a bit of fun somewhere with someone who can afford to give her a lovely time and then drop her back into her own world.'

'If you say so. But from what we heard the boys in blue 'ave been sniffing around a flat above a dingy wireless shop in a side street not far from here. Less than a ten-minute walk in fact.'

'Oh? Well that's a different kettle of fish. And you know for sure that it's to do with her disappearance, do you?'

'According to the talk in our local. They've already taken in a flash lad for questioning who was apparently one of the last ones to have seen 'er alive.'

'Blimey.' Charlotte shrugged. 'Well, that is different. And he's someone from the pub where you and Mum always drink?'

'So they say.'

'And did you know him?'

'Don't think so. It's always packed with lads when I'm in there. It could 'ave been any one of them,' said Eddie.

'Well . . . there you are then. I might be safer in the East End than in this lovely little country town after all.' She looked from her dad to her mum. 'And if this is what's worrying you – I've not only got Nathan, Gran and Granddad to keep a protective eye on me, but the lovely woman, Mrs Braintree who owns the house – and her son Donald, who's a sweetheart.'

'Good,' said Eddie. He looked across to Rita. 'Feel better now, love? Now that we've heard a bit more about madam living back in her roots?'

'I suppose so,' Rita shrugged. 'But you can't blame us for worrying, Charlotte, can you? You do hear of terrible things these days.'

'I'll be all right, Mum. And from what you've just said, it might not be any more dangerous in London than anywhere else. Who would have thought that the police would be crawling over Bridgeford?'

'So,' said Eddie, wishing to change the subject. 'You love the flat you've seen, you liked the place where you went for the interview, and you'll be moving out in a fortnight's time? Is that right?'

'Well . . . it depends.'

'On what?' said Rita.

'I only need to give the council offices here a one-week notice apparently. They've already got a junior who works in the post room who will fill my position and someone further down the line who'll fill hers. That's the system.'

'So you think you'll be ready to go in a week, do you?' Eddie sniffed and raised an eyebrow. 'Clothes washed, pressed and packed in just seven days? Never mind your bits and pieces that you'll want to take. Such as your bedding, for example, and your bedside table lamp that you've had since you was three years old and won't part with. Your fluffy bedroom rug that you love . . .'

'I'll be ready if you are, Dad. I'll need a lift down, obviously.'

Rita glanced sadly at her daughter. 'You've got it all worked out then? But we've not seen the place yet. What if we don't think it's good enough for you?'

'It is, Mum, trust me. Please. Just this once trust that I know more than you do.'

Eddie cleared his throat and looked sideways at his wife. This wasn't the kind of a conversation that she appreciated. Far from it. He knew that he had to be a bit of a peacemaker here. 'Let 'er make 'er own mistakes, Rita,' he said, 'and be it on her own head if she comes unstuck. She won't be able to say that you didn't warn 'er.'

'Oh, do what you want, Charlotte. You always have done in any case, in your own quiet way. But if we don't think it's good enough when we take you down next weekend I'm not leaving you there.'

'That's fair enough, Mum. I'll agree to that.'

'Good,' said Rita. 'Now then . . . you'd best write a list of things that we'll need to buy. Kettle, iron, teapot, cutlery, crockery, toaster . . .'

'I won't need all of that! It's furnished!' Charlotte laughed.

'I think you'll find that you will. Phone the woman who owns the property and ask what's included when it comes to the kitchen and the bed linen and bath towels and hand towels and tea towels—'

176

'Yeah all right, Reet,' Eddie interrupted. 'I think she's got the point.'

'Good,' said Rita, 'because in two minutes time *Coronation Street*'s on and I don't want to miss it. Annie Walker's upset Ena Sharples.' Eddie caught Charlotte's eye and winked at her. They had won the battle without too much of a fight. He had previously warned Charlotte that she had to play it just right because if her mother had laid down the law and not agreed to her plans, he would have had to go along with that. It was with a sigh of relief that he leaned back in his chair and tried not to worry if his beautiful daughter would be all right looking after herself. She was going, and that was all there was to it.

Fourteen

On the morning of her departure for London, once everything had been packed into two large suitcases and furnishings such as her fairly new record player, records and bedside lamp had been loaded into the family car, it was Charlotte who experienced butterflies in her stomach, and not her parents. They had by now got used to the idea of her going and were looking forward to seeing where she would be living.

Settled into the back seat of Eddie's car and on the way, she broke into a lovely smile and then said to her parents, who were chatting away in the front of the car, 'I can't believe I'm doing this.'

Eddie and Rita glanced sideways at each other, keeping their thoughts to themselves – thoughts that they had discussed more than once about how she would soon miss the home comforts and be back in Bridgeford appreciating the way of life instead of grumbling about the everyday boring existence there. Rita had by now had a change of heart, and instead of worrying about whether her daughter would cope in London after five years spent in a small country backwater, she felt rather proud of her. She wanted her to make a success of it. And having had time for it to sink in, she knew that she was only going to be three or four hours away at the most . . . depending on the traffic. And of course Rita also knew that her own mum and dad would take great care of Charlotte.

They loved their granddaughter to bits and they would certainly keep an eye on her. Deep down she realised that she had been a touch over protective when it came to her only child. Her only child who was now undeniably a lovely young woman.

Hugging her first teddy bear, which was worn and a touch misshapen but that she still loved, Charlotte was tired. All of the excitement and packing had stopped her from being able to drift off to sleep at her usual time the night before, so she rested her head back and, before she knew it, slipped into a welcome doze. She had been relaxed and excited at the same time at the thought of being in the centre of swinging London in the Swinging Sixties. Her mind had gone from one thing to another the night before, even to thinking about Twiggy who hadn't even sat her O-levels when she had been launched into stardom. She wasn't an East End girl it was true, but all three of the celebrated photographers that worked with models of her ilk – David Bailey, Terence Donovan and Brian Duff – were East London born and bred.

Ordinary young working-class men and women, who had made it to the top were now mixing with the offspring of the old rich. And apart from all of this, with London swinging it was true to say that there was a kind of new religion emerging: the talk was of everyone being able to develop ESP should they set their mind to it. Various stages of consciousness were being discussed in clubs, pubs and coffee bars and LSD was beginning to be passed around. Suddenly there was an abundance of new music and daring lyrics emerging, as well as flamboyant fashion. The culture was changing, and Charlotte wanted to be part of it all, if only in a very small way.

With the roads pretty clear, they were soon crossing the border from Norfolk into Suffolk and then Essex. Driving through to Wanstead and then Leytonstone and Stratford East, they finally arrived into Stepney Green and made for Lavender Square, where Eddie parked outside the grand

179

terraced house that faced the hedged green. Both Rita and Eddie remembered this romantic part of Stepney from their courting days when they had strolled through the old-fashioned back streets – a time when they had sometimes paid homage to the Prospect of Whitby down by the river Thames.

Properly awake after having dozed on and off for most of the journey, Charlotte looked at the front door to which she would soon have a key. A door that she would have every right to enter and leave at any time of the day. She could hardly believe it was happening, and from the expression on her parents' faces neither could they. It was an imposing house, as were those on either side of it in this exclusive terrace overlooking that treasure of a square.

Isabelle Braintree opened the door, smiling sweetly. She then stood aside and waved a graceful hand, beckoning in her new tenant and her parents. 'Please do come in. I have been so looking forward to your coming.'

'I hope we're not too early,' said Rita, a touch at a loss for something to say because she was so bowled over by everything, especially the grand entrance hall. And if the truth be known, she was also a touch intimidated by it all, as was Eddie. But neither of them showed their nervousness as they too smiled and in turn shook the hand of the graceful woman who was so obviously a lady of refinement, born and bred.

'Of course you're not too early,' Isabelle said. 'I expect you must be terribly dry after that long journey. Would you like a cup of tea or a cold drink?'

'No, we're fine,' said Rita, a touch shyly. 'I packed a picnic and we had that on the way. But thank you for offering.'

'Not at all. I expect you'd like to settle your daughter into her new home. I'll show you up to the apartment and then leave you to it, shall I?'

'That would be lovely,' said Rita. 'Thank you.'

As they trooped up the wide staircase, Isabelle told of how quiet the square was, day and night, and how she was sure their daughter would soon feel very much at home. She then briefly spoke of the other tenants before she opened the door into the apartment where Charlotte was to live. 'I'll leave you to show your parents around, Charlotte,' she said, smiling at the girl as she took her leave.

Gently closing the door behind them, Eddie exclaimed, 'I didn't expect it to be this good, Charlotte! Well done, babe. It's lovely.'

Rita went to the window where beautiful, lined William Morris flowery curtains hung and looked out across the square. 'I wouldn't mind living here myself,' she said.

'Nor would I,' said Eddie, joining her. 'Who wouldn't?'

By now Charlotte was inside her small kitchen and grinning like a Cheshire cat. She could see that a kettle, teapot and a tray with four cups and saucers had been set. There was also some instant coffee and a pretty tea caddy. In the small fridge there was a jug of milk and four small fresh cream buns. Seeing all of this she was almost brought to tears. 'She is *so* nice. Look at what she's left out for us.'

Eddie came into the kitchen and slowly nodded. 'You've fallen on your feet here, babe.'

An hour or so later, once they knew that their daughter was well and truly ready to be by herself and unpack at her leisure, the proud parents left to make their way to see Nell and Johnny. Charlotte hugged her parents goodbye, and could tell by the expression on Rita's face that her mum was no longer worrying about whether she would cope in London. After all, her parents knew that Nell and Johnny would keep a close eye on her welfare. And now, with her suitcases unpacked and her other special bits and pieces, such as her old teddy, Charlotte felt like shedding a tear one minute and shouting at the top of her voice for joy the next.

Now that she *was* alone, she slowly walked around the flat that was hers and only hers and looked at every tiny thing, touching almost everything with her fingertips as if to say hello. As she went back into the kitchen to make her first cup of coffee in her very own apartment, there came a soft tapping on the door. Excited to have a visitor so soon, even though she expected it was only her landlady, she opened the door wide with a smile on her face. But it wasn't Isabelle, it was Wendy from the flat above. The smiling woman was wearing a cheerful red blouse and a flowing white skirt, both of which she had purchased at a charity shop in Whitechapel close to where she worked. In her hand was a small posy of fresh flowers that she had picked from the garden with the permission of Isabelle. Charlotte stood aside and invited her in.

'Darling, I'm not going to intrude,' said Wendy. 'I just wanted to welcome you.' She smiled and then handed her the bunch of flowers.

'Oh . . . that's really nice of you,' said Charlotte, touched by the gesture.

'I won't stay,' said Wendy as she looked around her. 'I do so love this flat, but then I also love mine. You must come up for a cup of tea or coffee in a few days once you've settled in. Do you think that you might like to?'

'Of course I would, that would be lovely. Thank you.'

'Not at all, not at all.' She drew a slow breath and with a contented expression said, 'This is such a pleasant house to live in and the landlady is really very kind. Her son Donald is a bit on the odd side,' she whispered, 'but harmless enough. I think that he's a bit lonely.'

'Oh really?' Charlotte didn't think so. 'He seemed quite nice and normal when I met him and not in the least bit odd. That was when I came to look at the flat.'

'Well . . . there we are. Time will tell. I have a teeny-weeny inkling that he's rather taken to me as a matter of fact – despite the age gap.' She then laid a theatrical hand on her chest and speaking quietly, said, 'Please don't let on that I said so, Charlotte, will you?'

'I wouldn't dream of it,' said Charlotte, her heart sinking just a little. This woman seemed a touch on the barmy side.

'I don't think that he knows that I've realised this. I expect it's my perfume that draws him to me. It's the very original Evening in Paris. I was introduced to it by my grandmother decades ago.'

'It's a lovely scent.' Charlotte was now wondering if she was meant to offer Wendy a cup of coffee. She didn't want to but wasn't sure what someone else in her situation would do so, more out of politeness than anything else, she did say, 'I'm just going to have a hot drink. Would you like one?'

'That's very lovely of you but I've just had a coffee. Thank you. And don't get me wrong . . . I'm not saying that it wouldn't be nice to have the boy's company now and then but one doesn't want to lead him on. He's one of life's vulnerables I think. I suppose I could ask him in for coffee and biscuits. What do you think?'

'I don't know,' said Charlotte, her mind a blank. All she wanted now was to be by herself and adjust to her new surroundings.

'No, it is rather a tricky one, isn't it. But there, I mustn't keep you. You've got to unpack and all of that. But remember . . . I'm not far away should you need anything. Any teeny-weeny problem that you might need advice about. I am always happy to help if I can. I'm only just above your head. Isn't that marvellous?' With that the woman almost hugged herself as she smiled. She looked as if she had brought her conversation to an end. But she hadn't. She began again.

'Of course I don't take too much to heart the way that the innocent boy looks at me. I think that he thinks that I don't have a clue as to how he feels. I expect it's my perfume that he can't resist.'

'It's a lovely scent,' said Charlotte again, walking slowly towards the door ready to open it wide as a hint that it was time for the woman to go. She didn't want to know what Wendy was trying to suggest. Donald seemed fine to her.

'Of course, I really don't think that it should be me who makes an invitation. If my landlady's son wants to come in for a chat he should say so. Do you agree?'

'Possibly,' said Charlotte. 'I don't really know. I've not long come down from the country don't forget. I need time to adjust to London living again.'

'Well, of course you do, poppet. What was I thinking?' Wendy smiled sympathetically at her. 'But you'll soon be in the swing of things, my dear, don't you fret. And as for Donald, well, don't let his strange ways bother you too much. He can be worrying at times, I know. For instance we once had a little disagreement as to which of the two of us best remembered the tenant who rented the basement before the artist. Donald said he could remember a half-caste man. I said that no, it was definitely a young Irish man. And I'm sorry to have to say it, but the look of annoyance in his eyes did set me back a bit. I do believe that he's not a hundred per cent right in the head. I think his poor mother knows this too, but of course she's bound not to let on. If I didn't know him personally, I think that I wouldn't be too keen to come across him in a back turning in the black of the night. But there. I expect I'm just being silly.'

'Oh, I'm sure he wouldn't hurt a fly,' said Charlotte, her patience now running out. 'He's a very genteel type of a person.'

'Well . . . I have to say that there have been reports in the local newspaper recently of local prostitutes going missing. And he does sometimes like to go out very late at night to have a quiet stroll around, as he likes to put it. Let's not forget too easily the old proverb of a sly fox in sheep's clothing.'

With that, Wendy swanned out of the room and Charlotte was left to gaze at the open doorway, shocked by all she had said. She swiftly closed the door and then leaned against it, wondering for a few seconds whether she had done the right thing by moving into this house so quickly before finding out a little more about the tenants. But this thought was immediately wiped away as she looked around again at the lovely room that was now part of her new life. This was her very own pad with its own front door. The old-fashioned floral sofa with its feather cushions and two matching armchairs were homely, and looked absolutely right set around the ornate pine fireplace. A fireplace that was inset with an unlit gas-burning fire and surrounded by beautiful richly coloured patterned tiles. She brought Donald's face to mind again and told herself that perhaps she should keep him at arm's length. He *was* a touch out of the ordinary, but no more than that . . . even so, she thought it best to keep herself to herself for a while.

Back in her own attic apartment, Wendy pulled the chair out from under her writing desk that was in front of her window and sat down to make a few notes in her diary about the new girl. But as she listened to the song of a blackbird, she remembered that she hadn't fed her feathered friends. She went to the kitchen and fetched a brown paper bag in which she kept grated breadcrumbs. She then sprinkled a few on the windowsill for the pigeons, or the sparrows, depending on which of them got there first. It didn't bother her either way . . . she had done her duty and happily so.

Her voice low, she spoke to herself, as was her wont. 'I believe that Donald is someone who wouldn't mind eating baked beans cold straight out of the can.' She then smiled at the image of him when he had once been smoking an old cigar that he found in the silk-patterned smoking jacket purchased from a second-hand clothes stall in Whitechapel market. He really did have a lovely nature and he never minded telling her that some of his clothes were second hand. In actual fact he seemed quite proud to have found such bargains. She couldn't help but like the boy, even though he was a bit on the odd side.

Slipping into her seat at her writing desk by the window again, she wanted to see if she could work out for herself what star sign Charlotte might be. But then she glanced out and up at the clear blue skies, and decided there and then that since this was a lovely summer evening she would go out for a stroll. She had always got her best ideas when walking and thinking, and she did want to get on with the novel that she had been slowly writing over the years. Usually at this time of the day she wrote a little piece about each of the people that she had come to know at work and in this house where she lived. Donald, without a shadow of doubt, was the most interesting of everybody she knew because she couldn't quite fathom him. She still didn't know for certain whether he was highly intelligent or mentally disturbed. The word insane floated through her mind, as it had done before, but she brushed it aside as being far too melodramatic. She wrote only a short piece about him since she had other things on her mind such as her walk. She underlined the word barmy with a question mark. She had already begun to write on a clean page a little about the new girl, Charlotte, but kept it brief because she wanted to have a little rest before she got ready for her stroll.

She had been shopping that morning since this was one of her days off and had spent just over three pounds ten shillings in her favourite Oxfam charity shop in Maida Vale to which wealthy women gave almost-new clothes. Clothes that had been purchased in such places as Harrods, Selfridges and Liberty's of London. Today she had managed to purchase one complete outfit and several beautiful flowing scarves, which she adored. The outfit that she would wear this evening consisted of a purple and pink three-quarter-length summer coat and dress with one of the chiffon scarves to match.

An only child from a middle class family, Wendy had been

brought up in a privately owned house in Wanstead that had a lovely back garden, and she was quite used to dressing nicely. Sadly, both her parents had been killed in a car crash some years before, and just a few years after this her own husband had gone on that missing list, taking some of her inheritance with him. The adulterer in their marriage, he had left her for a girl called Eileen who cleaned the offices where he was working at the time. She felt sure he wouldn't stay with Eileen forever and, since neither of them had sought divorce, she took this to mean that one day he would want them to get back together again. Whether she would be able to forgive him for forging her signature on several of her cheques, robbing her of a substantial amount, she wasn't quite sure.

By now she was quite used to living alone and had almost given up the hope of ever seeing him again . . . but not given up entirely. He had been the love of her life and the only man that she had given herself to. To fill her lonely hours when not working at the local bookshop, she had her work as an Agony Aunt for a quarterly magazine.

To her mind, the people she worked with at the bookshop, as well her fellow lodgers, didn't know that she was an aspiring author. Thus, she would not suffer the embarrassment of failure, should she get rejection slip after rejection slip and never see all that she had written over the years in print. Her pseudonym as an Agony Aunt, Eartha Fire, was one that she would use once her novel was finished and ready to go off to a publishing house of good repute.

Glancing across the room at the outfit on a padded hanger that she would be wearing that evening, she decided that her stroll would be along the High Road to the rather pleasant hotel nearby across an old fashioned bridge where the riff-raff hardly ever went. The class of person who drank in the bar of the hotel was mostly from the City, on their way out to such places as Wanstead, Chingford, Chigwell and Buckhurst Hill. Very respectable areas. Whether or not she would meet up with a handsome romantic bachelor who would sweep her off her feet was anyone's guess. She had always felt that she would give her body and her love to a handsome man should one come into her realm, but they hardly ever did. But she wasn't too put out that she hadn't met someone to love and hold since she had been free and single again. To her mind it was all a matter of what might be in her stars. And now the stars, according to her ever faithful astrology ledger, did look strangely interesting . . . so long as she took heed of the teeny-weeny warnings of danger. From what she could fathom her stars were telling her to be cautious when meeting a stranger. She took this to be the new tenant – the girl called Charlotte – so shrugged it off.

Just as Charlotte was about to make herself a second cup of coffee she heard a soft tapping on the door of her flat. When she opened it her heart sank a little to see that Donald was standing there. He looked as though he might have been there for a few minutes plucking up the courage to knock. 'I hope I'm not disturbing you,' he said, going a little pink in the face. 'But I wondered if you would like this vase to put in the flowers from the garden that Wendy picked for you.'

'Oh, Donald . . .' said Charlotte, touched by his thought. 'That's lovely of you.' She thanked him and said, 'But are you really sure you want to part with this? It's beautiful.'

'Oh yes,' he smiled. 'I've brought it back to its former glory. I'm certain that it's genuine cut glass and now I'm wondering whether I should have brought some more cut flowers with me. There are plenty growing in our garden. There's an old plain white vase in the cupboard under the kitchen sink. It would be nice if you could have some blooms in your bedroom as well as in your sitting room. For the fragrance as well as the picture they make.'

'No, I'm happy with those that Wendy brought, but I do appreciate the vase. Thank you very much for thinking of me.'

He broke into a smile. 'That's perfectly all right. In a week's time I'll cut you some more flowers from the garden to put in the vase.'

'Really? Don't you think that you should check with your mother first before you go cutting her blooms?'

'It's my garden too, Charlotte. I do live here. I shall leave you with the vase and come back in a few days' time with some fresh flowers.'

Charlotte thanked him again and closed the door behind him. She was now wondering if the woman who lived above her was right. One minute Donald seemed such a sensitive soul and the next he wore an odd expression. He had told her three times about his clothes-pressing tactic of putting them under the mattress, but she had noticed that he was wearing a brand new white shirt with the cardboard under the collar still intact. Obviously he wanted to keep it perfectly in place, or possibly believed that this was why the cardboard was there in the first place. She had no idea.

A little sorry for him, she now felt a sense of guilt. She hadn't invited him in for a cup of coffee. But then she reminded herself that she had only just arrived in the house a couple of hours ago, and from his demeanour, she felt that Donald wouldn't have accepted the invite in any case. And it was too soon to set any kind of a pattern that might become a habit with anyone living in the house. Because of the style of house, the space on Charlotte's landing was smaller than that outside Donald's door. This didn't bother her in the least but he had said on the day that he had invited her in that he would exchange flats with her if she didn't think it fair. Of course she wouldn't hear of it. It was at this point that she had wondered if he was all the ticket. But he did seem very nice and innocent if not a touch child-like.

Going into her kitchen she heard yet another tap on the door and was reluctant to answer it this time. But then, telling herself that people were only being kind and friendly, she opened it . . . to Donald. 'I've just had an idea,' he said. 'Should I need to speak to you again I'll tap twice on the door and if you don't open it I'll know that you know that it's me and by not opening it I'll be given a message that it's inconvenient. How does this sound?'

'I think that's a clever idea, Donald,' she said, trying not to sound amused. He was certainly different from anybody she had ever come across.

'I think that it's best to be polite but not overly friendly when living under the same roof but in different apartments.' With that he bade her farewell again and was just about to take his leave when he had another idea.

'Oh, and by the way, should you get lonely in the evenings and don't feel like reading a book we could always play a board game. I've got Monopoly now and that can be quite absorbing.'

'That's really thoughtful,' said Charlotte. 'I *am* used to my own company, but should I for one reason or another start to miss the countryside that I'm used to, or my parents, I'll pop down and see you.' She instinctively held off mentioning that she hoped to spend time with her boyfriend.

'That sounds sensible.' Cupping his chin and still in thought, he said, 'In nice weather, incidentally, my mother sits in the garden. I know she won't mind if you join her for afternoon tea or morning coffee. And by the way, my mother feels that I keep far too many things in my room, so apart from this vase I might have some other bits and pieces that you would like for your flat. I'm a bit of a collector, which is all right, but I don't want to end up a hoarder.'

'Thank you for the offer,' said Charlotte. 'I'll let you know if there's anything I'm short of.'

'Good. To have reached this arrangement at the beginning of our relationship suits me down to the ground. So as not to intrude I shall leave things out here on the landing floor should I think them useful or decorative.'

'That sounds fine.' She smiled at him. 'And if I don't have a use for the things I'll leave them where they are.'

'Absolutely,' said Donald trying his utmost to be correct. 'Much better that we start as we wish to go on.'

Once the door was closed between them Charlotte looked at the vase and felt her stomach churn. Donald seemed sensitive and safe and yet her sixth sense was still warning her to perhaps keep her distance. He was a lovely person but also someone who seemed as if he was a penny short of a shilling, and until she knew what was what in this house, under this roof, she was going to keep herself to herself. Looking around at all of her belongings, bags and boxes on the floor and on the sofa, she decided there and then that what she needed was a bit of music while she unpacked.

Lifting her record player from the sofa to a side table where she could see that there was a socket she selected her favourite LP by the Beatles. While she had the Fab Four in the room with her she knew that she would feel at home. She decided to make herself another cup of coffee and perhaps light a cigarette before she began to unpack properly and settle in. She couldn't wait to sleep in the double divan bed with the big feather pillows. And she couldn't wait to see Nathan again.

A couple of hours later and tired from all of the packing up, travelling and unpacking, Charlotte was resting on the settee. She had phoned Nathan and looked forward to seeing him, but now she was drifting in and out of a light sleep while listening to her music. Feeling peckish she went into the small adjoining kitchen and found the Tupperware box that Rita had packed for her that morning before they set off. It was only now that she realised she hadn't eaten anything other than snacks since breakfast. While waiting for the kettle to come to the boil for another cup of coffee, she eased the lid off the lunch box to find it jam-packed with sandwiches. There was also a large wedge of Rita's homemade fruitcake, and a chunk of egg and pork pie, everything wrapped neat and separate in greaseproof paper. There was enough to feed two people. She silently thanked her mum for thinking of her and felt the prick of tears as it dawned on her that she had actually left home. That she would not be sitting at the dining table the next day for a meal with her mum and dad. This was it. This was what she had been dreaming of for so long. Drifting back into the sitting room with the evening sun streaming in, she smiled at her ever-changing moods. She loved the room. It was spacious, yet had a cosy feeling about it. There was a mismatch of patterns when it came to the wallpaper, curtains, fabrics and fitted carpet but it all seemed to come together to create a kind of comfortable, almost bohemian, mood. And now that some of her own bits and pieces were placed on shelves and on the waxed pine mantelshelf above the fireplace, it looked and felt homely.

Going over to the long sash window she glanced down at Lavender Square where it was peaceful and quiet. She then looked along the turning at the trees that were in full leaf. She felt happy in these surroundings. Happy and at home. Across the square she could see an old man who lived opposite. He was sitting at his window with a lamp just behind him to give him a warm light and was gazing out at nothing. He looked quite lonesome. Charlotte waved to him and at first couldn't catch his attention but, determined not to give up, she waved again and this time he saw her. He nodded his greeting at first and then showed a hand. She then turned away to leave him to his own private world and thoughts, wondering if he was as solitary as he seemed to appear.

The old gentleman, who had been pleased with her show of a hand, was a widower in his seventies who lived by himself in what was more of a bedsit than a flat or apartment. In one corner of his sitting room there was a paraffin heater that he used as a back up for when there was no coal to shovel into the grate of the fireplace. He was a lonely soul, and a friendly wave from someone opposite whose name he didn't even know meant a great deal to him. Rubbing his eyes he smiled down at his old dog and then prodded him with his slippered foot. 'Somebody nice has moved in across the square,' he said and then softly chuckled. 'Maybe I will get a nice picture of her when she goes out walking.' He looked across the room to his old Box Brownie camera on the shelf. 'I think I might need a new film soon.' He then pulled himself up from the chair and wrote himself a note on the pad he kept by the door, reminding himself to take his Box Brownie to the chemist so that the young man who worked there could remove the used reel and replace it with a new one. He had caught so much on his camera that would mean little to anyone else but everything to him. His most treasured picture of all was the one that he had taken of his wife just a few days before she passed away three years earlier, when she had had a soft smile on her face that spoke volumes. He knew that she had had enough of hospitals and check-ups, medication and torment, and had been ready to pass on to the next world.

Back in his chair by the window he looked down at his beloved square again and tears filled his eyes as he murmured how he wished that he had died alongside his dear wife. He was fed up with watching too much but never bored with his view. Even though he could see little reason for being alive he felt that there had to be a reason for him having been left to live alone without the love of his life. All he hoped was that that purpose would show itself soon so that he could be left to sleep in peace . . . forever. And for some unknown reason he felt that the girl who had moved into the house opposite and given him a wave was going to become part of God's bigger picture where he was concerned. It didn't worry him. It didn't excite him. It was simply a matter of fact. He wasn't sure why he felt this but he had given up asking questions of the Lord since his late wife became ill and wracked with pain.

*

193

Thinking about the old man, Charlotte felt that it would be okay to pay him a visit one day soon. She then went over to a small cupboard that was set into the wall next to the fireplace. It had a waxed pine door with a lovely old-fashioned brass knob that had been recently polished and shone like gold. Flicking down a small brass bow-shaped catch, she pulled the door open and the musty smell reminded her of her childhood. A time when her nan had been looking after her and let her rummage through her old photograph albums and little knick-knacks in a cupboard by her fireplace similar to this one. Smiling to herself she closed the narrow cupboard door, then turned around to look at her room again and noticed the dust that seemed to be dancing in the rays of the early evening sun. Again she went to the window and looked across at the old man. This time he showed a hand. This made her feel warm inside.

Later on, soaking in the big white old-fashioned bath before getting herself ready to meet up with Nathan outside Stepney Green underground station, Charlotte couldn't stop herself from smiling. Here she was in a strange house and sharing the same roof with people that she hardly knew. If anybody were to have told her just two weeks ago that this would be the case she would have laughed in their face. She could hardly believe the way things had gone or how quickly it had all happened. And apart from the fact that she was now living in her very own apartment, she and her childhood friend had not only met up again but had fallen in love. And the most wonderful thing of all was that she was back in the heart of the place where she had been born and bred. She had come home.

Closing her eyes and enjoying her soak in the warm suds scented by a Yardley bath cube, she heard the sudden crashing boom of brass band music coming from somewhere in the house and had a feeling that it was coming from the flat below hers. From Donald's room. She remembered that he had said that he was working on an old fashioned wind-up record player that he had found in a skip, and by the sound of things he had managed to get it working. Sighing at this first sign of trouble she tried to relax again, but the music got louder and the sound of crashing cymbals told her that enough was enough.

'You know what Granddad has always said . . .' she told herself. 'If you've got a complaint don't put it off because it's not likely to right itself. I wouldn't mind if I liked brass band music but I don't. And *that* is very, very loud!'

Deciding to take the bull by the horns she got out of the bath, pulled on her long thick white towelling robe and tied the belt nice and tight. She pushed her wet feet into her bath slippers and made for her flat door, putting the latch on so as not to shut herself out on her very first day. She went downstairs to Donald's door and thumped it with the heel of her hand, but with the noise from within resounding through the hallway she guessed that he wouldn't be able to hear her. Then, as if the Almighty had heard her plea, the noise stopped and she knocked again to try and catch him before another burst of music.

Opening the door to her, Donald was clearly taken aback. It was as if he had no idea that anyone else lived in the house. 'Charlotte. Goodness. There you are in your bathrobe and here I am wearing one of my father's old silk smoking jackets. I don't think anything like this has ever happened before.' He smiled incredulously.

'Donald . . . I'm really sorry to be a spoilsport but that music is very loud.'

'Oh dear.' He sucked on his pipe thoughtfully. 'I didn't realise just how powerful music could be. And if it's upset you enough to have you come down to complain I will certainly lower the sound. This is the very first time that I've managed to get the old wind-up going so I was carried away by my little success. I do apologise. My father always said that had we been born poor I would make a very good electrical engineer. This of course was when I was a lad, a grasshopper as he liked to refer to me. Last week I fixed an electric iron of Mother's that was getting far too hot. Just a small electrical fault but dangerous had I not detected it.'

Charlotte smiled warmly at him. 'No hard feelings then? My asking you to keep the sound down?'

'No, no. No hard feelings. I don't suppose you would like a cup of instant coffee while you're here? I was just going to boil a kettle. Up until last week I always percolated my coffee from ground beans but then I was given a free sample of instant and I found it rather nice. And far quicker to make than percolated.'

'No thank you, I must go and finish having my bath and then get ready to go out and meet my boyfriend.'

'Ah. Boyfriend. Then indeed I mustn't keep you. And will this boyfriend be taking you somewhere pleasant?'

'For a drink in the Black Boy pub on the Mile End Road and then to my grandparents and then to a Chinese restaurant just five minutes from where they live.'

Donald raised his eyebrows and drew breath. 'Chinese? Oh dear. The Chinese have been known to eat dogs, you know.'

Charlotte laughed. 'Not in our part of the world they don't. Anyway . . . thanks for being so good about keeping the sound down. I do appreciate it.'

'I do have a book on China and its people through the ages and I think you will find that I am right about what they eat and what they don't eat.'

'Well, I'm really not that bothered. As long as I eat what I want, who cares what other people do?'

'I suppose that is one way of looking at it,' he said, all thoughtful. 'But then—'

'I must go, Donald,' she said, before he could get in to another long speech, 'or my bath water will go cold.' With that she smiled, showed a hand and practically ran back up the stairs.

Once back soaking in her bath, she had to ask herself again if her landlady's son was all the ticket. She didn't think he looked much older than herself, maybe a year or two, and yet he spoke as if he was a worldly-wise old man. Clearly he wasn't a normal run-of-the-mill chap and all she could hope was that he was just an oddball and nothing more sinister than that. She felt a chill run down her spine, then berated herself for being mean-minded about the poor soul and allowing Wendy to sow seeds in her mind about his state of mind. He was all right. A bit bonkers but okay.

Fifteen

Sitting on her favourite padded tall-backed chair by the long sash windows in her sitting room, Wendy, drawing through her gold-rimmed ivory cigarette holder, was enjoying a smoke. Now dressed in her purple and pink three-quarter-length summer coat and dress and with her make-up on, she was recalling a time in her childhood – a time when she would have rather been at home than at a private boarding school. Her parents had wanted her to do well and eventually go on to university, but she hadn't wanted any of that. All that she had ever dreamed of was to one day own her own bookshop in London. Earlier on in life, when just seventeen and before she had married the bastard who had left her for another, she had got a job as junior book buyer at Foyles in the West End of London and taken cheap digs close to the store.

Her parents hadn't been happy about her stubbornness in getting what she wanted and her father had written several times during the early years telling her that unless she returned to the family home she would be left to herself; that neither he nor her mother would visit her. But then her father, who had always ruled with the rod, had simply refused to believe that all she had wanted when it came to a career was to sell books or be a writer. From the age of five, when she had been taken to join the local library, she had simply loved books. The look of them, the feel and the smell, and of course the content.

It was true that she was now sometimes a little on the lonely side, but she had her window and could look down on the square below and the houses opposite. She loved all seasons, but her favourite was when she could see the pink blossom on the trees that lined the narrow road. She loved the square, where she had now lived for a while, especially that lovely green below hedged by cherry trees and waist-high black wrought iron railings with a pretty gate on a latch.

Her self-contained apartment, as she liked to call it, was probably similar to others in this old-fashioned type of square where most of the period houses had been converted into separate dwellings. Donald had painted her walls and ceiling white just before she had moved in and now it was all looking a touch jaded, but she didn't mind.

She had taken to the new girl Charlotte straight away and felt that she would fit in nicely with the rest of them. She thought that the artist in the basement flat was a touch unsociable and preferred to keep himself to himself, which is what he did for most of the time. But he did show his face now and then when a barbecue had been arranged in the garden. She also liked her landlady, Isabelle, who she got on quite nicely with. Of course, being the landlady she lived in the best and most salubrious apartment of all four and who could blame her? She certainly didn't. Wendy felt that she was in tune with Isabelle even if she couldn't fathom her son Donald. He seemed content enough to maintain a solitary life, with no sign of a girlfriend in the wings. He was pleasant enough but even so, she had decided from the very beginning to keep a friendly distance.

Fortunately, he, just like her, preferred his own company for most of the time. And if he talked to himself, the way she sometimes did at times . . . what did it matter? She preferred to have a one sided-conversation with no one there to hear the private thoughts that she spoke out loud, so why wouldn't he? Once she had lit her second and final cigarette of the day, she poured herself a little more sherry from her beautiful cut glass decanter, which always stood on a tall side table next to her chair by the window. She so loved this time of the evening.

Her thoughts drifting from one thing to another, Wendy murmured, 'Of course I'm bound to get lonely in my room at times. Anybody would if there's nobody around to talk to. It's not something that I worry over . . . but I do find it offensive when people at work ask if I shouldn't get out a bit more.

'And as for my husband . . . I don't think I do want to see him now. The ball's been in his court for long enough and he's done absolutely nothing about it. He could find me if he wanted to.' She then looked around, saying to herself for the umpteenth time that she really should put back onto the hangers the clothes that she had been trying on.

'I just have to make sure that I look my best and that's all there is to it. I've always been this way. I wouldn't want to be like my landlady. An old wealthy Bohemian? I should say not.' She giggled at the thought of it.

'I wouldn't mind betting that Donald is the only heir, and I'm certain there's got to be a lot of old money floating about. He'll get everything. Lock, stock and barrel, and won't know what to do with it.

'And as for the artist who lives in a basement of all places . . . well, I simply cannot imagine what it must be like to live below ground. I suppose this is why he goes out almost every night. I don't know if he has a hoard of lovers or plenty of lady friends. He's always entertaining but never invites any of us to join in. But never mind . . . Each to their own as my father would always say. Each to their own.

'When I get a chance I shall speak to him again. I shall tell him that the cravats that he wears aren't really in keeping with our surroundings. If he wants to dress flamboyantly like an artist, he should live in Portobello Road. I've been there many times of course, and I know that most of the minglers are actors or writers or painters. I should think that he would suit that area far more than he suits this one . . . in my humble opinion.'

Her sherry glass empty for the second time and her second cigarette smoked, Wendy was now ready to go out into the Saturday evening for her stroll along the High Road. Checking herself in her gilt-framed full-length mirror on curling legs, she thought she looked glamorously sophisticated and younger than her forty-five years. With this thought in mind she left her apartment, double-locked her door, and drifted down the staircase. On reaching the first floor landing she was greeted by Donald, who was turning the key in the lock of his door and was dressed ready to go out himself.

'Goodness me . . . we do look smart in our sports jacket,' said Wendy as she lifted an envelope from her post in-tray and slipped it into her pocket. This was from her optician to remind her that her reading glasses were ready for collection. 'Are we going somewhere special? To meet up with a young lady, perchance?'

'As a matter of fact, Wendy, I am on my way to a very important meeting at the library. A local author whose first book has just been brought out in hardback is giving a talk and I am to conduct a signing session.' They then walked down the stairs together and out of the house.

'How terribly exciting,' she said as they stepped out onto the wide entrance decked with old and worn flagstones. 'You simply must let me know how it goes.'

'Yes I shall,' said Donald, closing the door behind them. 'I'm expecting quite a few people to be there, as well as the local press. It's something that I've been quietly arranging for some time. We need to let the outside world know that not all of the people who live in the East End work in the docks or in the factories.'

Walking down the few steps and onto the pavement, Wendy bade a middle-aged gentleman good evening and he returned the gesture with a smile and the old-fashioned lifting of his Trilby hat as he continued on his way. 'Well, indeed, we do need to back our local talent,' she said. 'I would have loved to attend the book signing myself, but I have another engagement so alas I shall have to miss it.' This was a fib but only a tiny one. 'But let's stroll nice and *slowly* along the High Road together until we branch off in different directions.' She hoped that her emphasis on the word slowly would put him off.

Donald raised a concerned eyebrow as he glanced at his wristwatch. 'As much as I would like to escort you, Wendy, I am sorry to say that I'm in a bit of a rush. I have to be there in advance of everyone else so as to make sure that the staff in the library have carried out my instructions to the nth degree. It is a very important evening.'

'Well, of course you must. You hurry along, my dear, and do give me an update tomorrow. It all sounds so terribly exciting.'

'I won't promise, but providing I am not called upon to give an interview to the Press or attend a photo shoot, then I shall call in on you and give a full account of how it went. How does this sound?'

'Marvellous. Simply marvellous.'

'Good. And please do have a very enjoyable evening yourself. I must say that you are looking very glamorous.' He then straightened and nodded politely at her before taking his leave.

Watching him walk away Wendy murmured, 'Mad as a March hare' to herself, then hovered for a few moments so as to give him time to get well ahead of her. The last thing she wanted was to have to walk along with her landlady's peculiar son who sometimes talked non-stop and about nothing of any consequence. She glanced along the wide pavement on this very pleasant evening and decided to take another route for her stroll. A route through the narrow back street. She slipped across the boulevard, as she liked to call the tree-lined square, and was surprised to see a young man on one of the benches. She felt duty bound to bid the lonely-looking soul good evening.

Smiling gently back at her, Kenny felt that this was fate on his side again. He knew exactly who she was, of course – Wendy from the bookshop who lived in the grand house, where he presumed Charlotte was now lodging. He had been toying with the idea of pulling on the old-fashioned doorbell of the house to ask Charlotte if she would like to go out for a drink with him. He wanted to find out why she had been nasty to him when they were kids on the street. And why she had only hung out with the fat Jew called Nathan at that time. He also wanted to know why she had always tried to humiliate him those years back when he had been out and about with the lads to whom he had been leader of the pack.

But an attractive older woman had come into his orbit. A bit of nice old, as his dad would say. The words, *a bit of fun with a bit of old*, drifted through his mind. He couldn't help smiling.

Drawing on his cigarette he pushed away thoughts of Charlie, and focused on this woman. Someone, who to his way of thinking, was mutton dressed as lamb – someone who had the look of a paid whore and someone that he might be able to have a little bit of fun with.

Kenny was bored yet agitated, and when this mood took him he was his own worst enemy. His need for excitement at such times took over, and right now he was in a kind of tormenting frame of mind with nowhere to go and no one around to give vent to his lust for fun. Except for this older woman, this bit of mature cheese, who was now settling herself on another of the benches. She wasn't a bad looker to his way of thinking.

Paying Kenny no attention, Wendy took out of her handbag her packet of cigarettes. She would, after all, have another smoke before she set off to see what the evening had in store. Of course she had noticed that the good-looking lad in the gardens was giving her the eye, but he was far too young and a touch too tall and lean for her taste. She vaguely recognised him as one of her customers from the bookshop and was aware that he was watching her. She turned to glance at him over her shoulder and then leaned back on the bench and drew on her cigarette. Smiling inwardly, she glanced at her delicate hands and manicured nails and the pretty new pale pink varnish purchased that day. She felt quite beautiful and more than ready for a romantic liaison. Soon she would make her way to her favourite pub down by the riverside for a gin and tonic.

She was so carried away with her thoughts that she didn't see Kenny approach, and only just heard him ask her if she would mind giving him a light. Glancing up at him, she was surprised to see that he didn't look quite so gaunt when standing and had quite broad shoulders for a lean young man.

'Be my guest,' she said, offering her rolled-gold slim Dunhill lighter.

'That's very kind of you,' said Kenny. 'Thanks very much.' He then lit his roll-up and said, 'Haven't I seen you in the second-hand bookshop?'

'Oh . . .' Wendy smiled. 'Well yes, I do work there . . .' She wasn't sure that she wanted to give too much away about her life, especially not to a complete stranger.

'I love second-hand books,' said Kenny. 'I much prefer them to brand spanking new ones. Don't ask me why.'

'I wouldn't dream of it,' said Wendy with a smile. 'I perfectly understand. I too prefer books that have been thumbed just a little.'

'It's not just that though,' said Kenny. 'It's the interesting books that you've got on your shelves. Stacks of books written by famous writers in paperback that are a brilliant read.'

Wendy patted his hand maternally and then squeezed it. 'Young man . . . you have made a woman old enough to be your mother very happy. I love my work in the bookshop. And mostly for the reasons that you mention.'

'Old enough to be my mother? Give me a break.' Kenny laughed. 'You can't be a day older than thirty and even though I'm only eighteen going on nineteen, I think I can tell that you're kidding me.'

'Well, I'm not. But I must say I don't feel my age and in fact I would go as far as to say that I actually feel more like a thirty-year-old. So in a way you are a very perceptive young man.'

'Well, that's really nice of you to say so.' He then cupped his chin and went all thoughtful before saying, 'Would you be offended if I asked you to come for a drink with me?'

'Of course I wouldn't be offended. I was only going for an evening stroll. I chose this purple and pink outfit for this evening because I felt that there might well be a lovely sunset that I could blend into. All dressed up in sunset colours with nowhere in particular to go,' she smiled. 'Everything matches. Even the shoes.'

'I know. I thought you were an actress when you walked in all graceful and natural like. You're a very attractive woman – but then I suppose you know that already.'

'Not really, but thank you for the compliment. And I must say that you're a handsome young man. You could easily find someone of your own age to partner you for a drink, I feel sure of it. A very nice girl at that. One who would enjoy sipping a gin and tonic in your company.'

Kenny offered a cheeky smile. 'So that's your favourite drink, is it?' he said. 'Good. Because when I'm a bit flush, as I am now, that's my drink too.' He lied.

'Really? What a lovely coincidence. And why shouldn't we go for a drink together? Yes, I would very much like to join you for a glass of our favourite. Thank you for asking – if you're really sure you wouldn't rather go to a pub with a girl of your own age.'

'I am sure,' he said, 'and I'll tell you why. Later on, I've to be at my nana's house to read a bit from her favourite novel before she drifts off to sleep. I love my nana and I'm the only one who sits with her. She's lovely but a very lonely soul.'

'Goodness me – what a kind young man you are.' Wendy then gracefully lifted herself from the seat and said, 'Shall we go?'

Smiling at her, Kenny offered his arm and together they strolled away from the square, taking the back route towards the Prospect of Whitby, a romantic kind of a riverside pub down by the docks. This was a place where each of them knew that they could sit on the timber balcony and gaze at the inlet from the Thames flowing by, and once the evening sun went down candles would be lit.

Quietly chatting away about this, that and the other to do with both of their make-believe worlds, they came into a narrow turning with derelict run-down houses on either side. This was a dead-end where bombed-out houses and a small factory showed the result of the war. Stopping in his tracks Kenny said, 'This is where I used to love to play as a kid.'

'Really?' said Wendy. 'How sweet. You would think that by now those buildings would have been razed to the ground, wouldn't you?'

'Well . . .' Kenny sighed. 'In a way I agree with you, but on the other hand it's a bit of history that reminds us of what that war did. Come on. We'll wander down there and we can cut through to the Prospect.'

Loving every minute of this impromptu nostalgic walk, Wendy allowed him to lead the way. 'I'm sure that this back turning should have been reconstructed with new housing by now,' she said, 'But do you know, I quite enjoy the thought of walking through a bit of our local if not our tragic history.'

'I know what you mean,' he said. 'And I'm glad you feel the same as I do. Not everyone goes in for nostalgia, do they?' He then stopped by one of the broken terraced houses without a front door and slowly shook his head. 'You might not believe this but my great aunt and uncle used to live here.' He was such a convincing liar.

Wendy was all ears and all heart. 'Oh, how sad. Well, look, before this lovely evening turns into the black of night, why don't we go carefully into the house for the sake of auld lang syne? Or would this be too upsetting for you?'

'No, I would like that very much. But I wouldn't dream of asking a lady such as yourself to go into an old place like that,' he said, all convincing.

'But you didn't ask, my darling boy – I am suggesting it. To be able to slip into your ancestor's home before this is all razed to the ground? It's an opportunity and an experience not to be missed, surely?'

'Well,' said Kenny, slowly shaking his head and sighing. 'Put like that . . .'

'We must do it!' she said, all excited.

Taking her hand, Kenny gently led her through the open doorway and into the semi-dark bombed house. 'Be careful,' he said. 'The floorboards could give way and we could end up in my great aunt and uncle's cellar.'

Once inside the passage and looking into a room that had once been a parlour and was covered in filth and dust, Wendy sighed. 'To think that your relatives once sat in there and ate their supper.'

Turning his head to look into her older but beautiful face, Kenny showed a sad expression and sighed. 'You know, I think you should write books rather than sell them. You have a way with words that gets you here.' He gently patted his chest where his heart was beating like mad. Racing in fact.

'Well as a matter of fact,' she said, smiling, 'I am a secret writer.' She looked across the room at a small cupboard with its door hanging open on just one hinge that was next to the fireplace.

'Honest to God?' said Kenny, now more than a touch

excited by the thought of possibly squeezing the last breath out of this woman. 'You really are a writer?'

'Yes. I write a column for a magazine now and then and I'm also—' She stopped in her tracks as she looked into Kenny's eyes and saw a different expression in them – and on his face. One that she found quite frightening. There was a kind of look of menace about him now. Menace and loathing. 'Are you all right, dear?' she just managed to say as she glanced sideways around this old derelict building.

Of course he was all right. He had clocked her jewellery and could see that she had on a diamond ring to die for. He smiled and then chuckled. 'Am I all right, she asks. Now what's that supposed to mean? You're not gonna start patronising me, are yer? After all, you're nothing but a cheap paid whore. A fucking whore. Who pays for the jewellery, eh? The rich men who like a woman who wears loose silk drawers?'

Stunned, and very frightened by his sudden change of mood Wendy glanced at the open doorway again and could see that to make an escape one would have to go via the narrow passage. 'I am not a whore, young man,' she said. 'I am nothing of the sort. I thought that we had made friends with each other. Not bosom buddy friends, granted. But then you know this and you're just teasing me for fun.' She forced a smile as she slowly backed away towards the passageway and the opening that led out into the street and fresh air. But Kenny had anticipated this and was casually stepping side-ways so as to block her. It was as if he was playing a game and thoroughly enjoying it. A game of scare and dare. His eyes narrowed as if he were in deep thought as he stared into her face. And he was chewing the inside of his cheek.

With her heart pumping faster and her stomach in a knot, Wendy did her utmost to keep calm even though she knew that the young man, who was, of course, no more than a stranger, would be able to see that her fingers were trembling.

Cold beads of sweat were now breaking out on her forehead as his cold eyes searched hers. He then spoke in a gentle but intimidating voice, with a smile to match. 'Teasing you?' he said. 'A fucking whore? Why would I want to do that? And do not patronise me.'

'I wouldn't dream of it. Why would I want to?' Wendy's throat was so dry she could hardly get her words out.

Grinning, Kenny stepped closer and cupped her chin. 'Nice jewellery,' he said. 'Nice gold earrings. You've got good taste for a whore.' He then gripped her neck between both hands and pressed his thumbs onto her Adam's apple with every bit of strength he had. He wanted this to be quick.

'You're no fucking better than the rest of 'em. You let men fuck you for a few quid. You and those like you 'ave turned our beautiful country into a place not fit for rats to live in. You fucking whoring bitch.' He tightened his grip and watched her eyes widen as the look of terror on her face fuelled his sense of power. He was getting rid of another whore who lured good men from their families. He squeezed so hard that he could feel himself trembling.

'All things from the soul shines out through the eyes,' he said, and then squeezed the last breath of air out of Wendy, who had never knowingly harmed a soul. He squeezed and she struggled . . . and then she started to choke on her own phlegm as her eyes widened. Then came the familiar sounds of dying that he had come to recognise and love. Trembling with a kind of passion, Kenny held his grip until her head flopped forward and her body was limp.

Exhausted both physically and mentally, he released himself from the corpse to let her drop to the filthy old floorboards in a heap as if she was a bag of dirty old laundry. Standing above her and drawing deep breaths of air he slowly regained composure. All of his energy spent, he dropped to his knees and placed both hands over his face, telling his make-believe master that this was it. This was enough. This would

209

be his last killing. He had done his duty and all that he asked for now was to live a quiet and ordinary life. After a space of time passing, Kenny glanced at his wristwatch and wasn't sure how long he had knelt beside the whore who had coaxed him to kill her. He dragged himself out of the room and into the dark and narrow passage and flopped down onto the staircase, where he sat with his head cupped in his hands in the stinking derelict house not that far away from where he lived.

'You're getting too chancy for your own good, Kenny boy,' he murmured as he tapped his head on the worm-eaten banister of the musty old staircase. A staircase that stank of mildew and rot and was under the shattered roof of a house that he imagined had once been home to some poor bastards, now dead, buried and forgotten. And then, with a sudden change of mood and a rush of self-esteem that seemed to come at times like this, he quietly congratulated himself for having done well. He was exhausted but proud of what he had achieved. He had rid England of another whore. He went back to the corpse and went down on one knee so as to carefully remove all of her jewellery. He took her purse and anything that would identify her so as to slow down the police efforts at uncovering her identity. But he had missed one important thing. In her pocket was the letter from her optician that she had picked up on her way out of the house.

Happy with all that he now had in his pocket, which he saw as payment for his deed of ridding the world of scum, Kenny used one foot and then the other to slowly inch Wendy's body towards a corner of the room. This was where he could see that the floorboards were broken and riddled with woodworm. Once she was in place where he needed her to be, he brought his heel down with an almighty crash onto the boards and then stood back to watch as the body of the woman, in a cloud of musty dank dust, dropped down into the dark cellar below. Pinching his lips together he then staggered to the doorway of the house and drew deep breaths of fresh air.

Once composed, he brushed away the filth and did his best to walk innocently into the warm evening, with the swirling leaves rustling along the pavement.

Kenny took the long route back home to his parents' flat on the new council estate where the small family had seemingly settled into a fairly peaceful way of life. He felt okay. He felt that he had done well. He felt satisfied that he and he alone had rid this country of another piece of shite. And now he was hungry and looking forward to whatever his mother had on the stove. She was a good old-fashioned cook, if nothing else.

Sixteen

Waiting for her son Kenny to come home while her husband was having a drink in his local with a few mates, Liza could not rid herself of the worry that had crept to the forefront of her mind. She knew that her son wasn't like normal lads of his age and she had a horrible nagging sensation in the pit of her stomach that something bad was happening. Her son had been in one of his dark moods again and she sensed that something was wrong, that her only child, now a young man, was very troubled. He had been too quiet since his return from Norfolk and had spent too much time curled up on his bed with the door shut. She knew that it would be useless talking to his father about her fears because he was so stubborn, and adamant that there was nothing wrong with the lad. But then, he hadn't been the one to give birth or breast-feed, and as far as Liza was concerned this was when bonding took place. The expression on her husband's face said it all when she had worried in front of him previously about their boy. He would have none of it. To him, Kenny was just a lazy little bastard who only worked when push came to shove, and that was the root of all his problems, laziness.

And now, as she sat on the edge of the kitchen chair looking at a pile of clean laundry waiting to be ironed, the distraught woman wondered yet again where her son might have got to. She also wondered what he might be doing or, worse still, what he might have already done. He hadn't been in for his favourite dinner of sausage toad, mashed potatoes and greens that she had put on steam to keep warm for him. Her gaze fell back to the ironing but still she couldn't bring herself to tackle it. Kenny had, and always would, draw her to worry, even though he was now eighteen going on nineteen. He was her son and she loved him.

He had been left so many times when a baby, and then as a child when she had gone out in the evenings with her sister to work the best and most lucrative streets in the West End – and for this she could not forgive herself. Pulling herself up from the chair where she had been sitting for over an hour, she decided to run herself a warm bath and pour in lots of scented bath oil. But just as she went into the bathroom she heard the key turn in the street door and knew that it was her son back from wherever he had been. She waited to see what kind of an expression was on his face. She hoped it wouldn't be the all-telling look of guilt as if he had done wrong. Something bad. Something really bad that would eventually lead to his collapse. This had always been her fear. Going into the sitting room once she knew that he was in there, she stood in the doorway and looked at him. He was pale and drawn and she could see that his hands were shaking. 'What is it, Kenny? What's the matter? What have you done?'

He closed the door of the sitting room and turned to face her, shock and fear showing in his eyes. This time he had gone too far and he knew it. He had killed someone on his own doorstep and felt that this could be his downfall.

The fear in his eyes told Liza that he had been bad again. She watched as he unbuttoned his jacket and when he caught her eye he shrugged apologetically as if to say, 'I've done it again, Mum.' She didn't know what it was that he had been up to when he came home in this kind of a state and neither did she want to. She loved her son so much it hurt. She couldn't bear the thought of him going to prison, and

213

somehow she just knew that whatever it was that he did before coming back like this had to be bad. Very bad. She wasn't going to ask. She never did. 'I'll run you a nice warm bath, sweetheart,' she said. Once in the bathroom she put in the plug and turned on the chrome taps, then dangled her fingers in the water to make sure that the temperature was just right for him. After a long soak he would no doubt fall into his bed and sleep like a baby until the morning. Sleep like a baby and weep in his sleep and sometimes wail quietly. She knew the pattern. She had lain in the dark listening to him enough times now to know. Her son was in the depths of hell and misery.

Charlotte, having been pushed into accepting an invitation over the phone from her granddad to go to his house for supper with Nathan instead of the lad spending his hard earned money at a restaurant, the young couple were now on the way there. Strolling along a back turning that was lit up by lovely old-fashioned iron lamp-posts and holding hands, she said, 'I feel guilty for caving in on the phone, now. It's not fair on you, never mind me. I should have been more adamant. Told Granddad that I wanted us to go for our romantic candlelit dinner. It's my fault.'

'The older generations are wily, Charlotte. My grandpa is, and so is my dad come to that. They always seem to manage to get their own way. But never mind, I can always book a table for two another time. We've got all the time in the world.'

'That's true,' she smiled. 'And I suppose I can't really blame Gran and Granddad. They hardly ever see me.' She squeezed his hand and then slipped her arm around him. The back street where Nell and Johnny lived was generally quiet at this time of the evening with the glow of indoor lights shining warmly through unlined curtains.

'I won't say that I have any regrets at having been brought

up in this part of the world, Charlotte,' murmured Nathan. 'But I would like to live in the suburbs one day. In a similar turning to this one but where it's more open. Wanstead is very nice and so is Woodford Green. Both are almost on the borders of Essex.'

'That sounds like a really good compromise. Living in Norfolk didn't do much for me, but I suppose I would miss the countryside now if we were to move back into this neck of the woods.'

Nathan quietly laughed. 'Now *you* sound like the older generation. *Neck of the woods.* That's your grandparents talking.'

Charlotte smiled back at him. 'My granddad actually. He's always saying it. But we are what we are and we can still learn from the old 'uns. Don't knock it.'

'I wouldn't dare. My dad would have my guts for garters if I pulled him up every time he came out with his old-fashioned clichés. But there are one or two that none of us would want to disappear.'

'Such as?'

'Well . . . how about "I love you more than all the tea in China"?'

Charlotte laughed. 'Is that what he said to your mum?'

'All of the time. And now I'm going to keep up the tradition.' He stopped in his tracks, placed his hands on either side of her face and said, 'But I love you more than all the tea in the world, Charlotte.'

'And I love you more than all the slingback shoes and handbags in the world, Nathan.'

Nathan burst out laughing. 'My God, that takes me back. I remember you saying that you wanted both those things all those years ago.'

Continuing on their way, arms around each other, he then added, 'I really did mean what I said to you when we were kids, Charlotte. That I want to marry you one day.'

'And I really meant it when I said you would have to go down on one knee.' She smiled. 'God, it seems ages ago, back then . . . when we were full of hopes and dreams.'

'When I was short and tubby and scared of my own shadow. When I loved you more than all the sand on the beach at Margate. And here we are, and I may not be the same shy boy but I still love you as much as ever.' Then, after a quiet moment he said, 'I hope you don't break my heart for a second time.'

Melting inside, Charlotte drew breath. 'I won't, and I think you know why.'

'Tell me just in case I don't.'

'I love you as much as you love me.'

Swallowing against the lump in his throat, Nathan could only just get his words out. 'May God let it last. And let's leave it there or I will burst into tears, I swear it. And then what would your grandparents make of me if I walk in with red eyes?'

'I hate to think.' Charlotte smiled. 'You're so sweet and so soft and I love you. I'm sorry we moved away from the East End and I'm sorry that you were so lonely without me.'

'It doesn't matter any more. I've got you back and I'm not letting you go. Ever.'

Gazing at him affectionately, Charlotte stopped in her tracks and turned to face him again. 'I think that in a way we did love each other back then and I don't think that we were too young to know . . . as the song goes.'

'No . . . and we're certainly not too young now. I'm crazy about you, Charlie. I always have been.'

'And you're sure that it wasn't the romantic candlelit dinner and the love songs playing in the background in that little restaurant last weekend that turned your head?'

'Of course not. I booked the table as soon as I knew you were going to be in London. I was determined to win you over.'

'Well, you have.' Charlotte broke into a lovely smile. 'And now you're gonna have to win my nan and granddad over.'

Almost at her grandparents' house now, Nathan said, 'I used to dream about marrying you, Charlotte. But I also used to think that that couldn't ever happen . . . unless your family were okay about mixed-faith weddings.'

'They'd get used to it in time. I've got an aunt who married her Jewish boyfriend. Nobody minded a bit, we're not like that. But how about your family?'

'I'm not sure. Dad, and maybe my grandparents, would be okay, but I'm not so sure about all of my aunts and uncles. But then I wouldn't much care what they thought. If two people are in love that's all that matters . . . isn't it?'

'Of course. We might be Church of England but we don't go to Sunday services, or any other come to that, unless it's for a wedding, or a christening or funeral. So we're hardly what you would call religious.'

Nathan quietly laughed. 'Absolutely! But I wonder about the grandparents, yours and mine. Maybe we should test the water this evening. See how they think about their only grand-daughter being in love with a Jew. A Jew that she might marry one day.'

'Is that a proposal then?'

'No. I said *might*. Time will tell.' He glanced at her face and smiled. 'We love each other and that's all that matters.' Then, stopping by an old tree, Nathan leaned against it and pulled Charlotte in close to him. 'I'm sorry if it sounds as if I'm rushing things. I'm just so bowled over by all that's happened and I do love you so much.'

Charlotte couldn't help but smile warmly at the expression on his face. He hadn't really changed at all. 'I've not had a boyfriend yet, Nathan, but you've had three steady girlfriends from what I remember you telling me. You're going to have to teach me a thing or two.'

Gazing into her beautiful face Nathan swallowed again,

overwhelmed by her loveliness. He could hardly believe it. He had in his arms the girl that he had so badly missed and had never stopped loving. 'I won't need to. We'll take everything one step at a time. Just don't leave me for a second time. I think I would kill myself if you left me again.'

'No you wouldn't. Don't talk like that. But I do know what you're saying. Ever since you turned up in Bridgeford I've not been able to get you out of my thoughts. Our time together as kids came flooding back.'

Cupping her face, Nathan sighed. 'I can't believe this is happening. I wasn't expecting to be in love like this, and I would be a liar if I said I wasn't scared. I'm bloody terrified. I don't want to lose you.' He blushed a little and then added. 'Please God . . . be on your toes.'

'Oh Nathan . . . I remember who used to say that.'

'My mother.' A look of sadness filled his eyes. 'May God rest her soul.'

Nathan then placed a gentle hand around her lovely soft white neck and said, 'I love you, Charlie. I love you so much. I always have and always will. And if I'm honest I would love it more than anything in the world if I could just curl up in that bed in that flat with you.'

'But you wouldn't want to rush me . . .'

'Of course I would, but I won't. I'll wait for as long as it takes.'

Clasping her hand in his they strolled onwards in a warm silence until they arrived at Nell and Johnny's door. Charlotte pressed the bell, wondering if her granddad was going to probe Nathan as to his intentions. She was his only grandchild after all.

When the door opened and Johnny stood looking at them she knew that he was trying to cover the fact that he was thrilled to bits to see them. She couldn't help smiling – he was so predictable.

'Oh, look what the ill wind's blown in,' he said. 'And what's the joke then?'

'There's not one, Granddad. I'm just pleased to see you.' She kissed him on the cheek.

'Come on in, the pair of you.' Johnny stood to one side and waved them into the passage. 'Your gran's been polishing the bloody brass and copper and washing the knick-knacks all day in your honour, Nathan. Go on through.'

Closing the door behind them Johnny followed in their footsteps, talking as he went. 'Gawd only knows how long she's 'ad that chicken and barley soup on the stove. She reckons she knew that famous East End playwright's – what's 'is name – mother who always cooked it for 'im. Your nan reckons that it was his mother who gave her the recipe in the first place. She's fibbing, but it's true that she always got on well wiv our Jewish neighbours.'

They went into the living room with Johnny still rambling. Charlotte knew that his shaggy dog story was her granddad's clumsy way of letting Nathan know that he had no objection to her courting someone of a different faith. 'I know she did, and the playwright you're talking about is Arnold Wesker.'

'Eh?' Johnny, who always smelled of Lifebuoy soap leaned back and stared at her face. 'How'd you know that?'

'The amateur dramatic group that Nathan belongs to put on one of his plays last week and he told me all about it.' She nudged Nathan to give him the cue to get in now. To make something of the fact that her granddad was trying to find something in common that they could talk about.

'What a coincidence,' said Nathan. 'That you should know the playwright who I happen to think is the best that we've got.'

'Go on?' said Johnny. 'Fancy that.'

Once they were in the kitchen, Nell turned away from her stove and wiped her hands on her pinafore and then offered her hand to Nathan. 'How do you do,' she said, too worn out to be anything more than polite right then.

'How does he do?' Johnny laughed. 'Mind your own bloody business.' He then looked at Nathan and slowly shook his head as he looked up to heaven. 'Anyone'd think that you were royalty, wouldn't they. Sit yerself down, son. Our kitchen's not a palace but it's clean and well paid for.'

'You sound just like my grandpa. He says exactly the same thing.'

'Does he? Oh that's good. Our little home is humble, but there's always a welcome mat at the door. That Formica table top's not so humble though – that cost a few bob when it was new. Personally, I would 'ave preferred to 'ave a blue one with little gold stars but the gov'nor wanted pale primrose and so that was that.'

'Take no notice of 'im,' said Nell, smiling. 'He rambles on like this all the time. Now then, do you both want a cup of coffee?'

'That would be very nice.' Nathan smiled and sat down.

'And what about you, Charlotte?'

'I'll have the same, Nan.'

'Right. Put the milk in the little saucepan, Johnny.'

'See what I mean? Do this, do that, skin the cat . . .' Still grumbling jokily, Johnny went to do as he was told.

Nell drew breath and then spoke in a whispering voice, '*Moan, moan, moan.* If only it was still the nineteen-thirties and I was still beautiful and young. I would be off with a secret admirer. I was always tall and slim.'

Johnny lit his Woodbine cigarette with his old chrome Zippo. Then, slipping it back into its worn leather pouch, he said, 'You're too blooming well thin. Pencil thin.'

'And you haven't seen better days?' said his wife. 'I don't know how I put up with him sitting in that chair day in, day out. Don't forget to warm the teapot as well. I don't want coffee.'

'No, I won't forget.' Johnny slowly nodded his head. 'God help you once I do pop my clogs.' He went back to his chores. 'Who'll be at your beck and call then, eh?'

'Here we go again . . .' Charlotte sighed and then laughed. She had heard most of what her granddad came out with many times before.

'I was a secretary once upon a time, Nathan,' said Nell. 'Always smart. Always on time. And I could type forty words per minute on a clanking old typewriter. Admirers? You should 'ave seen 'em. Queuing up at the door for a kiss and a squeeze they were. Of course, I couldn't afford to be independent the way Charlotte is now. What I wouldn't have given to be able to live in a little flat of my own.' Arching one eyebrow, as was her habit, she sighed. 'But she does remind me of myself when young, I will say that. Independent and rely on no one.'

'You still are independent, Nan. You earn your own little bit of money cleaning at the Moonlight Soap powder factory five mornings a week now, don't yer?' Charlotte smiled.

'That's true. So, are the pair of you gonna stop overnight? Nathan can go on the settee.' She turned to look at him and said, 'It pulls down to a bed again.'

'I hadn't thought of stopping over,' said Nathan, eyeing Charlotte. 'But it would be nice. Or do you want to sleep in your little pad tonight, Charlotte?'

'I don't mind.'

'It's a lovely invitation,' he said, trying to keep his options open. 'Let's see how we feel later on after we've been out. You might want to get back and Dad will be expecting me in so won't bolt the door before he goes to bed.'

'Well, you can phone 'im and tell 'im to bolt the bloody door, can't yer, so that's settled. And as we said, there's no need to waste good money on a restaurant. We'll 'ave chicken soup with toast and all sit round the table in the morning for a nice fried bacon, egg and tomato breakfast,' said Johnny before going to the sink with his own cup and saucer so as to wash it up before his wife started to nag.

Nell sat down with a sigh and then leaned back in her chair. Smiling to herself, she was dead chuffed that her granddaughter and boyfriend were happy to consider stopping over in their little abode. 'We could 'ave a game of cards. Play for pennies though and not shillings.'

'Play *what* for pennies?' asked Johnny.

'Pontoon.' Nell folded her arms and shot him a look of warning. 'It's what we *all* want to play before we turn in. It's all arranged.'

'No it's not, Nan. Stop telling fibs. We might play cards and we might not. We might stop over and we might not. We were gonna go to a favourite—'

'You're bound to wanna stop over, the way I've done that bedroom up!' Johnny cut in so as to have his way. 'I'm pleased with it. Would you like to 'ave a butcher's at the way I've done the spare bedroom up for madam, Nathan? All my own work that is.'

'Here we go,' said Nell, placing the flat of her hand on her forehead. Then, leaning forward in her chair she said, 'I don't wanna get a migraine, Johnny, so don't go on and on and on about that bloody wallpaper and paint.'

'I wasn't gonna! But I will say this and I'll say no more. That little cupboard, next to the old-fashioned fireplace up there that I painted in a nice ivory cream, does remind me of when I was boy.' He slowly shook his head, all thoughtful. 'I used to hide in my old gran's little cupboard which was very similar.

'When I was in that cupboard I imagined I was back there in the olden days with Oliver Twist and Charles Dickens and that. Then, later on in life when this place came up for us and I went into that bedroom . . . well, I was taken right back. Back to when my old granny used to look after me. I could smell the must. She used to let me rummage through her old photograph albums and that. Kept me quiet for hours that did.'

'Do you take sugar, Nathan? Only you look as if you've been on a diet. You was a fat little sod when a kid,' said Nell.

'Two please,' said Nathan, ignoring the fond insult.

'Charlotte's got a bed all to 'erself up there – home from home. When I was a kid I 'ad to share with two brothers. Which is why I appreciated it when I stayed at my granddad's. I used to lay on the bed and listen to the song of a blackbird. They were a happy couple, my old grandparents. Warm and affectionate as well as friendly. And they never nagged each other neither.' He looked slyly at Nell. 'My old granddad used to do all the decorating as well, and my nan used to keep the place lovely. Kept on top of the dust and that without you even seeing the duster in 'er fingers. You never saw dust floating in the ray of the sunshine coming in through the windows in that old house the way you do in this one. You only 'ave to open a door in this place to see it dancing. Ain't that right, sweetheart?' he smiled. He was tormenting Nell and he knew that she knew it.

'I wouldn't know, Johnny . . . my mind's not on dust all fucking day long, as it just so happens.'

Johnny winked at Nathan. 'If you don't keep on top of dust it'll choke you to death in the end.'

'Well, you'd better do the dusting from now on then, Johnny – instead of sitting on your backside and listening to sport on the wireless or the telly hour after hour. He never folds his clothes, Nathan, he just leaves them crumpled in a heap on the bedroom floor. Sometimes I wish he would go to sleep for years and then wake up the man he was when I first met him.'

'God help you once I've gone.' Johnny smiled with a certain look of self-satisfaction. 'You'll 'ave no one to nag and no one to make pies for. And if you don't make pies you can't brag about it down at the laundry doing your washing.' Taking the

Woodbine from the corner of his mouth and placing it on the edge of a saucer he was using as an ashtray he chuckled and then said, 'It sounds like a song, don't it?' He hummed a little tune and sang, 'Down at the old laundry rooms . . . da, da, da, and da . . .'

Half an hour later, once they'd drunk their beverages and the old folk had got used to the youngsters being there, Johnny and Nell were at it again, getting digs in at each other whenever they could. The banter was amusing whichever way it was viewed.

'I should 'ave married the first love of my life. His name was Chris. He was such a quiet chap. A real gentleman,' said Nell.

The two men of different generations looked at each other, suppressing their laughter. 'What 'ave I done now? Why are you trying to make me jealous by fetching up old tales of old boyfriends?' Johnny winked at Nathan.

'What 'ave you done? It's what you *don't* fucking well do. You never wash up, you never vacuum the place for me, you don't cook dinner and you don't do the ironing.'

'I keep the back yard looking like a little garden for yer though, don't I?' he said, trying to look as if she had hurt his feelings.

'And you don't clean the windows neither. Apart from that he's not too bad, Nathan. Some men are worse than him, I daresay. Not many. But some might be. A few. One or two.'

Rolling his eyes Johnny turned to Charlotte. 'You don't wanna be too late in bed, miss. Not tonight or tomorrow night. You wanna get an early night on both nights. You wanna be nice and rested so that you don't go in to your new job looking like somefing the cat's dragged in.'

'I don't start till Wednesday, Granddad. I went through the contract earlier when I was in my flat and saw the date. Then it clicked. I've been so bowled over by everything that's happening that I got confused.'

'We all do that at one time or another, sweetheart,' said her nan. 'Now then, if you get a bit chilly in the night, Nathan, you switch on the paraffin heater in the corner of the sitting room.'

'You can see a lot from the flames of a fire,' murmured Johnny, 'but there's still somefing cosy about a paraffin heater. All right, with a paraffin heater you might find steam inside the window but so what? On the other side of the road are only houses that are just like this one.'

'You find a reason and an answer to everything, Granddad.'

'Do I? Well thank you darling. It's nice to get a compliment now and then.' He shot a look at his wife.

'It wasn't meant as a compliment, it was said to shut you up,' sniffed Nell.

'And like I was saying, what if there is a bit of steam? If we can't see out the nosy bastards can't see in, can they?' Johnny grinned. 'I only 'ave to wipe a bit away to see what's going on out there though. I don't get much enjoyment other than to take the mickey out of the neighbours now and then.'

'As well as annoying the relatives if and when they deign to show their faces,' said Nell. 'But there we are. I try to get out as much as I can for a bit of company with people who smile. A smile doesn't cost anything does it? It's a good job that I've got the Women's Institute. That gives me a little bit of pleasure now and then.' She turned to Johnny again. 'You should get out a bit more instead of listening to bloody sport on the wireless all day long. I'm sick of strangers coming into my house through that bloody wireless. Talk talk talk. That's all those bloody sportsmen do.'

'Oh, come on. Don't be like that,' said Charlotte, 'he made the coffee and a pot of tea.'

'Take no notice, Charlotte,' said Johnny. 'Your gran's vying for attention. She's always going out. Once, if not twice, a week when she's not at work. To sit with a load of gossiping women.'

Charlotte looked at Nathan and rolled her eyes and then made a snap decision for the pair of them. 'Me and Nathan are gonna go out for a walk and have a few drinks in one or two of your local pubs. Do you still keep a key on a string or have you got a spare one for me to take, Nan?'

'Key on a string. It's the only one we 'ave got, thanks to your granddad not getting another one cut when he lost the spare.'

'Right – we'll be able to let ourselves in then. I know you both like to be in bed by nine so don't wait up for us. We'll help ourselves to some chicken soup then. Keep it simmering.'

'I should fink I'll be well ready to fall into my bed by then. By the time I've fed the pair of us, washed up, made up the sofa bed for Nathan—'

'Oh no!' said Johnny. 'I'm not 'aving you straining your back pulling that sofa into a put-you-up bed. No. I'll do that.'

Charlotte gave Nathan the eye and a message to move himself and try and show that he was expecting to go for a drink. She wanted to get out before they started going on again and he was only too ready. All he really wanted was to be alone with Charlotte. 'Right. So we'll be off then for a nice romantic evening together back in the East End. Don't wait up.' Charlotte smiled.

With that the couple made a quick exit before Johnny had time to suggest going with them. Once outside in the street Charlotte and Nathan burst into laughter. 'If nothing else . . . your grandparents are very funny,' Nathan just managed to say. 'God help you if you hadn't found that flat and had to live under the same roof. One night I can manage. But no more than that.'

'You and me both.' Charlotte giggled as she slipped her arm into his and strolled along feeling happier than she had ever been in her life.

Once she heard the street door close, Nell, in a provocative mood, put her hands together and closed her eyes, saying, 'Do me a favour, Lord . . . make sure that Charlotte takes to this new job and that they take to her. And if it's not too much to ask, could you please do something about this husband of mine when he's lying next to me in bed talking non-stop, snoring or grinding his teeth.'

'I don't talk non-stop and I don't snore,' said Johnny. 'And I 'aven't any back teeth to grind any more.'

'Well then, it must be an old nightmare from when you did that comes back to haunt me.'

'Don't talk daft. Now then . . . do you fancy a drop of sherry left over from last Christmas?'

'Why? What are you after?'

'Well . . . with all the romance in the air between them two . . . it's brought back lovely memories of when we were young. I thought we might go up for a cuddle. What d'yer reckon?'

'Fetch me a glass of sherry and I'll think about it.'

'Oh . . . so I can take that as a yes then, can I?'

'I don't see why not. I quite fancy a bit of the other between them fresh clean sheets I put on today as a matter of fact. And you'll do – I suppose.' She smiled.

'Well, at your age you're not gonna find anyone more handsome. So shall I take the sherry upstairs then?'

'Yes, please. That'll be lovely. A nice little drink before a nice bit of nookie and then another nice little sip of sherry afterwards.' She looked at her husband and recognised a certain smile on his face that she didn't get to see too often. 'You're still a handsome man you know . . . even if you are a torment.' She stood up and swaggered out of the room calling over her shoulder, 'And don't go too heavy on the aftershave!'

'Oh gawd . . . she wants me to 'ave a shave an' all. I wish I hadn't of said anything now. Still, there you are, Johnny boy.

She still finds you irresistible even though she pretends otherwise for most of the time. So we'll make the most of the hay while the sun shines, as they say.'

He peered into the small mirror above the kitchen sink to check whether he could get away with the six o'clock shadow without her noticing. 'Waste of blooming energy, shaving at this time of the day, when I'm not even going down the pub for a pint with the blokes.' He gave a pained sigh and turned off the gas under the saucepan, ready to go upstairs to their little bathroom.

'Johnny!' Nell's somewhat sweeter loud voice echoed from above him.

'Hello! What d'yer want now?'

'Fetch up the rest of the sherry. So I can be sipping that while you're 'aving a quick wash-down? I'm resting on top of the bed!'

Slowly shaking his head Johnny puffed air. 'Oh gawd . . . is it bloody well worth it for a bit of the other?'

Seventeen

Nathan had woken before anyone else in the house the next morning and not because he was uncomfortable in the makeshift bed but because he was happy to be there – to be in the home of the grandparents of the girl he loved. He was remembering the day when Charlotte had told him she and her family were going to move out of London to Norfolk. A time when he had been too gutted to think straight and had to hold firmly onto the only bit of bravery that he could muster then, when he was thirteen. Smiling to himself he wondered if Charlotte remembered what he had said when she left. Something that he had heard his dad say more than once. 'Everything, with the exception of a ring, comes to an end at some point.' And soon he would be slipping a ring on to her finger. He had loved her just as much then as he did now. He remembered her saying that her mother was going to buy her a pair of slingback shoes soon after they settled into the new house. Whether or not this came about, he didn't know. Five years had passed but the style she had thought to be the best thing since sliced bread was still in fashion, and he knew as he hugged his pillow what he was going to buy her at the end of the week on payday. Shoes *and* a beautiful leather handbag to match. He made a mental note to find out what size shoe she took and then wondered if Charlotte was awake yet. He could hear noises coming from the kitchen and he could smell bacon frying.

Charlotte, just like Nathan, was still in bed, but awake and thinking of him tall and broad and having to sleep on an old fashioned put-you-up settee that pulled down into a bed. Glancing at her wristwatch she could see that it had just gone nine o'clock and suddenly remembered that Nathan had told her nan that he had to be washed, dressed and fed by ten-thirty. He wanted to be back at home with his dad and go with him to see his grandparents. Of course she knew that Nell wasn't going to let him go out without a Sunday breakfast inside him. A fried breakfast without the bacon, though – Nathan, being Jewish, didn't eat it – would be a challenge for her. Nell was too old-fashioned for her own good at times.

Wearing one of her gran's thin cotton white nightdresses, purchased from Charlie's Cheap stall in the Mile End waste market, Charlotte felt a touch chilly even though it was summertime, but she could see that Nell, having crept in at the crack of dawn, had laid an old-fashioned thick candlewick housecoat at the foot of her bed. She pulled herself up into a sitting position, plumped up her big feather pillow and then sank back into it and smiled contentedly. There was a lovely warm glow inside her, partly because she was in a familiar room that held childhood memories but mostly because she was in love. In love with Nathan. All cosy in her grandparents' spare bedroom, she was making the most of the tranquillity before she was called down for breakfast. She thought of her flat, her very own flat that she couldn't wait to get back to. Thinking about the house and the people living there she felt a kind of sisterly warmth when she pictured Donald. Now she was regretting having been a bit short with him when she had gone downstairs to ask him to lower the sound of his music. She made a vow that once she was back in the house she would push a little note through his door thanking him for the welcome and the vase and his offers of help.

'I've not only found a sweetheart in Nathan,' she

whispered, 'but I think I might have found a brother figure in Donald.'

Contented and relaxed, she compared all of this with living in Bridgeford. It hadn't been dire by any means but she had been lonely for a long time and now she couldn't be happier. She had missed small things such as the old mix and match streets, courtyards and alleyways and the friendly housing estates. She couldn't wait to go to the Whitechapel Art Gallery again and she was looking forward to strolling through the back streets to the Tower of London, stopping for pie and mash on the way. These were things that had once been ordinary everyday occurrences.

She brought to mind the strong man who escaped from thick chains and all of the tourists who poured into the area at Tower Hill to watch him. People would arrive in their droves in nice weather and sit by the river on the small man-made beach. She couldn't wait to go back whenever she felt like it, and she looked forward to taking the tube to such places as the King's Road for general window shopping and Biba to treat herself to something small and inexpensive.

The best thing about it all was that she could now catch up on everything in London without having to make a day of it as if she was a tourist down from the country. She could go with Nathan to dance halls, pop concerts and coffee bars. And from what he had told her when they had spent time together in Bridgeford, being part of the theatre group and working with them nearly every other weekend, meant that he was always being invited to parties. Parties that were going on all over the place. And this is what she so wanted. What she was ready for. What she was in need of.

Pleased to have had a bit of time to herself, she left her cosy warm bed and went downstairs, hungry for one of her gran's great fry-ups. She knew that the newspapers would have arrived by now because her granddad always kept the owner of the corner shop on her toes when it came to the delivery boy. Pulling on the dressing gown left out for her, she tiptoed down the stairs, wondering if Nathan was still asleep on the couch bed. Going into the room that led into the kitchen she wondered no more. There, at the Formica-topped table her granddad and Nathan were reading the newspapers as if they were novels that they could not put down. On seeing her come into the room Johnny looked across to Nathan and raised his eyes to heaven.

'It's very quiet in here,' Charlotte said. 'What's up? The cat got both of your tongues? You all right, Granddad? All well on the home front, is it?'

'Not too bad, sunshine. I slept like a log. Your nan's all right. She's getting on wiv cooking the breakfast and that.'

'I know, I can smell it.' She glanced from Johnny to Nathan, who was looking sadly back at her. 'So what *is* the matter then? It's like a morgue in here. Is there something in the paper that's shocked you both? Has one of the royal family died or something?' She glanced at the paper that Johnny was reading and chuckled. 'You don't still read the *News of the World* and take it seriously do you, Granddad?'

'Show your paper to her, Nathan, son. Let her read the *Mirror* for 'erself. Give her the newspaper,' said Johnny.

Nathan glanced at Charlotte and then said, 'Come and sit down.'

'Why? What's happened?' She looked from one to the other.

'Women – they're all the same. Nosy by nature. Got to know all the ins and outs before they read up on a story.'

Leaning back in his chair, Johnny hunched his shoulders and then released a low sigh before quietly saying, 'A local woman's been murdered sweetheart. It's all over the front pages.'

Cutting to the quick, Nathan took a deep breath and then spoke quietly to her. 'It's the woman who lived in the house where you're renting a flat. They've taken your landlady's son in for questioning over it . . . according to one neighbour's account of it.'

'What!' Charlotte could hardly take it in, never mind believe it. 'Donald's been arrested for murder? I was there yesterday and all was normal. You've got it wrong, you must have. It can't be true. Donald's not that common a name in this neck of the woods, but even so—'

'Charlotte, it's true,' said Nathan. 'Come and sit down and read it for yourself.'

'No. I don't wanna read about a murder! I've only just got up!' She backed away and stood in the doorway to the passage. 'You read it out to me, Granddad, and read it properly! That's if it's something that I should know about.' She then called out to Nell who was hovering in the kitchen, too bewildered by the news to know what to say.

'Nan! Did you hear what Granddad said?'

'You don't 'ave to bloody well shout! I'm not a million miles away. And I heard it all. Sit down and listen to what they're trying to tell you. I'll fetch you a cup of coffee.'

Folding the newspaper that he had been reading, Nathan spoke in a quiet and tender voice. 'Charlotte, it's true. The body of a woman has been found. And it's a woman who was lodging in the house according to a neighbour who spoke to the press.'

'But the house where I'm gonna be living is just one in that, square. It can't be the only one. Gossips always get something wrong. Always have, always will.'

Nell came in from the kitchen and handed her grand-daughter the hot drink. A mug of coffee made the way she liked it best, half milk and half water. She then placed a hand on Charlotte's shoulder and tenderly patted it. 'We'll 'ave to phone your mum and dad, darling. They can come and fetch you. We'll help you pack your things up. You can't go back to that place now. And I know you don't want to live with us

233

two old fogeys. And nor should you want to. You're too young.'

'Nan? Stop it. Stop talking as if you're someone else. What's happened? What's got into the three of you? You're reading the Sunday papers, for Christ's sake. They always go in for shocking stuff whether it's true or not. You know that. Granddad 'as always said that they're jam packed with gossip and lies.' She turned to Johnny for a bit of support. 'Aint that right, Granddad?'

'You can phone the council offices in the morning,' murmured Nell sadly. 'To explain why you're going back home and why you won't be starting work there.'

'What are you talking about, Nan? Of course I'll be starting work there! And I'll be living in my rented flat! All my things are there. The press have got it wrong. I've paid the rent for my flat and I like it there! You know I do! I'm not going back to fucking Norfolk! I'm going to my flat and staying there!'

A horrible silence then filled the room until Charlotte, close to tears, murmured, 'It's gotta be a mistake. It must be another house in another square. Neither of you 'ave read your papers properly. And anyway . . . Sunday papers are always full of sensational gossip. You should know that! You know what you've always said about the *News of the World*, Granddad. But you still fucking-well read it!'

'Don't swear Charlotte. Not in front of me and your nan anyway.' He looked at his beloved granddaughter and felt his heart melting. 'It's been on the wireless, as well, sweetheart. On the eight o'clock news. I caught the tail end of a report but I didn't pick up on the area. But it's here in black and white.'

Charlotte stared into Nathan's face. 'Did you hear it on the wireless?'

'Yes.'

'But I was there only yesterday. There was a lovely

atmosphere in the house. They've got the wrong area. The wrong address. They must have done!'

Looking from one to the other of them, and seeing no change of expression other than serious and sad, Charlotte felt sick. 'Granddad . . . say something.'

Keeping his voice low, Johnny shook his head. 'And to fink that the landlady's son was in your room giving you a cut-glass vase for the flowers that that woman he murdered had picked for yer. It could 'ave been you lying dead in that old cellar.'

Charlotte glanced from one to other of them. And then in a quieter voice said, 'Did they name the woman?'

'Read it for yourself, Charlotte,' said Nathan. 'And calm down a bit.'

'It don't bear thinking about,' murmured Nell as she stared out at nothing. 'The wicked bastard needs to be hung, strung and quartered. Whoever he is.'

His full attention on his granddaughter, Johnny said, 'Sip your hot coffee, Charlotte. It'll help, I promise you.'

'According to the paper they're linking this murder with another two women who went missing,' said Nell. 'One of which was—'

'Yeah, all right . . . don't go into the sordid details,' said Johnny. 'Give 'er time, for gawd's sake.'

'I've read it twice over, Charlotte,' murmured Nathan. 'I can fill you in a bit later on . . . if you want.'

'No,' said Charlotte, her voice no more than a whisper now. 'Tell me now. I'll know if it's all bollocks or not.'

Nathan drew breath and then began. 'A woman was found in the cellar of an old house close by the river and not far from the square where your flat is. Some boys who were messing around in the early evening in one of the dilapidated houses. One of them shone a torch through rotting floorboards and saw the body. The newspapers are linking it with two other murders. Two women who had gone missing were dredged out of the river about a week ago. They hadn't connected them as victims of a serial killer but according to the paper, they are now.

'Your landlady has identified the dead woman. There was something in her pocket . . . a letter from an optician. This is what led the police . . . and then the morbid sightseers, to the door of the house. Apparently, the landlady's son was the last one to be seen talking to her, by a man who lives in the house two doors along. He made a statement. He got involved when he heard the lads yelling as they ran past his house about a dead woman that they had been found in a cellar.

'The police, according to what this paper says, had been keeping quiet about the two women they pulled out of the river until they knew more. Up until now they had no lead about either of the two prostitutes reported missing. The paper is saying that it's Jack the Ripper all over again, except that this one goes in for strangling his victims.'

'I can't believe it. I just can't take this in.' Charlotte's face was now paler than pale. 'Yesterday . . . I was there. In the house.'

'You can't go back there now, Charlotte. The place will be swarming with the press and nosy parkers. The boys who found the woman ran through the streets screaming the odds so it couldn't be kept quiet.'

'It's not Donald,' she said. 'I know it's not. He is odd but harmless. He wouldn't hurt a fly. I'm sure of it.'

Then, as tears filled her eyes she whispered Wendy's name. 'That poor woman. She was so lovely. I can't believe this. I can't believe that such a thing could happen. Not on our doorstep. And why would someone lure her away to a derelict house and then strangle her? The landlady's son's not stupid but nor is he that bright. He wouldn't 'ave been able to lure a mature woman like Wendy away. It doesn't add up.'

'Well, maybe the lad isn't all he appears to be, sweetheart. Maybe he's just clever enough to pull the wool over your eyes?

It didn't take him long to draw you in, did it? Flowers and a vase and you thinking what a nice gesture it was.'

'Your granddad's right, Charlotte,' said Nathan.

'I can't believe she's dead. Only yesterday she came to see me, and she was up there in the flat above mine. It can't be real.' Tears filled the back of Charlotte's eyes. 'This wasn't the way it was meant to be,' she just managed to say.

The sudden intrusion of the telephone ringing pulled them all up sharp. In a whispering voice, as if whoever was on the end of the line could hear, Nell said, 'You might be wanted for questioning, Charlie. That might be the police on the end of the line.'

'Silly cow! Of course it won't be the police!' said Johnny. 'How the bloody hell would they know where she is? They don't know she's here! They don't know our address!'

Nell pulled a face to show her dread as she picked up the receiver to the sound of her husband still going on in the background. She cupped the mouthpiece and told him to shut up and then offered the receiver to Charlotte. 'It's Daddy, love. He's in a right state. He's read the bit in the Sunday paper as well.'

'Tell him I'll call back, Nan. I'm only just about able to take this in. I feel sick. I'm going upstairs for a five-minute lie down.'

'Of course, you must do,' said Johnny. 'But it'll all come out right, you'll see.' He only just stopped himself from saying that she could move in with them. He knew that this wasn't the right time.

Taking the phone off his wife while she went and got herself a glass of water from the kitchen, Johnny told his son-in-law over the phone not to worry. That his girl would stay that night at theirs again. 'We'll keep Charlotte with us for as long as you want, son, don't you worry.'

But this wasn't enough for Eddie. 'She was one of the last people to have seen that woman alive, Johnny. The police are bound to want to interview her. Now if she doesn't go back to the house they'll put her on the missing list and the Bridgeford police will be on our doorstep in no time. The landlady's got our address, don't forget. She's got to either go back or at least phone the police and let them know where she is!'

'All right son, all right. Don't get aerated. She's safe and sound while she's here. But, yeah . . . you're right. All three of us will go for a stroll . . . back to the square and into the house. And then round to the local police station to let them know she's okay.'

'They'll want to interview her, Johnny, you can bet your life on it.'

'Of course they will. But we'll go with 'er, as will Nathan. She ain't done nuffing wrong so stop bloody worrying! It'll all turn out right. They've arrested the weirdo—'

'What do you mean? Weirdo?' said Eddie.

Well . . . Charlotte said something about 'im not being the same as everybody else, that's all. Harmless enough but a bit loopy.'

'Harmless? He's been taken in for fucking murder for Christ's sake! I'm driving down to fetch 'er home. Tell 'er not to go back to that house. Tell 'er that if the police do want to talk to her then they can come to fucking Bridgeford. I'm not having her approached on all sides by the bloody news-papers! This is your fault, Johnny! You and Nell! Encouraging 'er for months on end to move back to London!'

'All right, all right. Keep your shirt on. And stop worrying. We'll deal with it and keep you in touch until you get 'ere. Okay?' There was a silence. 'And as it happens, I don't fink there's any point in you rushing down here to London. She's got her nan and me and she's got Nathan. He's a sensible young man.'

After a quiet pause, Eddie spoke in a quiet voice. 'How do you know?'

'How do I know? Because he stopped over with us last night and we 'ad a lovely time. We got to know each other.'

'What d'yer mean? He slept over? Where exactly did he sleep over?'

'Oh gawd . . . you and your over-protective—'

'I'm not being over protective! I just want to know where Nathan slept!'

'He went on the couch that pulls down into a bed! And he thought it was very comfortable too. All right? What kind of a girl do you think my granddaughter is?'

There was a silence and then a long emotional sigh. 'I'm sorry, Johnny, but I'm all on edge. This 'as scared the bloody life out of me. I want her back here where it's safe. Fucking London. I might 'ave known!'

Closing his eyes, Johnny sighed deliberately and then said, 'All right Eddie. I'll tell her you'll call back later then, shall I? Or will you be out and in one of your posh friends' houses playing bridge?' The soft click and then dialling tone coming down the line made him smile. 'Bloody snobs, the pair of 'em.' He then turned to Nathan who was still in his chair at the table and blew air. 'What a turn-up for the books, eh?'

'I just can't believe it.'

Joining him at the table, Johnny shook his head and then glanced through to the kitchen where Nell was making egg and bacon sandwiches. He knew that she knew that no one was going to sit at the table with knife and fork and eat as if nothing had happened. Sandwiches were portable. And apart from this he knew that this was a sign that his wife wanted to be by herself. 'Who would have thought it?' He sighed again and said, 'Two lads mucking around in a broken house that they'd most likely gone in for a secret smoke and what do they find? A woman's shoe in the rubble close by to a bloody great hole in the floorboards where she fell to 'er death.'

'Pushed more like it. Once she had been strangled.'

'Yeah . . . all right son. Don't get too detailed about it.'

'If the boys hadn't have gone in for a secret cigarette she could have lain there rotting and never have been found until she was a skeleton.'

'Yeah, well . . . I s'pose your mind would fink like that. You being in the theatre world and all that. It was just as well that they were there, though. I'll give you that. If they 'adn't of run out screaming the odds are the police wouldn't 'ave been called and she would have rotted and turned to dust. Them bloody headlines about another serial killer makes my blood boil, though. Serial killer? Anything to sell their bloody newspapers.'

'It says that he's another Jack the Ripper. What do you think?'

'She was strangled, not slashed, son. As were the other two London girls who've been dredged up from the Thames. It does sound like an open and shut case and that's why it's probably not. That young man they arrested was the last one to have been seen speaking to the woman by a gentleman who was passing by. That's not evidence.'

'No . . . but another woman from another building in the square saw them from her window. She said that the accused and the woman murdered seemed quite intimate when chatting.'

'People say all kinds of bloody things at a time like this. And you can't believe all you read in the paper.' He was worried but wasn't going to let on. The woman wouldn't have taken much notice at the time, but once the police were milling around everywhere she no doubt was out there lapping it up. Giving evidence as a chief witness. Some people love a bit of drama on their doorstep. 'But we can't let Charlotte stay there now. Not after this. She'll have to either move in with us or . . . sadly, she'll go back to Bridgeford.'

Eighteen

Kenny, reclining on his single bed at home was enjoying his time in the sun that was shining through the small picture window in the family council flat. He too had read the headlines and the article and could not believe his luck. The witness, who had seen the whore with the weirdo, had not spotted him in the public gardens in the square because of the thick foliage that surrounded it on all four sides. He had once again got away with murder and it was fuelling his passion. Enjoying a cigarette and a cup of tea he laughed to himself. He really had put the cat amongst the pigeons this time. The bitch that he had once fancied rotten when a kid and who had chosen a Jew over him was more than likely shaking in her shoes in case she would be next.

He wondered if she would sleep that night knowing that not only had a woman who lived in the same building as her been murdered, but believing that she had been under the same roof as the killer. The weirdo. Grinning, he recalled the way the Jew boy, Nathan, used to be always pushing his old and wonky round National Health glasses up onto the bridge of his fat nose so as to focus. A wide smile crossed his face as he remembered when he and his gang of ruffians humiliated the slob, who was short-arsed for his age and as fat as an ugly pig. He could still picture the way Nathan's lips used to quiver when he was trying to get on the right side of Kenny's gang before the boots went in. They would form a chain across his path, their arms folded, and act as if they were the Gestapo before they gave him a hiding and brought him down onto the old cobblestone ground. Suddenly proud of himself for having kept up the good work of the pre-war Blackshirts and Oswald Mosley, he wondered why he hadn't focused on Jewish prostitutes.

He smiled at the thought of coming across Nathan again . . . in that old unlit cobblestone turning with lock-ups on one side beneath the railway line and a park on the other. He had given him a bloody hiding more than once back in the old days. His mind turned back to the headlines and the pathetic drip called Donald that they had taken in for questioning. He toyed with the idea of striking again before the weirdo had been given bail. He could just see the next headline that would put fear into every woman in London: 'Wrong man arrested!' Or 'Strangler still on the loose!'

He lay down again with his pillow over his face to stifle his chortling. His mum was in the kitchen and he didn't want her in asking what he found so funny. She could be an interfering cow at times and this was when he wished he didn't love her so much. He didn't know why he loved her, because she had been a whore in earlier years and left him at home with his dad, night after night after night. What he really wanted to do was ask her why. Why she had to go out whoring for money and why she had not been there to tuck him up in bed when he was small and needed her. Why he couldn't remember a bedtime hug from her. Why she had never sat him on her lap and told him a story by the fireside . . .

Covering his face with his hands and pressing until it hurt, he managed, as he had done a million times before, to stop himself from crying. Once again, as had also happened many times before, his sense of exuberance was fast turning into gloom, but the face of his dad was filling his thoughts. He had often been tormented by his dad when he was young for weeping like a big soft girl after he had been scolded for being naughty. Controlling his emotions the way he had learned to do over the years, he drew breath and then relaxed a few times over until he was ready for another cigarette. Smiling again, he applauded himself for ridding the world of another streetwalker. This was how he viewed Wendy. As nothing more and nothing less than a streetwalker. Done and dusted.

Not quite sure whether to go and do a bit of wheeling and dealing in Aldgate or not, he closed his eyes to think about it. He knew that a load of stolen cigarettes had been delivered that very morning to a disused shop that stank of rats and mould and was boarded up. He also knew that if he didn't get there before three that afternoon the gear would be sold to other punters like himself and he would miss out, but he wasn't broke so it didn't matter. He would get a fair price for the whore's jewellery straightaway from an old boy who had a little shop tucked away in the back and beyond of Aldgate. He was tired, though. Very tired. So, feeling more relaxed now that he had thought things through, he closed his eyes and pulled his bedclothes over him. There was nothing he liked better than to sleep in late on a Sunday morning, before or after he had read the papers.

Curious as to what might be happening in the house where he had seen Charlotte come and go and where the dead prostitute had lived, he did a few of his usual deep breathing exercises to help clear his mind. Soon he would go out and see what was what in and around that old fashioned tree-lined square. He felt as if he were a main player in a movie. The star actor, the scriptwriter and the director, all rolled into one. And the best of it was that no one had a clue that *he* was the so-called serial killer. He ran the words *serial killer* through his mind and then laughed at the irony. He was famous but nobody knew it other than himself. And this, he realised, was probably what was causing him to be at odds with himself. If he confessed he would be famous but locked up for the rest of his life. If he carried on being clever and got rid of a few more whores and stayed anonymous, he would always only be seen as Kenny the small-time thief and fence. He made a snap decision there and then to go out and cast an all-seeing eye over his patch and perhaps give a few teasing tips to one of the uniformed men on duty. Tips that would no doubt be taken as nonsense but that would hold vital clues, should there be an officer on duty that was as intelligent as himself.

As he arrived into an area not far from the square where he was heading, Kenny was delighted to see so many sightseers milling around the area in small groups. He wondered, as he stood watching them, whether he had been daft to cover one of his previous deeds too cleverly by dropping the corpse down the old and very deep well in Bridgeford. He then quietly praised the local lads who had gone into the old wrecked terraced house and discovered the body of Wendy. Between them and himself, they had caused quite a stir with the local people and the press by the look of things. He casually strolled up to a small group of people and asked what all the fuss was about.

'There's another Jack the Ripper on the loose,' said a small rotund woman in her late fifties, who wore her silvery grey hair pulled up into a bun and tied with a blue ribbon. 'Not that it surprises me,' she went on. 'There are more prostitutes in this area now than there was in the eighteen-eighties – more foreigners an' all. I'm not saying that they deserve to be ripped to bits or strangled but I wish they'd go elsewhere to work the streets. They're a bloody nuisance.'

'Do they know who did it?' said Kenny, a touch boyish.

'Who knows? The old Bill won't give nuffing away. Not even to us ratepayers who deserve to know what's going on in the parish that we pay for. Too many foreigners, that's the trouble. In they pour, month after month from all over the bloody globe. I'm sick of it.'

Leaving the rubberneckers to themselves, Kenny let it all go above his head. Clearly he was not going to be able to get anywhere near the tree-lined square or his favourite bench that he had now marked as his own by scoring his initials into one of the slats of wood. The police had cordoned off the entrance, which was via a small brick archway, and were only letting those who lived in the square pass through. Looking around at the small crowds everywhere he could see that the small Italian café where he had sat at a table chatting to Charlotte was full to overflowing. He smiled to himself. At least he had brought business into this little corner of London. Turning away from those who he considered nothing but nosy bastards, he saw Charlotte and a guy who was tall, broad, dark and handsome who he thought he had seen with her before but wasn't certain. The couple were approaching the archway into the square and of course he knew that they would be allowed in because Charlotte had taken the flat in the house where the dead woman had lived. Bored now, Kenny sauntered off, more than happy with the thought that he knew better than anyone else in the world what had happened in that old derelict building. He couldn't help but smile.

Once Charlotte and Nathan had shuffled through the police and reporters and were at the entrance to the house she was quickly up the steps and using her key to the front door. In the hallway she was immediately greeted by the very distraught Isabelle. From the look of her face and her red puffy eyes she had been crying nonstop. Holding out her arms as if she was greeting the only person in the world that was left to her, the distraught woman burst into tears.

Gently patting the woman's back as she held her close, Charlotte was close to tears herself. 'It'll be all right, Isabelle, you'll see,' she only just managed to say. 'Your lovely son could never be responsible for killing Wendy. He'll be home soon. You'll see. He'll be back here with us.'

'Oh darling . . . do you really and truly believe that? Honestly?'

'Of course I do,' said Charlotte, gently pulling away so as to be able to look her in the face. 'Just because he was seen talking to Wendy on the steps before he went off to the library to give his talk at the book signing doesn't mean that he killed her. It's ridiculous.'

'I know it is! It's quite mad!' The woman relaxed her shoulders and let out a sigh of relief. 'I am so happy to see you. When you didn't come back last night I thought the worst. Have you let the police know that you're all right, my dear?'

'Yes. I telephoned from my grandparents' house in Bow. I wasn't going to stop out all night but my granddad insisted that Nathan and I slept over. They don't get to see much of me . . .'

'And of course they would want you to stay. And you wouldn't have wanted to be here in any case. Can you believe that the police arrived and went into Wendy's flat to go through her most personal things? It was quite awful. What if they took away her diaries? I should hate to think that when I pass on complete strangers would read my most private thoughts. It's all too ghastly.'

Ghastly it might have seemed, but what Isabelle couldn't possibly know was that Wendy had written more than one entry into her diary to do with Donald. There was at least one that was incriminating when it came to this lovely woman's only son. Wendy had written a short piece about him, which was not unusual, but in this particular one she had underlined the word barmy and then written 'mentally deranged' with a question mark, in brackets.

'I would hate anyone to read my diary,' said Charlotte. 'I

shall have to be very careful not to leave mine around for my Gran and Granddad to peek into.' She smiled.

'Your grandparents wouldn't dream of such a thing, I'm sure. And of course they will see much more of you now so they won't have to read about what you are up to. They'll know. That is, of course, if you haven't decided to leave us because of all this horrid business?'

'No, of course I won't leave. I've not even stayed overnight yet but I love the flat. It's mine. You can rest assured I'm staying – no matter what.'

'Oh thank goodness!' Isabelle clasped her hands together and broke into a lovely smile. 'I am so relieved. All of a sudden all three of you had gone. The artist in the basement is away on holiday. He popped a note in my door before all of this dreadful business had happened. Poor Wendy. I just cannot believe it. I can't take it in. And of all people to arrest as a suspect? My poor innocent boy? He wouldn't harm a fly, Charlotte.'

'I'm sure he wouldn't. Come on, let's go into your kitchen and I'll make us a pot of tea while you get to know Nathan. He's a very close childhood friend who up until a week or so ago I hadn't seen in years.'

'Really? You do surprise me. I would have said that you hadn't ever been separated, you are so right together.' She then turned to Nathan and offered her hand, saying, 'I do apologise for going on. How do you do? I am most grateful for this visit. I can't tell you what it's been like. The phone hasn't stopped ringing and I've spoken to so many news-papers I can't take any more. So I've taken the phone off the hook.'

'Good for you,' said Nathan. 'That's exactly what I would have suggested.'

'Really? You would have done the self-same thing in my shoes?'

'Yes. Now . . . let's do as we're told by Miss Bossy Boots here and sit down while she makes us a hot drink.'

'Yes, of course we must. But you don't have to baby-sit me.' She sighed. 'I feel so much better now that Charlotte has turned up. Much better. Will you be stopping overnight, Nathan?'

'No. My dad will be worried. He's a widower and we live together in Bethnal Green. He will probably have read the papers by now and recognised the address as where Charlotte is going to live.'

'And do you like it where you're living?' asked Isabelle, doing her best to control herself and not to start crying again. 'I ask you this because the flat at the top that Wendy lived in will soon be available, and I think that the actor in the basement will be moving on quite soon, from what he's told me.' As hard as she tried, whether she even realised it or not, tears were trickling slowly down her cheeks and her neck. The poor woman was in shock but couldn't just sit still and do nothing.

Nathan, filled with compassion, gently squeezed her arm. 'That's very sweet of you, and I think that Dad would love to live in a house in Lavender Square. But try not to get things back to the way they were too quickly. You might make mistakes you'll regret later on. Wait until your son has been released.'

'Goodness me, you *are* wise for your age. And of course you're right. Donald will soon be back home with a public pardon . . . of course he will. He is such an innocent boy and not cut out for this sort of a drama. But if you and your father wanted to rent the flat I wouldn't charge you very much. It would be so nice to have some men around the place.'

Joining them at the polished pine kitchen table while the fresh pot of tea stood for a few minutes, Charlotte reached across and took hold of Isabelle's delicate white hands and squeezed them. 'Your son will be home tomorrow and, knowing Donald, even though it's only been for a short time, I personally think he'll be philosophical while at the police station and when he comes home too. He knows he's innocent. And this is the all-important thing. They can't find him guilty of a murder he didn't commit. He was at the library for the book signing.' Charlotte smiled warmly at the grief-stricken woman who was trying so hard to make sense of it all.

'But there's a problem, Charlotte . . . the signing was cancelled at the last minute and he came back. This is why they've taken him in for questioning. He was the last to be seen talking to Wendy. But he wouldn't harm her. They really liked each other, but only in a very platonic sort of way.'

'Of course he wouldn't harm her. It's ridiculous. He's not a serial killer and that's what they're looking for, don't forget. Two prostitutes have been dredged from the Thames, according to the newspaper.' Charlotte then left the table to pour out the tea. All kinds of things were running through her mind, in particular the time when the poor soul Wendy had turned to her for someone to talk to. When she herself had thought that the woman had been fantasising about Donald. Suddenly it all came floating back. Wendy had said that she had been touched by the way the sweet boy looked at her, and that he sometimes hung around outside of her front door. That he was one of life's vulnerable people.

Murmuring quietly to herself, Charlotte could hardly believe what she was thinking. But Wendy had said that she would ask him in for coffee and biscuits. That it would be nice for her to have some company. That it shouldn't be herself who made the first move. That if her landlady's son wanted to go into her apartment for a chat he should say so.

Caught up in her deep thoughts, Nathan's voice drifted into her consciousness as he said, 'Did either of you see the small piece in the *Evening Standard* about the young woman going missing in Bridgeford?'

'No,' said Isabelle. 'I don't take the *Standard*.'

Shaking herself out of the low mood she was slipping into when wondering if there might be more to Donald than met the eye, Charlotte paid attention to what he was saying. 'Dad did say something about the missing woman last week. I think I'll give him a call later on from Gran and Granddad's.' She looked into Isabelle's face apologetically. 'They won't rest if I don't sleep there until this is all cleared up.' Thoughtful again, she slowly shook her head. 'I'm *sure* I heard that she'd been found and was dead. Nothing about being murdered, though.'

'Oh . . . did you think that she had been murdered, Charlotte? Because if so maybe there is a link. And if so, they mustn't keep Donald in any longer. Do you think you might use my phone and call your father?'

At this point Nathan stepped in and with a firm tone to his voice said, 'I think that you've both had a bit of a shock and enough is enough. I take it there is a telephone in Charlotte's flat, Isabelle?'

'Oh, yes. And it's quite new. I got rid of the clunky old-fashioned one months ago. Why? Do you wish to call someone?'

'Yes. And don't worry about all that I said. It was just thinking aloud really. We'll sleep on it and if I still feel the same in a day or so I'll phone Charlotte's father and ask about the girl. You never know – there could be a link. A mass murderer could live anywhere in the world and pick girls off as and when he thinks fit.' The wicked bastard Kenny who had an evil streak was now on his mind. Charlotte had told him that he had been on the train from Bridgeford and then turned up in the Italian coffee bar close by.

Excusing himself from the table Nathan took the key from Charlotte that would let him into her flat. 'I need to make a call or two. It shouldn't take long.'

'You're perfectly welcome to use my phone,' said Isabelle.

'That's very kind of you but I've been brought up never to

bring work into the home and especially not to the kitchen table. And I would rather speak to my colleague about work in private. I think that you've both had enough for now, one way and another.' With that he took his leave, having no intention to phone work but to dial Eddie's number. He was desperate to talk to him because he felt that he was onto something. He sighed thankfully when he heard his voice.

'Hello, Eddie, it's Nathan. And before you ask, we're at the house and Charlotte's fine. She'll sleep at Johnny and Nell's again tonight. But listen to me. I want to know more about the girl that was reported missing in Bridgeford. Have they found her?'

'Why? What's happened now?'

'Nothing, I promise you. The police are crawling all over this part of the East End but telling us nothing. But I really do want to know if there's been any more about that girl. I've got a theory that is probably rubbish but I need to look into it.'

There was a short silence and then a sigh from Eddie. 'Apparently, and this is confidential information, Nathan, so keep it to yourself, one of the guys at the Freemasons meeting earlier on told me that the police are crawling all over the flat above the old wireless shop as well. Taking fingerprints and taking things away. I also heard that they lowered a bloke in a wet suit down into the well at the bottom of the garden.'

'So they're searching not only for clues but also for a body? Is that what you're saying?'

'Read it which way you like, but don't you dare breathe a word of it, Nathan. It's more than my life's worth. It's good for my business to keep in with the funny handshake lot.'

'Of course I won't say anything. It's just that . . . well I've heard of someone hanging around here who spent a bit of time in Bridgeford.'

'And you're putting two and two together. Be very careful, son, of what you accuse people of. I know what you're getting at and I can't say that the same thought hasn't crossed my mind. I should leave well alone if I were you.'

'Oh really? And what if it does turn out to be who we are both thinking about? Do we leave well alone until he strikes again? And what if it's your daughter that's found in the river, or in a cellar, or in a well at the bottom of someone's garden?'

There was a silence and then a sigh. 'I think that you're letting your imagination carry you away, son. Don't forget the old saying, don't let your heart rule your head. Kenny's not clever enough to have got away with murdering four women. You're barking up the wrong tree. Tell Charlotte I'm coming down to fetch her home at the weekend and until then she's to stop at her grandparents. Tell her to phone the office where she was gonna work and tell them she's not going to start after all. I want her back here. Understood?'

'I think I've got the gist of it, Eddie, yes.'

'Good. It's now your responsibility and not mine. I'm only the messenger. Rita has been going on and on at me, driving me fucking mad!' He replaced the receiver with a slam and all that Nathan could hear was the dialling tone.

'Well cheers for that, Eddie. Thanks for the advice.' He decided then and there to see Charlotte home to Johnny and Nell's place and then he was going home to have a good talk with his own dad. Tell him what he thought and ask his advice as to what he should do. For his part, he felt like screaming from the top of his voice that Kenny, the evil little shit from the past, was a very strong candidate for the murders. He would place his life and his possessions on it. The bastard had always been evil and it didn't sit right that he had drifted in and out of Charlotte's world in Bridgeford and now in this little part of East London. It could all be co-incidence, but he would rather have egg on his face than blood on his hands should another murdered woman be found. Never mind that it could be Charlotte.

Taking a deep breath and doing his best to maintain a calm

and composed manner, he went back downstairs and into Isabelle's flat. 'Sorry about that but I had to make that call.'

'Men and their work,' Isabelle smiled. 'My husband was just the same. I think all men are. Well, those who are not lazy, that is. I couldn't bear to have a man around the house all day long. It would drive me to distraction.'

'I think we should be getting back soon, Charlotte, so if you want to collect anything from the flat you'd best get it now. Your grandparents will be worried. And they'll be waiting to hear the latest hot news.'

Charlotte looked from Nathan to Isabelle and smiled kindly at her. 'Are you sure you're all right in the house by yourself? I could sleep here tonight if not.'

'No dear. I feel so much better for your visit. And of course my son will be let home soon. They can't possibly keep him in. There's absolutely no evidence to suggest anything other than that he is a quiet young man who likes to keep himself to himself.'

Catching Nathan's eyes, Charlotte felt her cheeks going red. She wanted so much to comfort this lovely lady. Her son had been arrested on suspicion of murder, after all, and history books were full of innocent people having been sent to the gallows. Justice did not always out in the end. 'I'm sure he'll be back home with you in a day or so. And meanwhile don't sit in the quiet. Put the television on, and let actors and presenters keep you company. It's what I would do. And I'll phone you from my grandparents' house later on to see how you are.'

'Oh, thank you so much, Charlotte. And do you really mean to come back to live here with us, after all of this?'

'I'll be back for good tomorrow. And that's a promise.'

'Oh splendid!' Isabelle clasped her hands together, joy and relief on her face. The poor woman needed a bit of sunshine in her life and Charlotte wanted to get back on track and live in the flat that she adored. Once they had said their good-byes and the street door had closed behind the young couple, Isabelle went back into her sitting room and sat by the fireplace where no fire burned, and burst into tears. The second worst thing for her was that the police had said that she wasn't allowed to go into Wendy's flat and they had cordoned it off. And now all that she had for company in this once cheerful house was silence and the ticking of her old-fashioned clock on the mantel shelf.

Nineteen

By the time Nathan got back to his own home he was shattered. He had gone with Charlotte by bus to Nell and Johnny's and spent a bit of polite time with them, and then left to catch another bus back home. Letting himself in with his key he called out to Jacob to let him know that he was back.

'What'sa matter with you?' his dad yelled from the back room. 'You think I don't know when someone comes into the flat? It's a poky hole, not a bloody mansion with me stuck in the tower. I even heard you turn the bloody key in the door!'

'What's rattled your cage?' asked Nathan, suppressing a wry smile. His dad always managed to make him smile or laugh, even when things were bad.

'The television aerial, that's what. I can't get a decent picture. You promised to get me a new one.'

'I did. It's down there in the corner, in that box under the newspapers. It was you who buried it, not me. Have you had anything to eat?'

'Of course I have. Why do you ask? You're not gonna drag me off to the hospital for an investigation of the bowels again are you?'

'I was going to suggest fresh salmon in beigels. I just passed by the bakers and by the smell of things there's a new batch just out of the oven.'

'Well, that's different. For fresh beigels straight out of the

255

oven I'm always hungry whether I've eaten or not. I don't know about the salmon, though. I don't trust that man with the salmon. I'm not sure that it's always as fresh as he says it is. I'll have cream cheese and gherkins in mine. So where did you sleep last night?'

'On a put-you-up in her grandparent's sitting room. Okay? Charlotte's a decent girl from a decent family.'

'I never said she was anything other than that. Did I say she was a loose woman? I think the world of that girl – you know I do. All she has to do is convert.' He looked slyly at his son to see what he made of the seed he had just sown.

'Forget it. We'll have a civil wedding if and when she accepts me. And before you say that your ancestors will turn in their grave, remember things are different now. Mixed marriages are all the thing. And anyway, we've only just started courting.'

Jacob tried to hide a smile by glancing out of the window. 'So you're going to marry the girl. Mazel tov. You've been in love for donkey's years so you won't be rushing in. I shouldn't keep her waiting, though. A lovely girl like that would soon find someone more handsome than you. She could have her pick of the lads.'

'You haven't bloody well seen her since she was thirteen. How would you know if she's grown ugly or not?'

'I can tell by the voice. A voice speaks volumes. And if she was ugly you wouldn't have come in at this time of night and you wouldn't have left an old man to sleep in this shit hole by himself. Put-you-up in the living room? Do me a favour. You crept into her bed, and if you tell me you didn't you're no son of mine. God gave you a tool to use so be thankful and make the most of it.'

Slowly shaking his head Nathan sighed with a smile. He was used to his dad and the things he came out with but, sometimes, he pushed the boundaries. 'Did you read the Sunday paper yet?'

'Of course I read the bloody paper. What else is there for me to do? I haven't even got a back yard to muck around in. There's nowhere to plant a bloody flower even. At least we had a back balcony and window boxes when we lived in the council flat. On the balcony I could sit on a kitchen chair and talk to God. You think he'll want to come visit me in this old-fashioned dump? I need a garden. Get married, buy a little house and put me in the attic room. I won't mind.' He gave his son a sly look, and added, 'I've got a bit put by for a decent deposit. You could buy a nice little terraced house with a garden back and front in Stamford Hill or Stoke Newington.'

Nathan filled the kettle to make a pot of tea and, ignoring the suggestion, said, 'What did you make of the headlines then?'

'The woman was a prostitute. What did she expect? You live life on the edge you have to expect consequences. Why did you bother to mention it? Have you been with her? Are you upset over it?'

'It's not something to joke over, Dad. And she wasn't a prostitute as far as I can make out. And what makes you think that I would go with a forty-five-year-old woman?'

'Don't knock age, son. She could have taught you a lot. So why did you mention it then? What's so special about that particular woman? And how do we know that she didn't fall down into the cellar? Did anyone see her being thrown down? Of course not. Bloody newspapers. They'll do anything to sell copies.'

'The landlady's son, in the house where Charlotte's renting a flat, has been arrested on suspicion of murder. Murder . . . of the woman who lived in the flat above Charlotte's. That's why I mentioned it.'

The silence that struck the room could have been cut with a knife. Jacob, for possibly the first time in his life, was lost for words. The seconds ticked by and then he asked, 'And where is Charlotte now, pray?'

257

'Staying at her grandparents. It's a long story. I'll tell you all about it tomorrow.'

'You'll be at work all day, tell me about it now. I'm an old man. I need to know now. I might be dead by the time you come home from work.'

Ten minutes later, father and son, each on an armchair and looking into the imitation flames of the electric fire, were silent. Nathan was thanking God that Charlotte had gone back to her grandparents' house and Jacob was wondering what the world was coming to. 'How could such a thing happen, Nathan? Didn't anyone realise that the lad was a nutcase?'

'Dad . . . I've told you all I know. Charlotte has met and spoken with him and she doesn't believe he's guilty. He's a bit odd but no more than that.'

'A bit odd is all it takes to find the next step to insanity.'

'So do you want I should go out and get some beigels or not?'

'I want. I told you that already. My God . . . what is the world coming to? A woman is strangled and then dumped in a cellar? What was she doing in that dump in the first place?'

'I don't know, Dad.' Nathan stood up to leave. 'I won't be gone long and I won't be long out of my bed once I've eaten. I've had it. I'm all in.'

Gazing at his father he knew that he was devastated. Jacob had lived in the East End boy and man, and knew every back turning and many people in the area. As a boy of nine he had picked up work delivering groceries from the local shop on an old fashioned bike with a carrying basket attached. 'Was the woman a foreigner?' he murmured.

'No, Dad. But even though she's been in the area for a while she wasn't born and bred here so you wouldn't have known her, and nor would Mum. It's horrible and I wish to God it hadn't happened, but it has. And Charlotte's smack bang in the middle of it. She'll be questioned as well, no doubt.'

'Of course she will. She had already moved into the flat where the murderer lives.'

'We don't know that he did it, and Charlotte thinks that he couldn't have. That he's too nice and too harmless. So if she phones don't put your opinions forward, just say you're sorry to hear what's happened and that I'll call her back.'

Jacob turned slowly in his chair to look up at his son and sighed. 'This is what it's come to? You telling me what to do instead of me telling you?'

Feeling sympathy for his dad who was genuinely upset by the news, Nathan offered a gentle apologetic smile. 'Of course not. I'm just a bit awry at the moment, that's all. You're my father and I would never disrespect you or not listen to your advice.'

'I should bloody well think not. And tell Maurice the baker not to put any bloody black pepper on the cream cheese . . . and no olives either. All of a sudden he wants to follow the Italians. Beigels are Jewish. They've always been Jewish.'

'Sure they have, Dad.' Nathan smiled. 'I won't be long.'

He left the flat and his dad, who was staring into those imitation flames again. 'My God . . .' the old man murmured, 'what is it coming to? And why all of a sudden does my world feel so small and vulnerable? I don't like it, Lilly. I don't like it one bit. So move over, darling, because I don't think that I'm long for this world either. At least I hope not. I don't want any part of it. It's changed, sweetheart. Everything that can be changed has been altered. God rest your soul, sweetheart, and stay a little bit warm for me.'

Charlotte, back in the safety of her grandparents' house, was trying to enjoy her favourite thing at the end of a tiring day, a lovely soak in a hot sudsy bath. Once she was out she was going to put on her pyjamas, and Nell's dressing gown, and go back down for a mug of Horlicks. Of course she hadn't been able to stop thinking about the double tragedy of Wendy having been murdered and poor Donald arrested for the crime. But right now she was nursing her head. Before taking some Dispirin it had been thumping with pain. All in all, everything had been too much for her. And while she was running everything through her mind, Nell and Johnny were down below speaking in whispers as if she would be able to hear them if they used their normal voices – which was quite possible.

'I don't fink she should ever go back to that place, Johnny, never mind living there. Not now. Not after all that's happened.'

'Tell me something that I don't know,' said Johnny as he slowly shook his head, deeply worried. 'But you know what she's like. Stubborn as a mule. And if we try and lay down the law she'll baulk against it – you can bet on that. She still insists that the landlady's son is too wimpish to hurt a fly, never mind strangle a woman.'

'Keep your voice down, Johnny!' she hissed.

'She can't hear us, you silly cow. And we're not just talking about one woman but *three* . . . by the sound of things. The two they pulled out of the river and kept quiet about and now this poor cow who done no harm to no one. What must she 'ave gone through? It beggars belief.'

'Don't go on about it. If Charlotte's chose to put on a brave face and push it to one side then we've got to do the same. It's gonna take years for 'er to get over this. Years. And what about his mother? What kind of hell is she going through? I feel as if I want to go round there and keep the woman company.'

'No . . . you can't do that. She don't know you from Adam and by the sound of what Charlotte's told us, she's a bit on the posh side.'

'So? What are you saying? That I'm not good enough to be in 'er company?'

'That's not what I said and you know it. All I meant is that we've gotta leave the woman to 'erself. She must 'ave some family. Brothers, sisters . . . cousins.' He shrugged.

'No doubt she 'as. But would you in her place phone relatives and tell them that your son's been arrested for murder?'

Johnny released a long low sigh. 'Dear oh dear oh dear. What a thing to 'appen. You know what I think? I think that all them bloody books about Jack the Ripper and the so-and-so strangler should be shredded or burned. To some people bastards like that become heroes, you know.'

'Don't talk rubbish.' Nell had heard enough. 'I'm gonna phone Rita to see how she is. I bet she's in a right state. I bet she's 'aving kittens.'

'Well go on then, if you must. You've said it enough times. Pick up the bloody receiver and dial the number before she comes down. We've got to try and keep Charlotte's pecker up. She won't wanna hear you giving a rundown on it. Enough's enough.'

'All right, Johnny. I'll tell 'er a few sidesplitting jokes, shall I? One or two of yours about the Irishman, the Scottish man and the Welshman. Once she's out of the bath.'

Johnny looked into Nell's face and waited but she just looked back at him wondering what he was waiting for. She finally said, 'Well, shall I then?'

'What d'yer keep asking me for? You always do what you fink you will in any case. Go on. Pick up the bloody phone and dial the number.'

Rita was watching television when the sound of the phone ringing in the passage pierced through the air. This was immediately followed by Eddie's urgent footsteps as he ran down the stairs from the box room where he had been getting up to date on his bookwork and filing so as to keep his mind off what was going on back in London. Within no time at all he had the receiver to his ear. When he heard Nell's voice he breathed a sigh of relief. She sounded okay. So Charlotte would be fine, too, was his take on it.

'What's new?' said Eddie, hoping for some kind of upbeat response.

'We've heard nothing more, sweetheart. But I thought I would just let you know that Charlotte's fine. She's having a lovely soak in the bath and then after a mug of cocoa I wouldn't be surprised if she'll be ready for her pillow early tonight.'

'Oh, that's good, that's taken a load off my mind. She can't go back to that house, Nell. I'm gonna come down tomorrow and fetch her and her stuff back.'

'Well, I can't stop you from doing what you want, Eddie, but I strongly advise you to leave it be. She's old enough to make up 'er own mind, and she doesn't want to go back to Bridgeford. Nathan's been a brick. He thinks the world of her and it shows.'

'So what then? She'll stop with you and Johnny then?'

'That's right,' said Nell, only half telling the truth. The truth being that Charlotte wanted to go back to the flat the very next day. 'Things will settle down soon enough.'

'If you say so. Can I speak to 'er?'

'She's in the bath!'

'Well get 'er to ring when she comes out of it!'

'Why?'

'Because I want to be sure she's okay.'

'She *is* okay. Leave it be. Rita's not being a mother hen so don't you be!'

'What d'yer mean? She's just as worried as I am!'

'Of course she is, but her motherly instincts are kicking in. She knows when to let go and leave it be. Charlotte will phone you if she needs to. She's doing bloody well so don't upset the apple cart.'

After a long sigh, Eddie finally gave in. 'Fair enough. I suppose you know what you're talking about, but I wish bloody Nathan hadn't of turned up out of the blue the way he did. She'd still be up here with us and none the wiser to all of this dark stuff – other than what's in the papers.'

'You can't keep 'er wrapped in cotton wool for all of 'er life, son. You've got to learn to let go. We all have to let go at some time or another. And this is *your* time to.'

'I s'pose you're right. You usually are. I'll phone you tomorrow for an update. Give 'er our love.' With that Eddie replaced his receiver and all that Nell could hear was the dialling tone.

'Silly daft sod,' she said. Then, as she replaced the receiver she had to swallow against the lump in her throat and will herself not to cry. Not to let go. Not to scream and kick and punch. Because this is how she felt, and had felt ever since she heard about the woman who lived in the flat above Charlotte getting herself strangled. It was all too close to home for her liking. Murders in England were few and far between and to have one happen on her doorstep was terrifying. She, just like hundreds of other women in the area, would not be sleeping too well for a while. After all, the young man who had been arrested could so easily be an innocent soul and the maniac could be still out there, ready for another kill.

Shaking off this dark mood that had crept in again, she put on a brave face for the sake of Johnny who she knew was worried sick and scared. Both of them knew that there was going to be no stopping Charlotte from going back to that house of horror and nestling down. Whether it was the right thing for her to do or the wrong thing – she was not going to be told what to do. She was a chip off the old block. Nell's block. Stubborn as a mule when she thought that right was right. And usually Nell wasn't wrong, and so all that she could hope was that Charlotte was doing the right thing by staying true to her plans, no matter what.

That night, as Nathan lay in his bed in the small second bedroom of the flat in Bethnal Green, he thought about

Charlotte and how much he loved her. He tried to imagine living with her in their own house. A house with a back garden where his dad could plant flowers and some vegetables and have a little shed at the back where he could potter about. Nathan was earning a decent salary now, and his dad had his local customers who still wanted a suit made to measure by a bespoke tailor. Jacob's old treadle sewing machine was still oiled and in good working order, and Nathan knew that between them all they would be able to afford a decent mortgage if he could find a modest house that suited all three of them. He also knew that his dad would insist on using his life savings as a deposit.

In his mind's eye, he could see Charlotte ironing his shirts to wear at the office while she listened to her favourite records, and felt a glow of warmth in his chest. But then, as had been happening all day long, Kenny managed to slip back into his thoughts and the old anger, now mixed with a gut feeling that the nasty piece of work was somehow involved in the murder, filtered through every vein in his body. But it wasn't to last long because the sound of his dad in the next room farting, snoring and moaning in his sleep was enough to wake the dead. He was used to hearing this by now and had his earplugs ready and waiting, but he couldn't sleep. He was exhausted but not sleepy. Something was in the air. Something deep down inside was almost telling him to stay awake and it had something to do with the woman who had been murdered. He felt like phoning Charlotte but knew that this was out of the question because it was late. He closed his eyes and left it all to God to keep a watch over those he loved. He then thanked Him for leading him to Charlotte, and thanked Him too for his dad's good health, sense of humour and determination to live until he was a hundred.

Nathan squeezed a silencer into each ear and then laid his head back onto his plumped up feather pillow, sighing as he brought his lovely Charlotte to mind. He was going to have to think of a different kind of a gift to give her now. Something really special. He knew that it was going to take a long time before the vision of that poor woman, lying in the cellar with her handbag empty and discarded and one of her slingback shoes in the debris, would fade away. He tried not to think about it any more. He so needed to sleep, he was exhausted. Just before he slipped into a well-deserved rest a gentle smile crossed his face. Of course he knew what he would give Charlotte! A ring. A beautiful diamond engagement ring with little earrings to match. It would take all of his savings and a bit of borrowed money from his dad, but he didn't care. In fact, he couldn't wait to go to an old family friend who had a lovely little jewellery shop in Whitechapel who he knew would give him a very good deal. And just so as to keep his dad in the picture, he would tell him of his plan and ask him if he would go with him to help him choose the ring. Blocking the thoughts of all that had happened, he waited for sleep and it wasn't long coming. Soon all was quiet in that little flat in the back and beyond of Bethnal Green.

Lying in bed and reading the book he had purchased a year or so ago, and that had become his bible, Kenny was in a tranquil mood as he underlined passages with a red ink Biro. He had read this book from cover to cover and yet could still find something in there that he felt he hadn't read before. Passages, names, places and characters. This was not the only published journal on the subject of past murders that had taken his attention ever since he was a young teenager, but it was one of the few where he felt that the author was closer to the truth than others had been. This particular account of the serial killings was also rather special in that he had bought it at the secondhand bookshop where Wendy had worked. A book that she had in fact personally sold to him. She had given him a smile that spoke volumes and that he had not forgotten. The typical smile of a teasing whore, he thought.

At that time, which now seemed like an age ago, he had felt that this had been an omen, that he was meant to read this account of what really happened in 1888. Once back at home in his bedroom, after he had taken the book out of the paper bag, it had fallen open at a page where there was an old bookmark, seemingly hidden. A bookmark that looked as if it had been lying within those pages for a very long time. He had noticed a sentence that had been lightly underlined in pencil. This read: *There lay dead the instigator of his first serious dark temper that had showed itself that evening. The gutter prostitute had spread a rumour that his manhood was little more than a pink newborn mouse. Small, soft and sickening.* Next to this Kenny had added his bit by scribbling: 'Jack then went on to rid the world of several East End whores. Paid whores. Prostitutes. Good man!'

Closing the book, Kenny rested back on his pillow with his hands clasped behind his head. He told himself that he had done well. That he would go on to do the work of the man he admired until he was forced to stop.

Content in his own terrestrial sphere of dark make-believe and happy that the half-witted idiot, Donald, had been arrested for crimes he had not committed, Kenny was ready for a nice long restful sleep. He felt not one iota of remorse over this latest murder because, as far as he was concerned, he had not only given fame to the trifling idiot who had been taken in for questioning, but he had also rid the world of another whore. How could he feel anything other than proud of himself? Proud, and content that all was going to plan.

Kenny's only real regret was that, having been born in a different time to that of his hero, he hadn't had the opportunity to meet him. But even this could take nothing away from his sense of triumph. So, with a feeling close to happiness, he drifted off to sleep with a smile of satisfaction on his face. He felt that he had done well. That if he were to be run over by a bus the next day, at least he would have left his mark and made the planet a little better for the elimination of the filthy whores who stalked God's pavements and dark alleyways.

Twenty

It was ten-fifteen and even though Isabelle was mentally and emotionally exhausted, still she could not sleep. She could think of nothing else other than her dear sweet innocent son being locked in a prison cell in a hostile environment. Of course he was innocent, but he had been arrested on suspicion of murder and there was nothing she could do about it. She had already written page after page of letters to newspapers and then screwed them up as being senseless drivel. She didn't want an apology. She didn't want justice. She just wanted her son back. Her gentle and somewhat naive son who she loved so much.

Now in her long, pale-blue soft cashmere dressing gown with nightdress beneath, she was sipping a mug of warm milk spiked with whisky, hoping this would help her to sleep. She had cried herself out and was now in a kind of nowhere land where she imagined that thousands of others had been before her. She was in shock. Drifting towards the sash window that looked out onto the square that was now lit by the old-fashioned iron lamp-posts, she wished for the umpteenth time that the clock could be turned back. That Donald had not gone out on that fateful evening.

Feeling as if she was the only one in the entire square who was awake and alone, she turned around so that her back was to the window and sat on the deep sill the way she had done as a child when her parents had owned this house. The house was so still and quiet and she could not take in the fact that the lovely Wendy was now a corpse in a coffin. Or that her own son was locked in prison under suspicion for Wendy's murder, and the pretty girl called Charlotte who had taken the vacant flat had fled to the safety of her grandparents' home in Bromley by Bow. Suddenly her beautiful house that had been her safe and happy domain for so long seemed as if it was her prison. Her cage. She glanced at the telephone on the stand in the entrance hall and realised that she had nobody that she could call just so as to hear another human voice. 'God please send someone to be with me,' she whispered, as tears slowly rolled down her cheeks and her neck. 'Please just for a few minutes let me have company in this house. Give me somebody to talk to. Sweet Jesus . . . hear my prayer . . .'

Whether or not it was from divine intervention that the doorbell rang through the silent house mattered not. Isabelle, not really thinking who it might be or how late in the evening it was and whether or not she might be opening the door to a maniac, was soon in the entrance hall and, with trembling fingers, was turning the old-fashioned brass mortise lock. She was so in need of company and the sound of a human voice, danger was far down on her list of priorities. At first, the shape of the tall lean man with bent shoulders under the dim porch lamp told her nothing. She opened her mouth to speak and then closed it again, feeling as if she were in some kind of a slow-moving film or a dark dream.

'I know it's very late, madam,' said the old man. 'But I saw that your lights were still on and I thought that it was important that we speak to each other in the quiet, now that the sightseers have gone. My name's Herbert Jenkins. I live across the square and I have something to show you. May I come in?'

'Of course you may!' His voice was like music to her ears. 'You're my neighbour who I sometimes wave to.' She stood aside and waved him in. 'How very sweet of you to come over. I can't tell you how I was so longing for company. May I offer you a glass of something?'

Closing the door behind him, the old boy nodded, smiled and shrugged. 'A drop of whisky would go down very well, madam.'

'Oh please . . . do call me Isabelle,' she said, showing him the way into the small and comfortable snug where she kept the drinks and glasses.

Once they were seated in the matching padded fireside chairs, Mr Jenkins said, 'So they took your son away and locked him up for questioning.' He slowly shook his head and said with a sympathetic voice, 'And you have been beside yourself ever since. The woman who worked in the bookshop and who lived in the top flat has been murdered, your son has been carted off on suspicion of murder, and the lovely young girl who waved to me from her window has gone away. And you are alone. They say that God works in mysterious ways, but you know what? Sometimes I think that God isn't always looking in the right direction at the right time.'

'Really? Why do you say this?'

He smiled gently at her and shrugged. 'Of course we wouldn't expect Him to carry a camera around twenty-four hours a day, would we?'

Isabelle smiled at him, totally mystified as to what he was going on about but she didn't care. 'Well no . . . I suppose we wouldn't,' she said.

'But maybe he should bring himself up to date a little because the camera doesn't lie. So, once we've finished our drinks, would you mind phoning for a black cab?'

'A taxi? But I rarely use them. I have a driver that I telephone whenever I need to be taken anywhere and that doesn't happen very often because I quite like a nice walk for one thing and there aren't many places that I go out to in the evenings so . . .'

'And this driver? If you were to call him now at this time of night. Would he come out?'

'Well, yes, I think he would – if it were important. Is it?' Isabelle was mystified, but even so she instinctively trusted this man and felt comfortable in his company.

'I think it's very important. I should like us both to go to the station where they are holding your son . . . or if not, to the nearest one to us.' He then pulled a white envelope out of his pocket. 'I went to the chemist today where a good friend works. He develops my films a little sooner than he might do for a stranger, and no matter if it's a day when the shop is closed.'

'Does he really? How very sweet,' said Isabelle, wondering where all this was leading. 'And you were saying that you would like me to arrange for my driver to take you and me to the police station?'

'Yes. But first of all I would like you to look at these three photos. I think this will tell us who did what to whom and who went which way.'

'Goodness . . . how mysterious.' Isabelle took each photo as he handed them to her, one by one. After a moment or two of staring at the first one, she said, 'But this is my son. This is Donald, walking away from the square.'

'That's right. I took it from my window. I wanted to finish the reel so that I could get the film developed. So I just took a few pictures from my window. I didn't realise, of course, just how important they would turn out to be. Take a look at the next one please.'

'Of course. This is quite fascinating. I *am* pleased that you called.' She then glanced at the next and her smile faded. 'Goodness . . . this is Wendy. Oh my goodness me.' Tears immediately filled her eyes. 'You took a photograph of her, on the evening that she was so brutally killed.' Frightened now as to this old man's state of mind she felt her fingers begin to tremble.

'It's okay. You've nothing to be frightened of. Now take a look at the third snapshot. The third, and the most important where your son is concerned.'

Studying the picture, hardly able to believe her eyes, the genteel woman who thought that she was going to lose her beloved son to the injustice of life and the law, gasped. 'Goodness gracious . . . it's Wendy with a young man.'

'Now . . . I said there were three but I have the ace card up my sleeve. Are you ready for it?'

'Well, yes I am. I don't know quite what to—'

Mr Jenkins held up a hand to stop her. 'Hush, hush. Don't get aerated. Be calm. Be patient.'

'Yes, yes I shall. But give me a moment.' Taking a few deep breaths with her eyes closed she finally said, 'That's much better.' And her smile said it all. 'Please do show me the final picture.'

'With pleasure,' he said and handed it to her. 'I think that you will agree that it's a very good shot. Very clear. You can see quite clearly that your poor departed tenant is talking to and walking away with the young man whose face is very clear and recognisable. That's not bad for an old-fashioned Box Brownie camera is it?'

Isabelle looked from the picture to the old man and then back to the picture and finally gazed into his face as tears rolled down her cheeks once again. 'Is this not evidence?' she said. 'Is this not proof that my son went one way and poor Wendy went the other with a stranger in tow?'

Smiling warmly at her, the old boy who had been the neighbour from across the square for years, said, 'Now will you phone for your driver? I think we have a very important ride to take, don't you?'

'To the police station?'

'Unless of course you want to phone and invite them into your house instead.'

Isabelle flopped back into her chair and gazed at her

saviour with the caring expression. 'I can't believe this is happening.' She swallowed, and dabbed the corner of her eyes with her lace-edged white handkerchief. 'I would very much like to go with you and my driver to the station. But will you promise me one thing?' she only just managed to say.

'Only if you promise me that you're not going to ask the impossible.'

'No, I don't think I am. Would you promise to stop me if I lose my temper and tell all of the officers on duty at this time of night that the law is an ass?'

Herbert Jenkins laughed again. 'If I must,' he said. 'If I must.'

'And do you think that I shall be fetching my son home tonight?'

'I would have thought so, but let's not bank on it. The wheels of the law can turn slowly or briskly depending on who might be on duty at the station. It could be an ass or it could be a true blue copper with a good brain between his ears and a bit of common sense thrown in for good luck.'

Isabelle slowly shook her head and looked at him again. 'If this is what I think it is – concrete evidence – then I shall insist on his immediate release. Insist on it!' Again she asked if the pictures were true evidence.

'Yes, Isabelle. You may rely on it. Let's not forget that it was I who took the photos to finish a reel. I who saw it all. And I who shall lay my hand on the Bible in the witness box. I have seen that lad before, hanging around and sometimes sitting on a bench in our lovely Lavender Square. I will say that I was curious once or twice but not enough for it to kill a cat.'

Feeling a weight had been lifted from her shoulders, Isabelle broke into a beautiful smile of relief. 'It isn't that far to Harbour Square police station, is it?'

'Hardly more than the stone's throw of a strong man. Why do you ask?'

'I think you know what I am going to say . . .'

'Well then, get your coat and we'll go. A walk in the late summer evening never did anyone any harm.'

'Except for poor darling Wendy.' Isabelle sighed.

'That's true. So let's go and do our duty to our country where the law is concerned while at the same time paying homage to that lovely woman who always waved to me from her window. May God rest her soul.'

'May God rest her soul,' whispered Isabelle to seal it.

To anyone looking out of their window that evening or to those who were walking through the square, the old man and the woman, who had linked arms and were on their way to see justice done, looked like an ordinary couple out for an easy stroll.

And not so far away Kenny was twisting and turning in his bed. The sense of being pleased and satisfied with his work so far had by now worn off. He had woken from a dark nightmare with what felt like a knot in his stomach that was getting tighter and tighter. He felt that something was in the air and that his old friend the devil was calling him. But he couldn't be bothered to get up, get dressed and go out in search of another disgusting whore. So he snuggled down again and left it to others to cleanse the streets. He had done his bit . . . for the time being. He would now take a sabbatical, he told himself, and then quietly laughed himself back to sleep. But it wasn't for too long that he lay curled up and slumbering. The long ring on the doorbell an hour or so later was enough to wake all three of them up, his mother, his dad and himself.

Just before his mother opened the door she crossed herself and when she saw the two officers standing there, one in uniform and one in plain clothes, she knew why they had come and who they would take away. Her Kenny. She had little idea what they wanted him for but she knew that it was something bad. His dark mood swings had worsened and she had spent too long worrying about his state of mind and bearing. And she wasn't too shocked that Kenny went with the men without fuss, argument or struggle. It was almost as if this is what he had been waiting for. What he had expected – even what he wanted. To go down in history with other maniacs of his ilk. The saving grace for his mother was that he had not been taken away in a strait-jacket but had gone quietly. It was over. And as tears slowly flooded her eyes, her chest felt as if there was a dark hole where her heart once beat. Her only son was going to be locked up in a lunatic asylum or a prison – for the rest of his life.

Epilogue

$\mathbf{B}$eing taken from his home in handcuffs and under heavy guard, Kenny had looked strangely passive for someone who most likely was about to be locked up. Instead of keeping his head down, as might be expected under the circumstances, he had smiled and nodded at the assembly of onlookers, almost as if he were the innocent victim rather than the homicidal maniac. In fact his demeanour had been one of a man of worthy exploits. But when the jeers and angry responses began, as the small groups crowding the pavements gave vent to their feelings, Kenny did little other than show two fingers and smile contemptuously back at them. As far as he was concerned, they should not be condemning him, but praising him for the good work he had done by cleansing the streets of whores who lured good men from their wives.

He could hardly believe that the locals were behaving as if they were appalled to discover a killer of prostitutes in the East End. To his mind they should have been grateful. But even more infuriating for him was that he had only just got into the swing of things, of cleansing the streets so that decent men, young and old, could walk in the dark without being approached and lured by women who were the scum of the earth. He just couldn't understand why the people weren't shocked to think that prostitution still was rampant in the area where they lived.

Nor could he believe that their parents, and theirs before

them, wouldn't have told them about his hero Jack. The so-called Ripper. In Kenny's opinion, the serial killer had done the community more justice than any court of law could. But from what he had read, instead of praising him they had been out for his blood like fierce hounds. But none of it really mattered now. Kenny was vaguely amused by the gatherings of people that had built into a trailing crowd and stopped the traffic from being able to pass. But he hadn't really expected more from people he saw as morons. He was pleased he had managed to show two fingers to his audience even though his hands were cuffed. And when he was bundled into the back of a Black Maria by the two officers who had been firmly holding each of his arms, he chuckled quietly as the yells and jeers grew louder. The louder it got the better he liked it.

The saddest thing of all was, that once the police vehicle drove Kenny away with droves of angry people running behind it showing their fists, his mother had been watching from her sitting room window in the flat on the second floor. Pale and grief stricken she had watched her son, her only child, being hounded by neighbours who had suddenly turned into a pack of wolves.

Watching as the crowd gradually dispersed, the distraught woman turned to her husband – her bewildered husband – and burst into tears. 'When did it all go so wrong? When did our little Kenny turn into someone who hated women so much to want to kill them?'

Comforting his wife, the man only just managed to say, 'I don't know. But I suppose that he wasn't like other kids. He never was quite the same as everyone else. He never had what I would call close friends . . . never seemed to need any. But he did need to be leader of the pack, though.'

Of course his wife knew that he was right, that Kenny had been different from other lads. 'So . . . we can't be blamed for it all, can we?' she pleaded. 'We are for some of it, and we both know what that is.' Of course her husband had to agree but only with a slow nod of head. He hadn't wanted to drag up a part of the past when he had turned a blind eye to his own wife prostituting herself for money, along with her sister. He didn't want to think about the time when their son had spent too much time at home without her. Sometimes the boy had sat watching the clock for over an hour waiting for her to come in. And now his son would be separated from them for good and they were going to have to learn to live without him.

Watching the Black Maria pull away, Herbert Jenkins, whose photographs had saved Donald, turned away from the assemblage of people and the press and police officers and walked slowly back home. He still couldn't believe that such a thing could have happened on his doorstep and to such a wonderful woman whose wave from the window he would sadly miss. But at least he had made a friend in Isabelle. She had all but pleaded with him to move out of his small rented rooms in the less grand house across the square from hers. She had insisted that if he agreed on the move then she would not take a penny more than the low rent that he had been paying for years. The lovely woman had pleaded with him so much that he could not refuse. Nor did he want to. His lonely life, it would seem, was about to change, and the only reason that tears were rolling down his cheeks was because the woman called Wendy was gone and he would soon be sitting at her window looking over at his. The twists and turns of life were known to be strange, but for this old man they were more than that. Now at least he would have someone to talk to. He would have Isabelle and her son, Donald. He would also be living above the lovely girl called Charlotte.

Eddie was gutted that Charlotte was not going to return to the safety of Bridgeford but he knew that there was nothing he could do about it. She was old enough to know her own mind and stand her ground – which is exactly what she was doing. She not only wanted to be back in her roots, but to be close to where Nathan lived. His little girl had flown the nest for sure. There was no point in trying to persuade her otherwise because it was very clear she was in love with Nathan and he was in love with her.

Eddie knew in his heart that it would not be long before Nathan asked him for Charlotte's hand in marriage. So it was with a saddened heart that he drove Rita back to Norfolk, knowing that his daughter was not just testing the water in London but had made up her mind that this was where her home was. He liked Nathan. He liked him a lot. So if he was going to have to lose his daughter at least she was going to be with someone he respected. He had known the boy's family for years so, even though it was with reluctance, he had to admit that things had turned out well for his only child. His cherished daughter. The one thing that he could take consolation from was the old saying, which he ran through his mind over and over while driving: 'You won't be losing a daughter, Eddie – you'll be gaining a son.'

Sitting in a big old-fashioned feather-cushioned armchair in Charlotte's apartment, as she liked to call it, Nathan knew, as he watched her fetching two coffees in bone china cups, that she was the one he wanted as a wife. He had been reminiscing again about their childhood and the time when she broke the news that her family was going to move to Norfolk. He could hardly believe that she was back and that he was with her in a lovely apartment in the house on the square, the kind of house that they had always dreamed of living in when youngsters. Quietly waiting for her to make herself comfortable on the two-seater sofa that matched the armchair, he sipped his coffee and glanced at her. A warm smile on his face he said, 'Charlie . . . you know that I love you and I know that you love me, but I can't carry on playing a guessing game of whether you were carried away on a romantic notion when I turned up at Bridgeford. I have to ask you . . . I just have to.'

'Well, don't look so gloomy,' she said. 'We've been through a horrible dark time, one way and another, because of you know who. Just say what you have to say.' She smiled at him and waited.

'I love you, Charlie. I always have and I always will. I want to marry you.'

Charlotte replied, with all the sincerity that was within her. 'I love you too, Nathan. And I want you to marry me.'

Nathan placed his cup and saucer on the side table and went over to her and got down one knee. 'Now I'm going to seal everything that I've said.' He took a small gift box from his pocket and flicked it open with the nail of his thumb. The solitaire diamond ring that his dad had helped him to choose looked beautiful, gleaming against the royal blue velvet lining of its box. He cleared his throat and then said in a quiet voice, 'Please will you marry me, Charlie.'

She couldn't help smiling at his way of proposing. So proper. So old fashioned. 'Of course I'll marry you, Nathan.'

And as he slipped the ring on her finger, tears filled her eyes and she said, 'It's beautiful. I love it and I love you. I think I always have and I know I always will.'

There really was no more to be said. But, since actions spoke louder than words, he took Charlotte's hand in his and, gently drawing her up and out of the chair, he led her out of the room into another. Into her bedroom and to the big old-fashioned double bed.